What Could Go Wrong?

What Could Go Wrong?

JESSICA FOWLER

This is a work of fiction. Names, characters, organizations, places, events, and incidents are either products of the author's imagination or used fictitiously. Any resemblance to actual persons, living or dead, or actual events is purely coincidental.

Published by Montlake, Seattle

www.apub.com

EU Product Safety Contact:
Amazon Media EU S.à r.l.
38, avenue John F. Kennedy, L-1855 Luxembourg
amazonpublishing-gpsr@amazon.com

ISBN-13: 9781662542152
eISBN: 9781662542169

Cover design by Debbie Clement
Cover image: © Ficus777, © Save nature and wildl, © Rayhan419923, © Irkhamster stock, © DOMSTOCK, © Jemastock, © SAHED STOCK / Shutterstock

Printed in the United States of America

To the author who told me I'd never make it, I remain fueled by spite.

1 MIRA

RUINED MY WEDDING

WORST DECISION I'VE EVER MADE

DO NOT HIRE HER

The bold letters shout at me through my phone screen as I compulsively refresh the page in the hopes that they might miraculously disappear. This scathing, one-star review came in a few months ago, and its placement at the top of my business listing has completely tarnished my reputation as one of the premier wedding photographers in North Carolina.

For there to be a permanent reminder of the worst day of my career stings, but for it to have been written by my best friend—or rather ex-best friend, Phoebe—is like pouring a bottle of Frank's RedHot on a gaping wound.

It would be one thing if I *had* ruined Phoebe's wedding, but besides the fight we had pre-ceremony, the day went off without a hitch. She and Cliff walked down the aisle, smashed cake in each other's faces in front of friends and family, and ended the night under a shower of sparklers as they drove off into their happily-ever-after. These, of course, were all facts I discovered while scrolling through the images my second shooter captured in my absence. Because yes, even after she ended our seven-year friendship and kicked me out of her wedding, I was still obligated to edit and deliver her gallery within my thirty-day window.

Working in the wedding industry as an event planner, Phoebe knew what a career-ending blow this would be for me. But considering she was the one to thrust me into this life of wedding photography, it was only fitting that she'd be the one to take it away.

I ignore the ache in my stomach as I slip my phone into my pocket and open the door to Finn's. The dingy dive bar has bad lighting and worse drinks but it's been my safe haven since the fight with Phoebe. A place where I don't have to be "Mira Maxwell, Luxury Wedding Photographer," and I can just be myself. A feat made infinitely easier by the red-headed bartender behind the counter.

"Hey, Mira," Hudson says cheerily, as I settle onto my favorite barstool, the one by the wall that gives me ample back support. His bright green eyes gleam under the fluorescents as he fills a few pints from the tap, setting each glass on a plastic tray.

"Give me a minute to run these over," he says, nodding towards the group of guys watching the baseball game at the back of the bar.

"Take your time," I offer, ignoring the vibration coming from my pocket. Since her review, I've been bombarded with cancelations and not-so-subtle texts from "friends" in the industry prying for details on the fallout. I've barely allowed myself to think about that day, let alone process the lingering trauma, so revisiting it for the sake of quelling the industry gossip mills or assuring clients that it was an isolated event won't be happening anytime soon.

No, instead I'm going to do what I've been doing every night since: avoid it.

"You look nice tonight," Hudson says, his words catching me off guard, as he takes his place back behind the bar.

Sure, we've flirted a little. But neither of us are one for compliments, at least none that are so forward.

"Not that you don't always look great," he stumbles, scratching at the scruff against his cheek. It's perfectly patchy, a sort of unrefined stubble that adds a distinguished flourish to his childlike sense of style. Much akin to a toddler who proudly dresses himself each morning, Hudson's ensemble tonight consists of green bootcut pants, a "Middle Earth Hiking Society" shirt that's faded and moth-eaten, and a pair of red-and-white checkered Vans. A stark contrast to my strictly black-on-black wardrobe.

"Really making a girl feel like she should shower more often," I say, digging in even further.

"That's not. I mean . . ." he says, adorably flustered.

"It's cool," I say, shaking my curls in his direction. With no editing queue or consultations to worry about, I actually had time to complete the entire six-step process that turns my wavy hair into manageable curls. "I'll take the compliment."

Hudson sighs a breath of relief as he reaches for a tumbler, setting it in front of me. "The usual?"

Although I've popped into Finn's a time or two over the years, I've become a regular. At first it was an excuse to get out of my apartment, to give my eyes a break from crying or editing the weddings left on my docket, but after Hudson and I became friendly, stopping in became part of my nightly routine.

"Haven't decided yet," I stammer, partly flustered but mostly stalling. Because as much as I enjoy Hudson's company, he's a terrible bartender. Truly. His concoctions are undrinkable. Last week, I saw him put olives in a tequila soda for what he called a "bit of whimsy." Needless to say, I'm willing to wait it out for Lilah, the bar manager, to make my drink so that I can *actually* drink it.

"I know you're going to order a whiskey sour. You always do," he says, stretching to grab a bottle of whiskey from the top shelf.

The reach pulls the fabric of his shirt across his broad shoulders, displaying a slew of toned muscles underneath awarded to him from weekend hiking trips and early morning kayaking. A patch of perfectly freckled skin peeks out at his midriff and I can't help but wonder how far down those freckles go.

When he catches me staring, I pretend to peruse the overhead menu. "I got a Negroni that one time."

"That's because everyone was ordering them, and you wanted to see what all the hype was about."

There's a knowing smile behind his eyes, a familiarity I'm unaccustomed to after years of keeping to myself, but Hudson has slipped past my defenses.

Unlike the mindless conversations I have to endure at weddings, curating responses to fit who my clients and the guests want me to be, there's never been an artificial moment with Hudson. He approaches even the most mundane questions with genuine interest, as if what I ate for lunch is just as fascinating as how tintype photographs are developed. What starts as one drink always ends up becoming hours of conversation, one subject flowing effortlessly into another, until Finn comes down from his apartment above the bar to kick us out and lock up for the night.

"Maybe I'm feeling adventurous today," I reason, all too aware of the door I'm opening.

Resting his palms against the bar, Hudson takes my cue, leaning into my personal space. I breathe in the earthy scent of him, a combination of pine and petrichor that makes my knees so weak I'm thankful to be sitting down.

"What type of adventure are we talking about?"

It's the same challenge we've volleyed back and forth over these last few weeks—to take this chemistry between us to the next level. But every time I contemplate stepping up, asking him to go to dinner or to see a movie, or do anything outside the confines of Finn's, fear stops me.

Besides not wanting to explain why I'm currently blacklisted from the wedding photography world, I haven't dated in years. Working in an industry that consumed my nights and weekends, companionship was limited to industry professionals and wedding party members who slid into my DMs—not really options with much viability for long-term success. Then again, after almost a decade capturing weddings and watching the subsequent divorces, I started to believe that love, the kind that lifts a person up and lasts a lifetime, might just be a fallacy. A hypothesis confirmed by the disaster that was Phoebe's wedding.

But sometimes with Hudson, I could swear I feel that *spark.* That pulse of electricity that makes me do stupid things like over-share or wonder what it might be like to wake up together on a Sunday morning before meeting friends out for brunch. I tried to ignore it, but the more we've hung out, the more that spark has grown until it's become perpetual fireworks every time I see him. But no matter how I feel about him, or how easily he evokes a Fourth of July celebration in my chest, I know better than to get my hopes up.

"How about the kind of drink that provides me with a momentary release from the burdens of reality," I sigh.

"I'm not sure we serve that here. But Lilah might know a guy you could call if you want the hard stuff."

"A whiskey sour is fine," I assure him, nervously playing with my newish bangs. I cut them in a panic after the review hit, hoping that a change in appearance might lessen the gnawing discomfort in my stomach whenever I looked in the mirror. But I still saw the same scared girl who flinched every time her phone buzzed. The same girl who couldn't help but wonder if there was truth to Phoebe's words.

"I finally finished those books you gave me," Hudson says, pulling me from my thoughts.

"How'd you like them?" I ask, watching as he combines three parts sour mix with one part whiskey in a metal shaker, little droplets of whiskey and juice flying out with every pump of his arm.

"I really enjoyed the dragon classifications."

"You would," I laugh. From magic regeneration sources to made-up native species of plants, no matter what series I throw at him, Hudson always finds an element to geek out about in every smut-filled fantasy series I recommend.

"And let me guess. Yours was when Tarwyn sacrificed his soul for Alia?"

"Please," I scoff, offended at the accusation. "I'm not that much of a romantic."

He raises an eyebrow. "Aren't you though?"

I flinch at the misconception. People always romanticize my job, believing that being surrounded by love and laughter on the "happiest day of their lives" must be like working in a fairy tale. But in reality, it's enduring twelve-hour days, being subjected to endless passive-aggressive comments such as "don't miss that moment" from relatives, and generally running around capturing choreographed ceremonies with hardly any real emotion whatsoever. But I could never say that. At least not to Phoebe, who made me feel ungrateful anytime I complained.

"If you really want to know," I say, leaning into the reason I started bringing him books in the first place, "my favorite part was when they broke the armoire."

A redness creeps up his neck at the mention of the most intense sex scene of the novel, as he drops a handful of maraschino cherries onto the countertop.

I reach for my drink, readying myself to take a sip, before Lilah saves me.

"Hudson, could you grab a few PBR cases from the back? We're running low." Her words are quick-fire and instinctual, like a mother catching her child about to touch a hot stove.

"Sure thing, boss," he replies, heading towards the back room. The second he's out of sight, Lilah grabs my glass, dumping the contents into the sink behind her.

"You have no idea."

"Can you believe this is the last drink I'll have to remake for you?" she asks, measuring the correct amount of whiskey, lemon juice, and egg white into the metal shaker. Pouring it into my glass, she pops a few cherries on top to keep the illusion that it's the same beverage.

I take a sip, relishing the perfect ratios. "Please don't tell me you're leaving. I can't survive on beer."

"Me? No. I'm probably going to die here. Hudson, however, is moving on."

I almost choke on a cherry at her words.

"He's leaving?" I ask between coughs.

"He didn't tell you? Tonight's his last shift."

My stomach sinks at the thought of losing him. Even before everything that happened with Phoebe, photography was an isolating job. I didn't have coworkers to complain to, and most of my days were spent at the computer. The only human interaction I had each week came from paid clients who just wanted me to smile and tell them they looked beautiful. Without Hudson, I'll have to go back to doom-scrolling from my Finsta until 2 a.m. I shudder at the thought.

"Do you know where he's headed? Another bar?"

"I think he's focusing on his day job," Lilah says, wiping down the counter.

Of all the topics we've discussed—his childhood dog Frodo, his weekend camping trips, how he's been to too many Future

Islands shows to admit to another human, his distaste for gin, and his absolute obsession with *The Lord of the Rings*—Hudson has never mentioned having another job. And the omission makes me wonder what else he might be keeping from me.

"I'm going to miss him," I admit, sipping my drink grimly. If I'd known that was the last terrible beverage Hudson would ever make for me, I would have savored it.

"Me too," Lilah says, spinning a cocktail shaker like she's Tom Cruise. "I make triple the tips when he's on shift."

"Really?"

With dark hair and latte-colored skin and a collection of teeny-tiny crop tops, Lilah looks like she was born to be on one of those posters they tack up in the bathroom of a biker bar.

"Apparently, being a hipster with dimples is more lucrative than being angrily sexy nowadays," she says as Hudson rounds the corner.

"Talking about me?" he asks, setting the cases of beer down by the cooler.

"I don't think anyone would use the word 'angry' to describe you," Lilah counters, mixing a cocktail for herself.

"But 'sexy'?" he asks, running his hands through his hair. His dark auburn curls are matted against the back of his neck as if he's just woken from a nap, and I hate to admit that I've fantasized about leaning across the bar and untangling them with my fingers. But no matter how often his expressive green eyes have met mine over the mahogany bar or how many nights he's ended his shift early to sit next to me and watch whatever garbage TV is playing on the beat-up box attached to the wall, I know better than to ruin the last good thing in my life.

"Actually, I was just informing Mira here that you're off to greener pastures."

"Jeez, Lilah, way to make it sound like I'm dying."

"But you *are* leaving?" I ask, hoping my voice doesn't sound as heartbroken as I am.

He rubs his hands nervously, the humor in his expression softening, before he meets my gaze.

He leans across the counter, his hand resting beside mine. Our fingers aren't even touching, but the exchange is intimate, igniting a warmth in my core that usually only comes from a round of Fireball. "I was going to tell you."

"I get it," I say, moving away from him. "Gotta go where the money is."

As much as it hurt to hear it from Lilah, he doesn't owe me an explanation. It isn't like I'm his girlfriend. Hell, by most standards, we aren't even friends. I'm just a girl from the bar.

"Mira," he says, his voice low, and I hate that he can see the emotions I'm trying so hard to hide.

"It's fine, really," I assure him, putting on my best customer service smile, the same one I wear anytime a guest taps me on the shoulder and asks "Did you take a photo of that?" as if I would miss the wedding cake. "So if this is your last shift, does that mean another round of knock off, knock backs?"

"Hell yeah, it does!" Lilah says, a mischievous grin stretching across her face.

Hudson furrows his brow, an annoyed gaze meeting mine across the mahogany bar. "You had to bring that up?"

"Consider it your penance for not telling me you were leaving," I reply, knowing his hatred of the tradition. Unlike most places of work that would gift coworkers cake or a hand-signed card on their last day, Finn's has a game.

The rules are simple. The departing employee must take a shot every time a drink is ordered in the last hour of their shift. Considering there are only a handful of customers in the bar, including myself, I doubt Hudson will even get a buzz.

"And that's why I chose a Monday night," Hudson boasts, as if he's outsmarted the system.

"Don't worry, I called in reinforcements," Lilah says, just as the bell over the door rings. We all turn to stare at the two guys who walk in, glassy-eyed and giddy.

"The smoke shop bros?" Hudson says, panic in his eyes. "They cleared an entire case in two hours last week."

"Imagine what they can do on half-priced Mondays?"

"There's no such thing as half-priced Mondays," he counters.

"There is tonight!" Lilah says, pouring tequila into the line of shot glasses on the bar, preemptively handing him one.

I can't help but laugh as Hudson slides a glass towards me, tequila spilling over the top.

"What's this?"

"I just figured since you're the one who got me into this, it's only fair you suffer through it with me."

"I don't think that's how it works."

"I'll allow it," Lilah chimes in, already pouring two beers for the brothers.

Hudson stares at me with bright, hopeful eyes, like a kid waiting for the neighbor to come out and play. "You said you were up for an adventure, right?"

And I know it's now or never. If this really is our last night together, I don't want to miss my chance at finding out what could be.

"Fuck it," I say, picking up the glass in front of me and clinking it on the counter.

"To new adventures," Hudson says, offering me a new challenge. One I'm eager to see through.

"To new adventures."

2 HUDSON

After Lilah called in reinforcements to make sure I'd be shit-faced by the time I left tonight, I was annoyed, especially since it's the first time I'll have my apartment to myself in weeks. But sitting crammed into the lone booth at Finn's with Mira, her sultry hazel eyes catching mine from across the table, I'm perfectly content staying here until the sun comes up.

Her thick black eyeliner is sharp at the edges, and her lips are a deep, artificial red, stained by the cherries she's been eating directly from the jar, and I want to lean across the table and taste them.

"Hudson, is that true?" Lilah says, breaking my daydream.

"What?" I ask, realizing I've entirely missed the conversation.

"Mira said you've never seen *Survivor*," Lilah clarifies.

"Why watch it on TV when I can just take my wilderness bag up to the mountains for the weekend," I reply, my tongue heavy in my mouth as my words come out slower than I intend. I've never been a big drinker, just one or two beers on a night out, but tonight, thanks to Lilah, I'm a bit wrecked.

Considering Mira has matched me shot for shot, I expect her to be just as unsteady, but watching as she effortlessly keeps up with the quick changes in conversation I can't help but wonder if Lilah started replacing her tequila with water at some point.

"I've never seen the appeal of camping," Lilah says between bites of pizza. "I hate having to walk the ten steps to my own bathroom in the middle of the night. I can't imagine trying to find a place to pee in the woods, in the complete darkness, with the animals and serial killers. It's not fucking worth it."

"I dunno," Mira says, twirling one of her curls around her finger. "I like the idea of disconnecting. Isn't that the dream, to throw your phone in the lake and go off the grid for a weekend?"

"You'd really want to spend an entire night in the wilderness? With no Netflix?" Lilah asks.

"With the right person, it could be nice," she says, her attention shifting to me. "S'mores and stargazing. Sounds like it could be a fun adventure."

Was that an invitation? A suggestion for me to ask her to go? I have to admit I've thought about it a million times. Bringing her to my favorite spots. Of setting up camp and teaching her how to start a fire. Of cuddling under the stars. Of waking up in the morning with the scent of firewood in her hair.

Heat rushes through my chest and down my body at the thought as I reach for one of the discarded pizza crusts in the center of the table and shove it in my mouth to keep from blurting out how I feel about her. A challenge that gets harder every time her leg brushes up against mine under the table.

"I bet Hudson would be more than willing to share his sleeping bag with you," Lilah says, causing me to choke on my bite.

"How about a round of water?" Finn asks, patting me on the back. Unlike other proprietors who never come around, Finn lives upstairs and stops by almost nightly to check in on his crew.

I take a glass and swallow down half, glaring daggers at Lilah, who ignores my non-verbal threat while chatting up one of the smoke shop guys.

"Thanks, man," I say gratefully. Because without Finn and his generosity, I'm not sure I would have survived these last couple of months. Unbeknown to anyone, I didn't get paid to be here. I just needed a place to hide out from my problems, to be myself without having expectations thrust upon me, where I didn't have to make everyone happy all of the time. Being the kid of a CEO, even a laid-back mountain man like my dad who believes in four-day work weeks, still comes with stressors, including taking over Elite Elevation when he retires. A job that I'll be starting next week. A role I am nowhere near ready for. But no matter how many times he's assured me that I'm qualified to step into his shoes, I still feel inadequate.

My father achieved so much by the time he was thirty. He'd bought a house, got married, had a kid, made a name for himself at the parks department, and turned a lowly website for outdoorsmen to swap gear, locate the best trails, and find other like-minded individuals to go on excursions with, into a multimillion-dollar company. And he did all this while still managing to cook healthy dinners, make sure I did my homework, and take me on monthly camping trips. So, the fact that I'm sitting here as a twenty-eight-year-old, second-guessing how to ask the girl I've been flirting with for months out on a proper date, goes to show how far from ready I am to take over a company.

"She'll say yes," Lilah assured me at the start of my shift, listening to me practice my opening line.

"How are you so sure?" I asked, wiping down glasses.

"Because that girl has been eye-fucking you since she started coming here."

"You don't know what you're talking about," I said, shooing away the idea. Growing up with a full head of red hair and a face full of freckles made me very aware that I was not the most desirable of my classmates. Combined with a build that is more scrawny than solid from years of long-distance hiking, and a wardrobe that consists of tattered graphic tees I purchased in high school and whatever free swag I get from work, I don't fit the mold for anyone's sexual fantasies.

"Stop selling yourself short," Lilah argued, her voice stern.

"I just can't tell if I'm reading into it. Maybe she's just friendly with everyone."

Lilah snorted. "Mira never smiled before you started working here. And now she giggles all the time. It's weird."

"She does not," I argue.

"Ugh," Lilah groans, done with me. "It's simple. She likes you. You like her. Ask her out, or better yet, ask her to go home with you?"

"You really think I'm cooler than I am, don't you."

"That's where you're wrong, my friend. I don't think you're cool at all."

"Thanks for that," I said, pulling out my phone to see what time Mira was coming in tonight.

The day I gave her my number I turned my phone off silent for the first time since I bought it, not wanting to risk missing her text. I was halfway up Roan Mountain when it came in, slipping off the trail to take advantage of the limited cell service. I expected a vague "hello" or "what's up," even a good-hearted dig at my weekend plans since Mira had made her lack of camping experience well known, but the message on the screen wasn't a message at all. It was a photo. A selfie of her holding a purple blazing star stalk, one of the variety of flowers I'd explained were in bloom this time of year. Her cheeks were pink as she smiled into the lens, exposing the leather straps of her camera harness against her shoulders. And I loved that she'd stopped to send this to me even though she was at work. That day, instead of hiking to the peak, I spent the rest of my daylight hours getting to know her better, making camp where I wouldn't lose contact.

Although she kept up a protective armor at the bar, her texts were more uninhibited. Honest. And I felt as if I'd finally earned my way into her inner circle of trust, a privilege I never wanted to lose.

"Have you told her you're leaving yet?" Lilah asked, slicing limes for that evening's bar service.

"About the trip? Or from Finn's?"

"Either. Both," she said, knowing that this week was the end of a chapter for me, one I'd been ready to turn the page on for quite some time now.

I shook my head. "I feel like my particular brand of family drama is a lot to dump on someone. Especially when I haven't bought her dinner yet."

"Mmm. You've bought her plenty of dinners," Lilah offered, having taken advantage of my DoorDash account herself a time or two.

"You know what I mean."

"What's that thing therapists say? Relationships are built on a foundation of trust? You'll never know if you can be together if you don't tell her the truth."

It wasn't like I was trying to keep things from her, but once people find out who I am, things always get weird, especially with potential suitors. Explaining that I'm the son of a CEO has opened the door to questions I don't love answering, like what my net worth is or if I own multiple properties. It's as if who I am as a person takes a backseat to what I can offer them, so I tend to omit that part of my life. I've enjoyed being Hudson the bartender rather than Hudson the nepo-baby.

"You're right," I sighed, opening another bag of limes.

"I usually am," she grinned, mixing another batch of basil and rosemary syrup for our cocktail of the month. "So tonight then?"

"Tonight."

But as I sit here, staring at the clock, knowing that we only have a few minutes left before Finn is sure to kick us out, I'm still nervous.

"Do it!" Lilah mouths to me, nudging my shoulder, as Mira listens to one of the brothers regaling her about the financial security of investing in Pokémon cards.

I'm not sure if it's Lilah staring me down, or the regret I'll feel if I don't make my move, but I find myself reaching for Mira's hand across the table, stealing her attention. This isn't the first time we've touched, but tonight the exchange is charged, and when her thumb grazes along my skin a flame ignites inside of me. I resist the urge to interlace my fingers with hers as her copper eyes glow under the fluorescents, the color mesmerizing like chalcopyrite in stone.

"Did you need something, or were you overcome with the urge to hold my hand?" she asks, as I find my words.

"I was wondering if you might want to—"

But before I can finish my question, Finn cuts me off.

"Closing time," he says, shooing us out of the booth. "You don't have to go home but you can't stay here."

Lilah groans, gathering the remaining glasses onto the tray as the smoke shop guys scoot out the booth and towards the door. But Mira hangs back. She adjusts her hair, the messy chestnut curls bouncing right back as her fingers move through them.

"I'll be right back," I tell her, forcing myself up out of the booth to gather my things. Behind the bar, I toss my sling bag over my shoulder, grab my jacket and say a final goodbye to Finn.

"Don't be a stranger," he mutters dryly, as he counts out the night's till.

"I won't," I promise, as I turn towards the booth and find it empty.

I try to tell myself that it's for the best. That I should get through this week. This trip. That I should settle into my new role, my new routine before I bring someone else into it. I can always text her or stop into the bar for a nightcap. It's not as if I'll never see her again, right?

I rationalize the decision with myself, as I make my way outside.

The street is quiet, the sticky summer air already clinging to my skin as I throw my bag over my shoulder and turn to head home. But to my surprise, I find Mira leaning against the wall, one combat boot kicked up on the brick. Now that she's standing in front of me, I notice that her baggy black jeans hang low on her hips, accentuating her hourglass figure, her cropped baby tee stopping just above her belly button. My fingers long to touch the exposed skin there, to know if it's as soft as I've imagined.

"After-party at my place?" Lilah shouts from down the street, but I don't move, content to stay here in this moment with Mira.

"You want to go?" she asks, pushing herself off the wall to stand up straight in front of me. Even in her platform Doc Martens she tops out at five foot four, but there's an intimidating air about her that I'm certain has put quite a few unruly groomsmen in their place. Her body is so close to mine I can feel her heat. She smells like citrus and honey as I breathe her in.

"I definitely don't need any more alcohol," I admit, grateful to feel a little more sober. "Did you want to?"

Mira shakes her head.

We've never lingered past closing, Mira always declining my offer to walk her to her apartment, but tonight she's staring at me as if she has nowhere else to go.

"What were you going to say earlier before Finn kicked us out?"

I swallow hard, finding my courage.

"I thought, now that I'm not your bartender anymore, you might want to get a drink. Together. Not here."

"Hmm," she says in mock contemplation. "So you being my bartender, that was the only thing holding you back?"

"Oh yeah. It's like doctor-patient relationships. Very frowned-upon within the libations community."

"Good to know," she giggles, and this time I notice it. The unabashed glee that radiates from her as she takes a step closer to me. Her eyes are focused, locked on me like I'm the last slice of cake at the deli counter as I stand perfectly still, afraid I'll spook her with any sudden movements.

"So what do you think?" I ask, realizing she technically hasn't given me an answer. "Are you free next Friday, because I can get a reservation at—"

I can't finish my thought because she's twisting her fingers into my shirt and pulling my mouth to hers, the salty taste of tequila on her tongue. Of all the times I've imagined this moment, it never scratched the surface of how it actually feels. Of the soft press of her lips against mine. The warmth of her tongue as it slides into my mouth. The sensation of sugar and salt against my tastebuds.

My hands instinctively find her waist, as I guide her back to the brick, placing a hand against her head to protect it from the rough stone.

I pull back for a moment to take her in. Her dark curls are frizzing in evening humidity, her hazel eyes darkened, and her cherry lips are swollen. God, she's beautiful.

She only gives me a moment before she threads her fingers through my hair, bringing my mouth to hers. And when her nails scratch against my skin, pulling at the nape of my neck in a way that makes my entire body ache, I can't control the moan that escapes from my mouth. Embarrassment rushes to my cheeks as I ready myself for mockery, but she pulls harder. *Fuuuuucck.*

As good as she feels, I'm desperate to know what noises I can elicit out of her as I slide my hand beneath the thin fabric of her shirt. The bra she's wearing is just as thin as her shirt, as I run my thumb along her hard nipples. Her breath hitches as I lightly squeeze one between my fingers, and I swear I forget place, time, and all other earthly things that ground me until a car whizzes by, its horn honking as it passes.

"Get a room," the driver shouts as they roll through the yellow light. The interruption is enough to remind me that we aren't in any position to take this further. Not here at least. And not when there are so many things I need to tell her.

"You said you finished those books I loaned you, right?"

"Yeah, last night," I say, taking a moment to process the subject change.

Her lips curve into a seductive smile. "With you leaving and all, it's probably best if I get them tonight, don't you think?"

And even though I know it's the wrong decision for so many reasons, I grab her hand and lead her to my apartment.

3 MIRA

My phone's ringing. The incessant beeps and chimes are as pleasant as a baby screaming in a fancy restaurant as I roll over to silence it.

Had I known that hangovers would be even worse at twenty-nine, I would have partied more in my college years. I can barely open my eyes, my lids heavy with sleep, as I extend my arm over towards my nightstand. But instead of finding my secondhand dresser, covered with unread books and half-empty water glasses, there's nothing but empty space beside me as I almost fall out of the bed.

It takes about two seconds for me to realize that this is not my apartment. And I am not wearing any pants.

Hesitantly I glance over and see a mop of red hair and freckle-covered torso wrapped in heather-gray sheets lying beside me. Hudson's face is adorably smushed into the pillow, his lips are curved in a giddy smile, and the night comes back to me in pieces.

Lilah calling the smoke shop guys to order as many two-dollar beers as they could stomach. Helping Hudson consume the line of tequila shots she poured even after he officially clocked out. The rush of adrenaline when I pulled him in for a kiss. The heat of his breath against my neck when we reached his apartment. The way my body completely relaxed as his hand worked its way into my jeans, like an artist who had mastered his craft. And then . . . nothing.

There is a hole in my memory, a hazy blackness that makes me regret those last couple of shots. Of course my first opportunity for a non-self-assisted orgasm in almost a year is lost to the ether of my brain. Fan-fucking-tastic.

It's fine, I reason to myself. We can do it again. After I borrow a swig of his mouthwash, fix my face, and pretend that the morning glow and peppermint breath are one hundred percent natural. But if I'm going to be able to do any of that, I need to silence my damn phone.

Pushing myself off his surprisingly comfortable bed, I locate my jeans in the middle of the floor and wrestle my phone out of my pocket. I have every intention of ignoring the call, letting it go to voicemail, and dealing with whatever drama is waiting for me on the other end after an orgasm and breakfast, but in my haste, my finger slips, and I'm greeted with loud, incoherent sobbing.

"Mira? Mira, my . . . wedding . . . is . . . ruined!" a panicked, female voice exclaims, and my heart drops. The lingering PTSD from Phoebe's wedding evokes instant anxiety inside my chest, as I take refuge in the bathroom.

"I'm sure it's not," I say, closing the door and turning on the light. I take stock of my reflection in the mirror and surprisingly it's not terrible. My makeup from last night is primarily intact, a few black smudges beneath my eyes, my lipstick is gone, and my hair is a tangled mess, but overall the damage isn't that bad. Taking a step back, I see the words "Protect the Shire" printed on the oversized t-shirt I'm wearing, the hem falling just above my knees. Of course Hudson outfitted me in *Lord of the Rings* pajamas.

"Mira. Please, you have to help me; I don't know what to do," the voice says, reminding me that they're on the phone. I check my caller ID, expecting to find a frustrated client name, but see that it's my college roommate, Meredith Graham—who, according to the countdown she's been posting on social media all year, is getting married in a few days.

This isn't my problem. It shouldn't be my problem. And yet I default into crisis management mode.

"Tell me what happened."

After a decade in the wedding industry, I've learned that photography is more than taking pretty photos. It's putting out fires, metaphorically and literally. Seriously, brides should stick to LED candles.

It takes ten minutes of crying and two deep breathing exercises before I'm able to discern the details of what's caused this epic meltdown. The wedding photographer Meredith hired is currently in labor, and the backup is bedridden with the flu. With only three days until they walk down the aisle, and all the other decent photographers in the area booked for the season, I am her last resort.

"Can I have a minute to think about it? I just woke up," I say, reaching into the medicine cabinet in search of aspirin. Instead of the usual hydrogen peroxide and nondescript Band-Aids that I find in single guys' bathrooms, I'm greeted with a plethora of high-end skincare products. The pricey kind people steal from Equinox. I'm never one to judge a good skincare routine, but given that Hudson is typically sporting a rugged five-o'clock shadow, I find this a bit odd.

"Oh shit. I'm sorry. I remember you used to be a night-owl and I spaced on the time difference," she explains. "Honestly, I thought I would be leaving all this on your voicemail."

"Nothing like getting a jump-start on the day," I assure her, unscrewing the Tylenol bottle and popping two pills into my mouth. I swallow them down with a handful of water, then splash my face. Reaching for the hand towel, I find that it's embroidered with tiny foxes playing in a field of flowers. I imagine Hudson walking through a big-box store and spotting it on the shelf, coming up with names for each of the fictional foxes.

"I wouldn't ask if it wasn't an emergency," Meredith says, pulling at the soft spot in my heart.

When I first started my career, I was so excited for my friends to get engaged, to be able to be a part of their day as more than just a guest, and give them a lifetime of memories to cherish through my work. But watching Phoebe burn bridge after bridge, having to restructure her social circles anytime a so-called friend was unhappy with her event planning services, made me implement a rule to never cross professional and personal relationships. Of course, Phoebe convinced me that she was an exception to the rule, that nothing would ever come between us, that no other photographer would ever be able to capture her day the way she envisioned, so I caved. I fell for her flattery and put my faith in our friendship. But I know better than to repeat my mistake.

"I know it's last minute, but I'll pay double."

"Meredith?"

"Really. My fiancé is rich. Like super rich. Please."

With clients canceling left and right and bills piling up, I need the money.

"Where is it again?" I ask, already regretting considering this.

"Wyoming," she replies, her voice a bit more upbeat. "At Grand Teton National Park. Have you heard of it?"

"Yeah. I've heard of it," I say, knowing that it's a dream destination for any wedding photographer.

"So, will you do it?" she asks, her voice pleading.

I take a moment to consider my options.

Meredith and I haven't been close in a while, and if this wedding goes well, I could rebrand. Change my business name to something cutesy like Picture Perfect or Always in Focus, and start over far away from the blights of my past.

I'm about ready to pull the trigger when my shirt catches on the cabinet, pulling it open and causing a bunch of items to tumble onto the floor.

"Shit," I say, bending down to clean up my mess.

It's not until I'm tossing everything back underneath the cabinet—a Dyson Airwrap, bottle of vanilla-scented body spray, and a box of tampons—that I realize that none of these items belong in a bachelor pad.

I try to consider all the logical reasons why Hudson might be in possession of such a selection.

He has a female roommate? But it's a one-bedroom.

He has a sister who likes to stash stuff at his apartment? But he said he was an only child.

Closing the cabinet, a nagging feeling pricks at me as I gather my clothes from his bedroom and tiptoe into the living room.

The morning light exposes everything I failed to see in the dark. Scented candles, throw blankets, ornamental bronze elephants, and carefully curated coffee-table books that accessorize the small space. Combined with the fact there isn't a single piece of *Lord of the Rings* memorabilia hanging from the walls or sitting on the bookcase, my unease quickly turns to suspicion. And then I see it—the undeniable truth of what I've feared.

Nestled between *InStyle* magazines and golden bookends are framed photographs of Hudson with his arm lovingly draped around a beautiful brunette. In one, they are laughing together on the beach as she kisses his cheek. In another, they are sitting on the slopes in snow jackets. And the last one is a black-and-white print of them kissing in front of a fountain.

Hudson has a girlfriend—a live-in one at that.

My stomach churns from more than just mixing liquors last night.

One-night stands I can handle. Ghosting, sure. But making me complicit in his infidelity is absolutely unacceptable.

"I can get you on the first flight tomorrow," Meredith says, as I bite back the rage burning in my chest. "Does that work for you?"

And even though I know that saying yes is probably going to be another mistake, the opportunity to escape to the other side of the country, to get away from this city and everyone in it who's betrayed me, feels like kismet.

"I'm in."

4 HUDSON

Rolling over, I breathe in the scent of cinnamon and citrus. After weeks of daydreaming about what it would be like to kiss her, touch her, taste her, my senses are buzzing with her proximity. The fact that she's taking up space in my bed and not in my dreams is a reality I haven't entirely accepted yet as I reach out to pull her close. But instead of finding the warmth of her body, I'm left with nothing but cold sheets.

Opening my eyes, I see the light on in the hallway and listen to the sound of her footsteps against the hardwood floor.

"You jonesing for coffee already?" I ask. My head is in that liminal space between drunk and hungover as I check the time. It's early—barely six. I've gotten maybe two hours' sleep, not nearly enough for my body to metabolize the remaining alcohol in my system.

Pushing myself out of bed, I make my way to the kitchen, stopping when I see that the door to the bathroom is open and an array of items are scattered on the floor—Katherine's things—and the sight sobers me like a cold shower.

"Mira?" I ask, right before I hear the front door slam.

My heart pounds as I run, barefoot and shirtless, down the hall. The elevator is already making its descent to the lobby as I open the emergency exit door and sprint down the stairs. All those years of traversing mountain terrain have prepared me for this as I jump two at a time, hoping to shave off enough seconds to catch her.

As I throw open the door, the security guard offers a shake of his head and I know that I've missed her.

"Fuck," I mutter, dragging a hand down my face.

Despondently, I take the elevator back up to my floor, ruminating on all the things I could have done differently. I should have told her the truth at the bar, the door, anywhere between Finn's and my bedroom. And when we got back to my place and she slipped off her jeans, exposing a pair of black lace panties that matched her bra, I could barely formulate thoughts, let alone explain my unorthodox living situation.

Before I started dating Katherine I'd only slept with one other girl, and when I found out that sharing a sleeping bag at wilderness camp was more of a rite of passage than a legitimate proclamation of feelings, I was heartbroken for a month. So no matter how much I liked Mira, or how badly I wanted to get her off, the thought of sleeping with her without being upfront about my situation felt disingenuous. Using all the willpower I could muster, I excused myself to the bathroom.

I had to tell her the truth. That I was still living with my ex. That I was about to be a CEO. That I had real feelings for her. When I exited the bathroom, I found Mira half-asleep on my bed, an arm underneath the pillow, and this premature ending to the night felt like a gift from the universe. I even optimistically DoorDash-ed a carton of eggs in the hopes of waking her up in the morning with a batch of my signature pancakes. Seeing the eggs now, carefully placed in the entryway of my apartment, I want to throw them against the wall.

Retreating to my bedroom, I grab my phone from the charger and open my text chain with Mira. My fingers hover over the keys as I contemplate what to say.

~~I know what this looks like . . .~~

~~I can explain . . .~~

~~I'm single. I swear . . .~~

Everything I type sounds like complete bullshit. Another excuse from another asshole. But I have no idea how to explain the situation without writing a dissertation on the last three years of my life. This is definitely a conversation I need to have in person. And on any other day, I would go sit at the bar and wait for her to show up. I'd wait all week if I had to. But today, I have a plane to catch.

Panicked, I call the only person I know who might have practical advice for this situation.

The FaceTime chimes as Lilah answers it with an aggressive "This better be an emergency."

She's still in bed, the camera held up above her head, the dim light of her phone exposing her sleeve of delicate floral tattoos.

"It is," I say, hoping she can discern the desperation in my voice.

"You know you can have condoms delivered, right?" she groans, pulling the covers over her head.

"Why would I call you for that?"

"I asked you to bring me cranberry juice for my UTI a week ago. Thought this might be a tit-for-tat situation."

"It is not," I reply, shuffling over to the dresser to throw on a shirt. It's a tie-dye green-and-black tee from Elite's annual Adopt-A-Highway cleanup.

"I think I fucked it up with Mira," I say, my voice on the verge of cracking. I should be calling Lilah with good news, sharing my excitement about what happened last night—omitting the more scandalous details, of how she felt like velvet between my fingers or that I had to name native bird species when her teeth bit against my neck to keep from exploding against her in the kitchen, which were secrets only for me. But the last thing I expected was to have to explain how I lost her in a single evening.

"I'm sure you're overreacting," she says lackadaisically. "Premature ejaculation happens to a lot of guys when it's been a while. If you just explain you had one too many—"

"Jesus, Lilah, that's not what happened," I argue, sitting on my bed. Staring at the empty space she occupied earlier, I wish I could savor it.

"From the text Finn sent me last night I heard you two were practically fucking in the street. I can't think of any other reason things would go south unless . . ."

She sits up, understanding washing over her face. "Hudson! Tell me you didn't."

"I wasn't thinking." I shake my head shamefully. "We were kissing and she suggested coming here and I didn't want the night to end."

The expression on her face is the same one she reserves for underage kids attempting to order a Long Island iced tea. "Did she freak out?"

"I didn't even get the chance to tell her. She ran out before I could."

"Ran out last night or this morning?"

"This morning," I replied regretfully.

"So you guys hooked up?"

"No," I clarify, "she fell asleep."

"Thank God for that," Lilah sighs. "At least she doesn't have a reason to key your car or burn your building down. This is solid drink-thrown-in-the-face territory at best."

"That's not helpful," I groan.

"I want to be sympathetic to your plight, but I told you to be upfront with her."

"I know. And now I need you to tell me how to fix this."

"Maybe she had to run out for a job. She works weird hours, right?"

"She did get a call," I say, remembering the sound of her ringtone blasting through the room.

"Maybe she had one of those sunrise photography sessions or something. I'm sure she just overslept. This freakout could be for nothing."

I bite my lip.

"What?" Lilah asks, reading my uneasy expression.

"She went to the bathroom," I say, sneaking a glance at the products still scattered on the floor, and then I remember the decor in my living room and I'm hit with another wave of nausea. "Oh God. And the photos."

"Yeah. You're fucked," she states, with the finality of a detective on a crime show. I bury my face in the pillow and let out a frustrated sigh into the feathers. It isn't until I breathe in that I realize that this was Mira's pillow, and the spike to my olfactory senses only intensifies the pain in my chest.

"What do I do?" I ask, my words muffled by the pillow.

"Not smothering yourself would be a start," she argues as I sit up. "Look on the bright side, at least Katherine didn't barge in. Now that would have been bad."

"True," I reply, grateful she left on the earlier flight.

"The woman basically declared squatter's rights to keep herself in your apartment. Could you imagine if she found out you were into someone else? She'd freak out."

"She's not that bad," I counter. Or at least she never used to be.

I met Katherine right after I moved to Raleigh from Charlotte, running into her at one of the networking events my father insisted I attend in an effort to get me out of my comfort zone. When she found out I was new to the city she offered to show me around some of her favorite places, and I eagerly agreed.

An introvert by nature, I prefer being outside in the quiet, watching human interactions more than partaking in them, but I never complained when Katherine forced me to go out with her. I went to dinner parties and stayed up past my bedtime at clubs with music that made my head hurt. I changed myself to fit into her lifestyle the best I could, so when she came home and announced that she wanted to open the relationship, the words "I think we should break up" sprang out of my mouth faster than a sprinter at the starting line.

Katherine tried to save face, explaining that it was just an idea, a fad she thought might be fun to try, like buttered coffee or aerial yoga, but I didn't believe her. I could tell that she wasn't happy and, if I was being honest, I don't think I ever was.

I thought I could start over, discover what I actually wanted from a partner, but our breakup was put on the backburner when, a few days later, my stepbrother and Katherine's best friend Meredith announced that they were getting married. Between engagement parties and family luncheons, Katherine and I were expected to be together. And with the wedding set for June, only a few months away, we made the decision to keep our breakup a secret.

In the meantime, I hoped Katherine would pack up her things and find a new place to live. But even for a real-estate agent, finding accommodations in her price range that would accept her mediocre credit score was harder than getting into Harvard.

Every day was another disappointment, and I regretted agreeing to the stupid ruse in the first place. Especially when Katherine started to blur the lines of our arrangement; using me as an emotional dumping ground to vent about work or sitting on the couch for longer than necessary in the evenings, in the hope that I'd go to bed with her.

And that's why I started working at Finn's. To put distance between us. To allow the reality of our breakup to settle in. And she got the message, finding an apartment she can move into the day we get back from Wyoming.

I was elated. Ready to have her out of my space, my life, to start something new. To start something with Mira. But of course, I fucked it all up.

"This is the worst timing. I leave in . . ." I check the time on my phone. "Two hours."

"How about this," Lilah says, sitting up. "If she comes in while you're gone, I'll assess the situation and report back."

"And if she hates me?"

"Then I'll explain that you're a good guy."

"Why are you saying that like it's a bad thing?"

"Because in your case it is," Lilah huffs, and I hate that she's right.

Standing up for myself is a character trait I never grew into. It's the reason I found myself in this mess in the first place. As much as I would love to blame Katherine for this turn of events, this mess is my own doing.

"Thanks for talking me down."

"Anytime," Lilah says, giving me a half-smile. "As long as it's after ten."

"Noted," I reply, ending the call.

Lying back on my bed, I stare at the stupid blackout curtains Katherine installed even though I've always loved waking up to the sunrise. I want to tear them down and burn them. But I know I'll probably just fold them up and place them in one of the many moving boxes coming on Monday.

Taking a deep breath, I open my text chain with Mira and cling to the hope that she doesn't hate me as I type a message.

Are you okay? I heard you on the phone and then you ran out. Just wanted to check in.

I sit there for a few minutes waiting for a reply. I know I should wait it out, but staring back at my words, insecurity washes over me as I send another message.

I hope that you don't regret last night.

And then another.

I'm sure you have questions. And I'd love to talk about what happened. Hit me back when you can.

Each time I hit send my stomach tightens and it's like I'm a teenager again, staying up and waiting for the girl to call me back. It's pathetic. But I'm not above it. I would sit there all day if I could, staring at my phone, but instead I push myself up. Opening my closet, I grab my duffel bag from the floor. The faint scent of campfire and pine clings to the fibers as I throw it onto my bed.

Typically, I'm an avid packer, laying out my items weeks in advance and checking off each on a predetermined packing list, but this time I haven't even done laundry. Fumbling through my dresser, I make do with what I have, tossing a few pairs of shorts, a couple of t-shirts, and some outerwear items onto my bed. I roll each item tightly for the best space efficiency, and head to the closet to grab the tailored tan suit I'm required to wear for the ceremony. The drab color and starched collar make me throw my purple floral Vans that I love but my mom hates in the suitcase too.

When I'm done, I set my bag by the door, doing a final walk-through of my room before I hear my phone buzz. I practically dive for it, hope blooming in my chest.

"Hey," I say, answering it without looking.

"Ready for your trip?" my father asks, his husky voice muffled by the sound of printers and chattering in the office.

"Just finished packing," I admit, a dead giveaway of my frantic mental state.

"Really?" he asks, concerned. "I'd assumed your suitcase would be sitting by the door since last week."

"Yeah, well, I haven't really been looking forward to this trip. You'd think destination weddings would be banned as a form of corporal punishment."

"I can still get you on our flight to Peru if you want," he says, the same offer he's given me all month. And for a second I consider it. Maybe wallowing in Machu Picchu wouldn't be such a bad idea.

"Mom will only make my life hell if I don't go," I reason, knowing that she'd probably come track me down and put me on a plane back to Wyoming herself if I didn't show up.

Growing up, my mother and I didn't have the best relationship. While I took after my dad, who enjoyed quiet mornings reading and afternoon bird-watching, my mother preferred shopping for designer goods, scheduling lavish spa experiences, and pretending to be better than everyone else around her. Unlike other moms who made an effort to be involved in their child's life, mine never baked brownies for my bake sale or offered to chaperone any of my field trips. Hell, she wouldn't even drive me to see *The Lord of the Rings because the showtime interfered with her standing nail appointment.*

So, when my parents got divorced, I hoped that she'd just forget about me, leave me behind as a product of her old life, but she insisted on including me in her new family.

Instead of spending my summers with my dad, traveling the country to find the best hiking trails for Elite Elevation, I was stuck at my mother's house on Lake Norman. And she and George would go off to dinner parties, or charity events, or weekend rejuvenation retreats, and I would be left to deal with my annoying, machismo stepbrother, who even though he was two years younger than me was determined to make my life a living hell.

"If you change your mind, the flight's nine-thirty. I know the team would love to have our best content creator there."

"You really need to hire an in-house photographer," I argue, for the millionth time. "Phone photos, no matter how advanced the technology becomes, will never beat a real camera."

"That can be your first order of business."

"Right, because hiring a full-time content creator is always on the top of the transition docket."

"If you think it's important, then it should be," he says confidently.

I always knew that I was going to work for my dad's company, not only because it was expected of me but because I genuinely love its mission. Providing a community for nature lovers to connect, to developing technology to make camping and exploring accessible for all, and traveling the world to promote environmental conservation. It's my dream job. But come Monday, I won't just be an employee, I'll be the head of the company. And even through the rigorous training process and assurances that he'll always be there if I need anything, I don't feel ready.

"I know you're nervous, but I have complete faith in you. You've always treated everything with care and respect, and I trust you're going to do that with Elite."

"You know, I wouldn't be offended if you decide retirement doesn't suit you. I'll happily go right back to product development."

"Please," my father chuckles. "After spending the last twenty years watching our customers experience the world, I'm excited to go out there and experience it for myself."

Although he's hiked some of the most breathtaking trails in the world, I know that my dad wants to actually immerse himself in the wild; instead of having to bring a hotspot and satellite phone with him everywhere he goes in case there's a work emergency he has to deal with. And more than anyone he deserves that.

I hear his assistant calling for him in the background.

"Look, Huds, I gotta run. But tell the Tetons hello for me?"

"Will do, Dad," I say as he ends the call.

And although I should be worried about how I'm going to run one of the top outdoor equipment companies in the world or spending the next four days with my ex, my mom, and my stepfamily, all I can think about is Mira.

5 HUDSON

The winding Wyoming roads glimmer underneath a sky of shimmering stars, and the blue-hued horizon lines are the picture of peace, but I can't appreciate any of it. Between flight delays, picking up my rental car, and my incessant need to check my phone, my anxiety is at an all-time high.

After watching Mira start a heated debate with other drunken patrons at Finn's over *Back to the Future Part III* being the superior film in the franchise, I know she isn't one to avoid conflict. I'm certain that if she hated my guts, she'd tell me to fuck off before promptly blocking my number. So, her going radio silent has me unsettled.

I try not to think about worst-case scenarios as I pull into the parking lot of the ranch, my headlights cutting across the dark abyss of the property announcing my arrival to everyone partying out on the lawn.

By the time I cut my engine, Katherine is already running down the path towards me. Her long brown hair is tied up in a loose knot at the base of her neck, and the pale pink dress she's wearing clings to her body, billowing around her knees.

"Hudsy, you're here!" she shouts, wrapping her arms around me; her breath pungent with the sweet scent of liquor.

"You don't have to lay it on that thick," I say, giving the group a wave and stepping out of her grasp.

"I'm just excited to see you," she says, as if we didn't see each other two days ago before she left. "Come on, let me show you to our room."

I suppress my groan as she takes my hand and leads me down the path, past the main cabins, and towards the two-story barn at the far end of the property. I knew that cohabitating goes hand in hand with the whole pretending-to-still-be-together thing, but now that the reality of it is dawning, my chest tightens. We haven't shared a bed in months, a fact my chiropractor keeps reminding me of—since my couch, as pricey as it is, is not suitable for long-term slumber. And in my Mira-induced packing daze, I forgot to bring my sleeping bag.

We walk through the lobby of the barn, traveling down the hall until she stops in front of the last door on the left. When she opens it, I'm elated to see that in addition to a queen-size bed there is also a set of wooden bunk beds. Dropping my bag on the floor, I go to claim my space on the bottom bunk as Katherine pulls me backwards and onto the bed. She's in my lap before I can process the movement, her long tanned legs on either side of me.

"What are you doing?" I ask, hoping that she'll come to her senses and get off my lap of her own accord.

"I missed you," she pouts, attempting to run her hands through my hair. I catch her wrist delicately, moving off the bed and across the room, a feat made infinitely harder by how cramped the space is.

"Why don't we go back to the party?"

"Really?" she asks, staring up at me in disbelief. More than anyone, she knows I'd rather build profit-margin spreadsheets than go to a party with her friends, but if doing shots with Meredith and Grant gets me out of this room, I'll do it.

She plops down on the bed, pouting. "But we agreed to be *together* this weekend."

"No, we agreed to sit in our assigned seats and walk down the aisle without causing a scene," I say in the same tone a parent would use to explain to a toddler why they can't bring the pony home with them.

She doesn't say anything, her eyes staring down at the floor, crossing her arms across her chest. "I didn't get the apartment."

"What?" I ask, the words knocking the air from my chest.

"I couldn't come up with first month, last month," she says, picking at her perfectly manicured nails. Being a real-estate agent, Katherine's income fluctuates with the economy, and with the housing crisis in full effect, sales are slow. My mother offered to refer a few of her friends to Katherine's firm, but she quickly learned that millionaires are the most indecisive people when it comes to buying houses.

"What about your savings?" I ask, leaning against the wall, unsteady.

"Between the dresses and the flights, and the bachelorette party . . . It all adds up, okay?"

This can't be happening, I reason, as my brain tries to come up with possible solutions.

"Which apartment was it? I know your credit isn't great, so if they need a co-signer . . ."

"I don't want you to do that," she argues, but I'm willing to do anything.

"I'll call them. I'll—"

She cuts me off. "They already gave it to another applicant."

Irritation bubbles along my skin. It took us weeks to find an available apartment in her price range and now it's gone. Just like Mira is gone from my life because I can't stand up for myself and kick my ex out like a normal person.

"What happened to that big commission payout? With the Franklin property?"

"I got a call from them yesterday," she whimpers, wiping her nose. "They said that their decorator doesn't have a vision for it."

"You know what," I say, pulling out my phone, "let me buy you a place. I'm sure you can find a condo or townhouse. I'll even let you broker it. Give you the commission."

"You can't be serious?"

"I'm about to be CEO. It comes with a significant salary increase. I can swing it," I say, as there's a knock on the door.

I recognize Adrian immediately. Of all the people in Meredith and Grant's friend group, he's the one whose company I enjoy the most. Our paths sometimes crossed at Elite during his time as a customer service rep, and he always knew how to read a room. It also doesn't hurt that he's dating Finn's sister Vanessa, who is just as kind and loyal as her brother.

"Meredith sent me to tell you two to stop making out and come back to the party," he says in his thick Irish accent.

"Give us a minute," I say, turning back to Katherine, who's wiping at the corner of her eyes.

"Let's talk about this later, okay?" she says as I make a mental note to call my accountant first thing in the morning.

Eager for a drink, I follow her and Adrian back to the main cabins.

The cabins are lit with string lights as music blasts in the air, a rhythmic dance track that makes me ache for the wildlife that calls this place their home. A plastic table is set up on the patio, red Solo cups lining the edges. One would think that a twenty-six-year-old might want to celebrate such a momentous occasion in a more dignified fashion, but as Grant and his cousins slam back beers during a particularly rowdy game of flip cup, it's safe to assume that nothing about this week will be classy.

When my stepbrother announced that he was getting married in Wyoming, I was shocked. Not only by the fact that Grant had found someone to commit to, a feat I believed to be impossible due to his lifelong string of casual, noncommittal flings, but to see the words "hiking boots required" on the wedding invitation was so out of character I believed it was a prank.

"Hudson," Grant slurs, throwing a rough arm over my shoulder. At six foot two he towers over me, an attribute he likes to accentuate any chance he can get. "Taking time away from pitching a tent with the hobbits to have some actual fun?"

"Came to give Meredith my best wishes," I say, moving out of his grasp. Digs like this don't hurt me anymore, especially since I discovered that Grant's reading level isn't high enough to comprehend Tolkien.

"Maybe she can give you some fashion advice in exchange," he says, thumbing my shirt.

"Why? Because I can't have my ensemble clash with your Vineyard Vines. What is that, the ultimate douchebag collection?"

The insult slips out of me, my threshold for bullshit at an all-time low tonight.

"Ouch," Adrian shouts, as Grant shoots me a death glare.

"Better than shopping at the lost and found," he shoots back.

"Can you stop ragging on your stepbrother?" Meredith says, coming out of the cabin and taking her place beside Grant, who immediately softens at her presence. "I like Hudson's style. It's hipster librarian chic."

Unlike his usual type of shallow, materialistic, and vapidly dumb hookups, Meredith is down to earth, insanely kind, and enchantingly endearing. And I swear he becomes twenty-five percent less of a dick whenever Meredith is around.

She waits for Grant to apologize, and he mumbles a quiet "Sorry" and refills his beer.

The apology is flat, but it's more than I've ever received from him before, so I take it.

"Hey, are you feeling okay?" Grant asks Meredith, as I take note of her downturned expression.

"Yeah, I'm just stressed. Do you remember how I told you about my great-aunt and uncle?"

"The doomsday preppers from Iowa?" he asks, raising a concerned eyebrow.

"Yeah. They just showed up without warning," she says, reaching for his drink. "I guess they didn't understand how the online RSVP system worked, or they chose to ignore it. Either way they've completely fucked up the room assignments."

"Can't they crash with your grandparents?" Katherine asks, coming up the stairs. Her eyes don't meet mine as she grabs a Solo cup from the table.

"Other side of the family," Meredith explains, nervously playing with the ends of her braids. "I do have an open room for them, but I had it reserved for the photographer."

"We can get the photographer off-site accommodation. You know I have the points, babe," Grant says.

"I know, but she's my friend. And I promised her a good time. Exiling her to another hotel feels like I lied to her and—"

"She can stay in our room," I interject eagerly.

"Really?" Meredith asks, clearly wondering if my suggestion is genuine or merely drunken.

"Why not? We have the bunk beds."

Not to mention that having a buffer between Katherine and me would make this week bearable.

"And you're okay with this?" Meredith asks, turning towards Katherine.

"How can I say no to the bride?" she says sweetly.

"Oh my God, thank you," Meredith squeals, giving my arm a squeeze. "You're saving the wedding!"

"It's my pleasure," I say, patting myself on the back. At least I can get a little space this weekend.

My father raised me to believe that every sunrise brings the promise of a new adventure, but this morning is nothing but agony. My head hurts, and my back is killing me thanks to spending the last six hours sleeping on top of the giant saltine cracker disguised as a mattress.

Slipping out of my bunk bed, I find Katherine starfished in the center of the queen bed, wearing the same clothes she had on last night. Drool pools at the corner of her mouth as she cuddles a pillow with one arm and holds her phone in the other.

The room is already stuffy, the heat of the day creeping in through the windows as I move to close the blinds. Forcing us all here in the middle of a heatwave might not have been on purpose, but it feels on-brand for the torture Grant has subjected me to over the course of our sibling-ship.

At least there is one silver lining to this otherwise agonizing trip, and that's being within driving distance of the Grand Tetons *and* Yellowstone. I'm contemplating which one I want to hit first when I hear a soft knock at the door.

On the other side is Meredith's aunt, Vivianne.

Her wavy, honey-brown hair is long and unkempt, a few braids threaded throughout, and she's dressed in a layered ensemble that rivals one of my grandmother's patchwork quilts. I've only met her once before, at Meredith and Grant's engagement party, but much like her niece, she has a welcoming energy that puts everyone she comes into contact with at ease.

"I'm sorry if I woke you," she says quietly, giving me a once-over.

"Nope, just getting ready to start the day," I say, stifling a yawn.

"You two get in a fight?" she asks, peeking past my shoulder.

"Something like that," I say, closing the door further behind me. "Did you, uh—need something?"

"Oh yes," she says, as if she had already forgotten. "Meredith wanted me to ask you if you could pick up a few people at the airport. She and Grant have a final tasting with the caterer and we're short on cars."

"Sure," I reply, eager for a chance to get off-property. "Let me just get dressed and then I can head out."

"Excellent!" Vivianne says, clapping her hands, causing the metal of her bracelets to clank together. "And, Hudson, you should stop by my cabin later, get yourself a reading. Your energy is very askew since the last time I saw you."

"Is that good or bad?" I chuckle, having absolutely no context for her statement.

"We'll have to find out, won't we?" she replies ominously, heading back down the hall and cornering Grant's uncle about his unaligned chakras.

I go to take a shower but abandon my attempt when I can't get the water to a temperature above freezing. Luckily, Katherine is still asleep when I come out, and I throw on a change of clothes and make the trek to my Jeep. After walking back last night I discovered the only place on the property that has any cell service is the Activity Center, located at the end of the parking lot. Pulling up outside the café, I open my phone and check my messages.

There's a few from my dad, the team in Peru asking for photo approval, and a friendly check-in from Lilah, but none from the name I want to see. Opening the Instagram app, I go straight to Mira's profile, checking for any signs of life.

Her colorful, documentary-style imagery fills my screen. It's easy to understand why people would hire her to capture such an important day. The photos jump off the screen, each still embedded with genuine emotion. Scrolling through is like peering behind an intimate curtain, as she shares stories with the world we'd otherwise never see. I check the date on her latest post and find it's from a few weeks ago and breathe a sigh of relief. At least she's been avoiding everyone, not just me.

I'm about to log off and head to my Jeep when I hear the high-pitched voice of my mother calling for me.

"Hudson, dear, could you come here for a second?"

Her dyed blonde hair is pulled back with a clip, and she steps out of the black SUV dressed in a gray sweatsuit that I'm sure cost more than my entire wardrobe. The trunk is open, bags stacked on top of each other as she waits for me to walk over. She gives me a quick hug as my stepfather lumbers out of the driver's seat. They spent the weekend in Salt Lake, rejuvenating before the wedding as if it were their own.

"Do you mind helping with our bags?" she asks, shoving her sunglasses on top of her head. "George's back isn't what it used to be."

Based on how many hours my stepfather spends on the golf course, I'm certain there is nothing wrong with George's back.

"I'm supposed to pick up a few people from the airport," I argue, not in the mood to play concierge.

"I can go," Adrian offers, popping up beside me. "Vanessa just got in and I'd love to be the one to greet her."

I want to blow him off, but if Mira was the one waiting at the airport, I would want to be the one to pick her up.

I hold out the keys to him. "Bring it back in one piece."

"Will do," he says, snatching them from my hand and sprinting to the Jeep.

"Hudson, please. I need to settle in and shower before dinner. I smell like plane," my mother says, already heading away from the car and towards her room.

Hauling her designer luggage up the hill, I watch enviously as Adrian pulls away from the ranch.

6 MIRA

"This will not be another Phoebe situation," I assure myself, ignoring the in-flight movie I selected to quell my pre-wedding jitters.

Thanks to the last-minute ticket Meredith purchased, I was up at the crack of dawn, and now I'm on a budget airline, squeezed into a middle seat, as the women either side of me argue over whether the book or the TV adaptation of *Outlander* is the superior representation of the story. Swiping Biscoff cookie crumbs off my jeans, I open my phone and familiarize myself with the itinerary Meredith sent me. Unlike other weddings, where I am only expected to show up for my contractually agreed-upon services, Meredith insisted that I be a part of the entire four-day celebration that includes a chartered excursion down the river with a private chef and access to a range of amenities, before the wedding on Friday.

Consider it a vacation, Meredith texted along with an info packet. Participate in whatever activities you'd like, no camera involved.

I tried to tell myself this was a good thing. That I should take time to disconnect, relax, and use this time to figure out if I really wanted to keep being a photographer.

Growing up, I was always the girl with the camera. Snapping shots of my friends at school, of my family members on holidays, and even the occasional self-portrait, determined to immortalize little moments that might have been lost to time or memory. But my love for the craft didn't start until I found a stack of *Life* magazines at my grandparents' house. I began to study the importance of horizon lines. Of how composition and light could make an image could feel muted, yet alive. Glamorous, yet subtle. And how even an otherwise mundane moment of life could be turned into something beautiful.

I won my first photography award during my senior year of high school, after capturing a man feeding the ducks at a local park. I waited hours for that photo, watching the day go by, hoping that I'd catch a perfect moment before it vanished. I'd almost decided to pack up for the day when a man pulled out a bag of breadcrumbs from his pocket and leaned over the bridge that framed the lake. I waited until the sun dipped along the water, a few of the birds mid-flight, and the flutter of breadcrumbs hung in the wind before I clicked my shutter.

And it was at that moment I knew that this was what I wanted to do with the rest of my life.

I had my first gallery showing during my freshman year of college, curating a semester's worth of shots into a cohesive showcase for a local coffee shop. It wasn't fancy. There were no champagne toasts or artists' banquets, but I was allowed to hang my photos on the wall and earn eighty percent of the profits from the sales. I thought the experience would be a stepping stone into fine-art photography, but as I finished straightening the last frame Phoebe came up to me, wild excitement in her eyes. Her presence there that night had been happenstance, coming in to meet with a client. But when the client pointed to my photo of a mother helping her daughter cross the street and said she wanted a similar vision for her wedding photography, Phoebe wasn't one to disappoint.

I explained that weddings weren't really my thing, that I'd never been one of those girls who dreamed of that special day, but after

Phoebe explained how much money I could make in a weekend, I thought why not give it a shot?

Within a few months my calendar was full, my bank account bursting, and I was dropping out of college to work as a full-time photographer. Even though it didn't look exactly as I imagined it, the wedding world was exhilarating. Every couple was different. Every venue was a chance to try something new. I was pushing creative boundaries I didn't know existed. Each booking felt like a high-stakes challenge and I fell in love with the thrill of it. But as the years passed, weddings became predictable, following the same tired patterns, and I could feel myself burning out.

I missed the slow, steady pace of creating art. So when I told Phoebe I wanted to take a step back she said she understood, that she'd help me make the transition out, but I never expected her to expedite my exit by blasting me online.

I sneak a peek out of the window as the flight attendants ensure our seats are ready for landing and the pilot announces our descent into Central Wyoming Regional Airport. The snow-capped Rockies are on full display across the sprawling landscape. The massive mountains are grander than the East Coast ridges I'm accustomed to and although I should be eager to have a new scene to capture, the idea of picking up my camera feels exhausting.

The plane's tires screech against the asphalt, launching my body forward and knocking my head into the hard, plastic monitor. Rubbing the tender spot on my forehead, I unbuckle my seatbelt and turn on my phone. It immediately springs to life, vibrating and beeping aggressively as I check my messages.

Most of them are from Meredith, checking to see if I've landed, if I think sunrise photos would be better than sunset, and if I think the first look could take place in a meadow she's found on AllTrails. The photo she's attached looks magical—a wildflower-covered hillside that, according to the reviews, is only a half-mile walk to the ceremony site. Totally doable in a wedding dress.

Closing the link another message comes in—this one from Hudson.

> Last text I swear. Could you let me know you made it home safe? Please. I'm worried.

I know I should block his number. Cut him from my life completely. But a small part of me can't help but wonder if I'm overreacting. It's totally possible that Hudson's in the middle of a lengthy breakup, or he's non-monogamous. Who knows, maybe the woman in the photograph died and he isn't emotionally ready to part with her things. But the other part of me, the one that's all too aware of how far men will go to take what they want, forces me to put my phone back in my pocket, knowing that it could never just be a one-night thing with him.

I wait for the passengers in front of me to exit before I bend down to dislodge my camera bag from beneath the seat. It takes three tries and an accidental elbow to my seatmate until I'm able to hoist it up onto my shoulders. With multiple cameras, lenses, flashes, batteries, and my emergency kit, the pack weighs nearly fifty pounds. A weight accentuated by the hot, heavy heat coming in through the landing door.

"Ugh," I groan, as the sweltering, stagnant air hits me like a wall.

"Damn heatwave. It came out of nowhere," the lady behind me says, removing her jacket and fanning herself with a magazine. "They say climate change isn't real, but I've been living in Wyoming all my life and I've never dealt with this before."

"How long is it supposed to last?" I ask, hoping they're like a Southeast snowstorm, melted and done with by the end of the day.

"Honey, this one is supposed to last two weeks."

After enduring summer days with ninety percent humidity, I'm sure I can handle some dry heat. Stepping off the plane, I'm quickly humbled. Between the black asphalt, the jet engines, and the blistering sun, I'm legitimately concerned that I might spontaneously combust like an ant under a magnifying glass.

Walking through the smallest airport I've ever seen in my life, I attempt to locate the rental car office, which I discover is across the street, two buildings away. By the time I make it over, there's a pedestrian traffic jam outside the small office. The air inside is as stifling as outside, the only airflow coming from an overworked oscillating fan, its blades caked in a thick layer of dust and grime. I stand there for what feels like an eternity. And by the time I finally get called to the front, my clothes are completely soaked through.

"I have a reservation for Maxwell," I say, pulling up my confirmation email and displaying the modest Hyundai hatchback I chose on the app.

The middle-aged woman, whose name tag reads Evelyn, looks exhausted. Her hair is pulled back in a low bun at the nape of her neck, her striped shirt is wrinkled, and her skin glistens with sweat as she types my name into the computer.

"I see you in the system," she replies, cautiously clicking on her mouse. "But it's not pulling up that vehicle for you."

"That's okay. I'll take anything. I can even drive a manual." The statement is a bald-faced lie, but if it's between that or nothing, I can watch a YouTube video in the parking lot and figure it out. How hard can it be? Men do it.

"Let me see," she says, doing another search.

"Seriously, I'm not picky," I assure her, desperation creeping in. I'll drive a Hummer, a delivery van, anything that will allow me to blast the AC, sit in silence, and stop at the first fast-food establishment I see to feast on fries and a fountain Diet Coke.

"I see the issue now," she says quietly, as if not to alert the customers behind me. "It appears that we are entirely out of cars."

"What?" I shriek, fingers gripping the plastic countertop, trying to glance over at her screen. "How is that possible? I made the reservation yesterday."

"Unfortunately, that just holds you a spot; it doesn't guarantee you a vehicle. With all the tourists coming in for the summer, those online bookings can be dicey. But I assure you, you won't be charged, and any deposits you made will be returned to the card on file," she replies with a smile, as if this will solve all my problems.

"I don't care about the money. I need a car. Please."

"Where are you headed?"

"Majestic Ranch."

She bites her cheek in contemplation. "Best I can do is suggest using an online service, but with the influx of visitors, they've been taking a few hours, and you'll probably have to carpool."

Working in customer service, I know that she has no control over the number of cars on the lot, that stranding me here is not her fault, but I've lost my ability to stay cool, physically and mentally, and I need to get out of here before I have a full-blown meltdown.

"Do you want me to try to check the app for you?"

"I'll figure it out," I snap, rolling my luggage behind me and out the door.

I have no idea where I'm heading, I just need to move, to feel in control of something, as I pull out my phone and open every rideshare app I have. The few accessible dots are already heading away from the airport and the next ride won't be available for at least an hour.

Going to my clients when there's an issue is a professional faux pas, but I don't know what else to do. According to the GPS, I'm almost a hundred miles away from the wedding venue, so walking is out of the question. With no other options, I text Meredith.

Stranded at the airport. No rental cars. Still available to pick me up?

I settle underneath the plastic awning and wait. Hopefully her phone isn't out of range—or worse, on Do Not Disturb. Taking a deep breath, I focus on the gentle breeze rolling in over the hills, the sound of birds chirping in the trees. It's an exercise I've had to use many times on the job, reminding myself that this moment will pass, but today it does nothing to alleviate the ache in my chest that I've made another error in judgment. My throat constricts, that scratchy twinge of restrained tears, as I reach for the water bottle I purchased pre-flight and chug it down. Standing up to throw it in the recycling bin, I hear my name being called across the parking lot.

"Mira?"

A familiar figure jogs over to me, and I take a moment to scan my internal catalog to place her. She's tall and thin, with sandy blonde hair and an approachable smile. "Oh my God, I thought that was you," she says, giving me a hug. Her ears are adorned with dainty gold jewelry in multiple piercings, and a few fine-line tattoos peek out underneath her matching activewear set: a moon, a collection of stars, and a postage stamp. After photographing hundreds of faces over the years, they all start to blend together, but after a beat, I place her.

"Vanessa," I say. "I haven't seen you in ages."

"Not since that freshman-year party where I blasted the same Modest Mouse CD on repeat until the neighbor from upstairs came down and broke it."

"Excellent night," I recall, the memory coming back to me. She lived across from Meredith and me in freshman year, and we spent quite a few nights bingeing *New Girl* and cramming for our chemistry final. "You here for the wedding?"

"You're looking at an official member of the party posse," she replies proudly, holding out her arms as if she's a Miss America contestant.

"Come again?"

"Meredith decided that a wedding party was too formal, so she designated us a 'party posse.' Our job is to keep the party going at all times."

"Please tell her to trademark that. I'm sure she could make a killing on merch," I say, already thinking about the line of rhinestone sweatsuits and sashes she could sell on Etsy.

"I will relay the message," she says, glancing behind me as if looking for someone. "You didn't come by yourself, did you?"

"I don't typically bring dates when I'm working," I reply, as if I'd have one to bring anyways.

"Wait! You're the new photographer," she says excitedly, bouncing on the balls of her feet. "I'm so pumped. I was worried, you know, because sometimes photographers only care about making the bride look good, but you're going to make everyone look fantastic."

"I'll definitely try," I say before glancing down at the rideshare app on my phone that is still searching for a driver.

She stares at my bags beside me. "Are you waiting on a ride?"

"Oh well, I don't know, really . . . my rental didn't pan out, and according to Uber, I'd be better off calling a horse for hire. I texted Meredith, but—"

"The service is shit at the ranch," Vanessa says, cutting me off, "or at least that's what my boyfriend Adrian said. He's over there." She points towards a gangly guy standing next to a bright yellow Jeep, who gives a little wave. "He got in last night."

"You didn't fly in together?"

"Last-minute work thing," she says, with a shrug. "But some of the posse was on my flight. And we may have started the party a little early."

She hands me a mini bottle of tequila from her bag. It's the same brand Hudson and I drank on Monday and the taste of it lingers in my mouth.

"You don't have to shoot it back now, but you never know when you might need a pick-me-up."

"Thanks," I say, slipping the bottle into my bag.

"Look, I know there's not a ton of room," she says, looking towards the Jeep, whose backseat is already crammed with three people, "but if you don't mind riding in the back, we can totally give you a ride."

Taking another glance at my phone, the estimated wait time's gone up an hour.

"I'll take it."

"Yay!" Vanessa squeals, waving over her boyfriend. "Adrian, a little help please?"

He meets us in the middle, picking up my bag effortlessly and placing it in the back. He's taller up close, a little under six feet, his dark hair matching his even darker eyes.

"Thanks, babe," Vanessa says, standing on her tiptoes to give him a kiss on the cheek. They work together, dark and light blending harmoniously, and I wonder if this is how Hudson and I looked all those nights at the bar—opposing elements.

"Who's our new friend?" a mousy brunette asks from the backseat.

"Oh shoot, I didn't realize you didn't know each other," Vanessa says apologetically. "Mira, this is Angie. And that's her girlfriend Jocelyn."

Jocelyn gives me a friendly wave, her jet-black hair short, cutting right at her chin.

"And I'm Derrick," the beefy bodybuilder next to them says, extending his hand for a firm shake.

"Nice to meet y'all," I say, climbing over the tailgate and settling into a bench in the back. The protective covering around the sides of the Jeep has been removed, and I pull a hair tie from my wrist, ready to get wind-whipped. I twist my thick hair into a messy bun on the top of my head and dig into my bag to find my sunscreen. Since I spend most of my time in dark rooms in front of a computer screen, I am hyper-aware of how my sensitive skin reacts to sunlight. From dressing in layers, covering my shoulders, and never going anywhere without at least three different travel-sized sunscreens in a variety of SPFs, I'm well prepared for the next two hours of full sun exposure.

"Oooh, can I have some of that?" Derrick asks, turning towards me, his muscles practically bursting from his shirt.

"I appreciate a man who knows the importance of SPF," I say, handing over the bottle. He squeezes a dollop onto his arm before evenly distributing it over his toned and tanned biceps.

"One of my friends showed me this video of truck drivers who spent like thirty years on the road, and the entire left side of their body was all fucked from sun damage. It haunted me. I want to make sure I stay hot forever."

I'm uncertain if the comments are being made in jest or sincere, but as long as it keeps him from getting melanoma, I consider it a win in his favor.

"Everyone buckled in?" Adrian asks in a thick Irish accent, and slowly inches the Jeep out of the parking spot.

"As best as we can be," Angie says, giving me a sympathetic smile as she holds up her broken seatbelt, as if our situations are similar. At least she has Derrick and Jocelyn keeping her in place. I, on the other hand, only have the strength of my weak forearms and a couple of bungee cords over my shins to protect me from certain death.

The ride is brutal. Between the bumps, the heat, and the whining pop blasting on the radio, I start to believe that I died on that airplane and landed in hell. The only thing grounding me to reality is the view.

Wyoming is so different from the tobacco roads of the Carolinas. It's all true American farmland: bold and beautiful, with wooden fences and hearty cattle. Actual buffalo roam on green and yellow pastures, and picturesque valleys with roaring waters cut through the topography. Fields of wildflowers sprawl down the cliff sides, framing the towering Teton Mountains that are on display. It makes sense why West Coast photographers are always winning so many awards; they never have to make shabby barns look chic.

We drive a few more miles until the dusty roads dissipate, and we're transported into a dense forest. I know we're getting closer to the park when we pass multistory lodges and vacation rental properties around every bend. I stare out into the distance, admiring the way the light streams through the branches, illuminating the forest floor. There's no cell service here, and for the first time in weeks, my phone falls silent. I consider the possibility that taking this job might be just what I need.

The tires kick up gravel as Adrian pulls onto a dirt road, but through the trail of dust behind us I see the hand-painted sign for the "Majestic Ranch and Resort," the letters written in blue paint, faded from years in the sun. The chains holding it up are rusted, and the metal bar it's attached to is bowing under the weight. I hold my breath, waiting for the broken-down stables, crumbling farmhouse, or other unsightly horror that awaits me, but I'm overcome by the beauty of the place.

Six identical cabins sit at the edge of the property, the timber fresh and pungent with the odor of cedar. Burgundy Adirondack chairs and well-strung hammocks are placed around a firepit, and I can't wait to sit and relax with my book as I watch the ducks slowly skimming along the blueish-green pond. In the distance, cattle roam across sprawling green grass speckled with yellow-and-white flowers, and Douglas firs lead the way to the snow-capped mountains sparkling in the distance. It's a view that could sell a thousand postcards, and I resist the urge to take out my camera to capture it.

"You survive back there?" Adrian asks as he hops out of the car, opens the tailgate, and lends me a hand to climb out.

"Still in one piece," I reply, rubbing at the indentations on my shins from the bungee cords that acted as my seatbelt. Hoisting myself up, I grab ahold of the crossbars, tossing one leg over the side to climb out of the back.

"I got you," Derrick says, grabbing me by the waist and setting me onto solid ground. I barely have a moment to acclimate to my surroundings or the fact that a strange man just hoisted me like a rucksack before Meredith's voice is calling for me across the lawn.

"You made it," she squeals, skipping towards us.

She's in a white peasant skirt and matching crochet top, her skin sun-kissed, her honey-soaked hair falling down her back. She looks exactly like she did in college, barefoot and carefree. The only noticeable difference is a thin gold nose ring that glints under the sunlight.

Her arms wrap around me excitedly and I find myself melting into her embrace.

I can't remember the last time I saw her in person. Has it been five years? Or seven? I try to recall as regret pricks my conscience.

Nowadays, our friendship mainly consists of sharing the occasional meme and obligatory "Happy Birthday" text, but I don't hold it against her. Choosing a career that took up my nights and weekends made it practically impossible to hang out with anyone with a normal work schedule. And when the invites stopped coming, I didn't take it personally. So being welcomed with open arms makes me appreciate this trip for what it is: a second chance. And I'm not going to blow it.

"I'm so sorry about the car situation," she says, releasing me from her anaconda-like grip. "I just got your text. Service out here is spotty, but I'm glad these guys were able to scoop you up."

"It's not a problem at all," I assure her as Derrick comes up beside me and swoops Meredith up into his arms. She squeals playfully as he spins her around.

"Anyone up for a whiskey tasting?" Grant asks, pushing open the cabin door and holding up two bottles of liquor, one in each hand.

"Hell yeah," Derrick says enthusiastically, setting Meredith back down on the ground and heading towards the entrance of the cabin. Angie and Jocelyn follow close behind.

"Adrian? Vanessa? A little pre-game before the boat ride?" Meredith asks, taking slow, backwards steps in the direction of her cabin.

Adrian defers to Vanessa.

"I would but I need to settle in," Vanessa says. "It takes me forever to unpack."

"How many suitcases did you bring this time?"

"Only three," she says sweetly.

"You packed light. I'm impressed," Meredith jokes, and I can't help but wonder how many girls' weekends I've missed out on. How many times have I put my career first? And for what? To please Phoebe, to make her proud of me, to prove that my work ethic is just as strong as hers? If only I could have known that it was all for nothing.

"Mira?" Meredith asks, pulling me from my spiral. "Want to relive the glory days with me?"

As much as catching up would be fun, I know better than to let myself blur the line between friend and client again.

"I'm feeling a little jetlagged. Think I'm going to take a quick power nap before tonight," I explain as I watch Meredith's mood deflate. "Is that okay?"

"Yes, yes. Go get settled. But I do want to carve out some girl time for us this weekend. Maybe tonight after dinner?"

"It's a plan," I say, already readying excuses to get out of it as I watch her disappear behind the cabin door.

Realizing I have no idea where to go, I try to spot other lost guests with luggage, but all I see are adventure seekers carrying fishing rods and dragging well-worn kayaks towards a building at the edge of the ranch.

A large, sun-stained sign outside the building reads "ADVENTURE STARTS HERE," a mantra accompanied by a collage of photos showcasing visitors participating in a slew of different wilderness activities. I step inside. Shelves of commemorative water bottles, keychains, and magnets are scattered throughout the space, and a gaggle of children run past me, their sopping-wet swim trunks dripping onto the carpet, as groups huddle around a wall of brochures completely oblivious to the idea of personal space. Caution tape splits the space in half, creating a barrier between the guests and construction workers who are hanging drywall on the other side. A large, laminated banner hangs overhead, depicting renderings of the updated building, proclaiming the mess the "Majestic Ranch Expansion Project."

Between the shrieking of children and the pounding of hammers and drills, I'm overstimulated and eager for my room key.

"Climbing, rafting, or kayaking?" the woman behind the desk asks me, utterly unfazed by the chaos surrounding her. She can't be older than twenty. Her honey-colored hair falls over her shoulders in a messy braid, tendrils sticking out all over the place, and the purple shirt she's wearing has a rainbow on it with the words "Hiking My Way to Happiness."

"Neither," I reply, hoping I'm in the right place. "I'm checking in for the Graham wedding."

"Oh, another one! You guys have been coming in all day." She picks up a clipboard. "What's your name?"

"Mira Maxwell."

She eyes the sheet skeptically, and turns to grab one of the plastic keychains hanging on wooden dowels behind her head.

"You'll be in room seven," she says, handing me my key. "Each room has its own patio, but since yours is on the first floor, we highly suggest locking your door after every entry and exit."

"Stragglers?" I joke, having watched too many true-crime documentaries.

"Bears," she corrects. "With the heatwave they've been exploring a little bit further than usual. We can normally shoo them off before they make it to camp, but it's always good to be vigilant."

I mentally add *Check for bears* to my nightly routine.

"You'll be in the Big Barn, which is about a half a mile down the ranch," she continues, handing me a brochure and a map. "It has its own separate parking lot, so feel free to drive down."

"I don't have a car," I say, a reality that's continually biting me in the ass.

"Oh," she replies, biting her cheek. "Do you have a lot of luggage? We do have a golf cart, but I'll have to radio one of the guides to get it."

"Just the two bags," I say, shuffling the weight of my backpack on my shoulders, a weight that feels ten times heavier as I think about carrying it a half mile.

She presses a button on her walkie-talkie, speaking through the static. "Bo, I have a guest here who needs to go to the Big Barn. You got time? Over."

"Negative on that. On a search and rescue for a missing cell phone. ETA forty-five minutes."

She gives me a sympathetic glance before one of the screaming children knocks over a rack of plastic license plates.

"It's fine," I assure her, backing out towards the exit. "Gotta get my steps in."

"Well, if you need anything, give us a holler," she says cheerily, already bending down to pick up the mess on the floor.

I snag a brochure for the property on my way out, flipping past all the expected upgrades in the coming years to examine the map. The Big Barn isn't that far, barely longer than my daily walk around my neighborhood, but as I take a step forward the wheels of my luggage catch on one of the many minuscule rocks embedded into the dirt path and I regret not waiting for the golf cart.

I've only made it a few feet, dragging the suitcase behind me, when Derrick jogs over from across the lawn.

"You need some help?"

By the size of his biceps, I'm certain Derrick could carry me and my luggage effortlessly across the entire property but asking for help is a short circuit in my customer-service-oriented brain. I'm not the one to have problems, I'm the one who solves them. But as I stare at the path ahead, the sun blazing down on top of me, I give in.

"Would I be an asshole if I said yes?"

"Absolutely not," he says, reaching for my suitcase. The sweet scent of liquor is pungent on his breath as he closes the distance between us. I'm instantly aware of how big he is as I crane my neck to make eye contact.

"Actually," I say, removing the camera bag from my back. "If you could carry this, I can manage the rest."

Considering I only packed four outfits and my toiletries, my luggage is significantly lighter than the gear on my back.

"Why don't I carry both?" he offers, hoisting the bag over one shoulder.

The maneuver is effortless, and I wonder how easily he could toss me over those shoulders. Not that I would ever consider allowing him to do that. After the disastrous night with Hudson, any romantic interests, even casual ones, are off the table for the foreseeable future. Or at least until I'm more confident in my judgment. With my current track record, Derrick is probably a serial killer—or worse, hiding a wife and kids at home.

"How do you know Meredith and Grant?" he asks, as we make our way towards the main building.

"Meredith and I were placed together our freshman year at Appalachian State. Lots of late nights being homesick and drinking too much cheap vodka."

"For me and Grant it was high school baseball camp and Patrón."

"I haven't officially met Grant yet," I confess. "What's he like?"

Unlike other clients who I get to know during engagement photos or pre-wedding Zoom meetings, my only knowledge of the groom has come from an hour of online sleuthing as I waited for my flight. According to his LinkedIn, the only social media account of his I could find, and the snippets Meredith has posted on her Instagram, he's in asset protection at Harding International Finance, was treasurer of his fraternity during his time at UNC, and is a four-time champion of his fantasy football league. Not really a lot to go on.

"Loyal. Hilarious. Smart, way smarter than me," Derrick remarks. "We've been friends for over a decade. He's practically my brother at this point."

"I bet you have quite a few stories you could share then."

"Oh, plenty. But I'm hoping to tell the most embarrassing ones over champagne at the wedding." He laughs with his whole body, and there's a boyish demeanor under his suit of muscles.

"So, you're giving a speech then?"

"Being Grant's oldest friend and all, it's expected," he explains. "I'm sure the girls have theirs all written out, but I'm planning on winging it."

"You totally should," I reply a little too enthusiastically.

Drunken toasts are one of my guilty pleasures. Listening to judgmental fathers, weepy best friends, and plastered groomsmen tell inappropriate and explicit stories in front of family members makes eight hours of surviving on appetizers worth it. The experience is like being in a reality TV show where the characters change but the secondhand embarrassment always hits.

"Just don't drop the mic. I've seen my fair share of them shatter. And the subsequent tears that come with the fifteen-hundred-dollar replacement fee is not worth the one second of cool you think it embodies."

"Eh, probably won't even use one."

"Really?"

"My voice carries," he says, projecting into the nothingness ahead of us.

"Theater kid?"

He lifts a *you've got to be kidding* eyebrow at me.

"Fire department," he retorts. "In my line of work, speaking up is a necessity. You have to be able to warn your coworkers about structural issues or falling debris, and I'm proud to say I've never needed the megaphone once."

I imagine Derrick putting on one of the red plastic hats they hand out in elementary school on fire safety day and committing to the bit. We fill the rest of the walk with mindless chatter, discussing his adult kickball league and my favorite wedding destinations.

Derrick sets my things down on a picnic table in front of the Big Barn, the red paint of the building a facade of rustic charm.

"Thanks for the help," I say, eager to go inside and take a nap.

"Anytime," he replies, running a hand through his hair. His movement is slow, an obvious attempt to show off his muscles, as if the half-shirt he's wearing is leaving anything to the imagination. "And if you need anything else, an extra towel, a helping hand, I'm right upstairs, in room fifteen."

He grins cheekily and I don't know whether to be appalled or impressed by his audacity.

"I'll make note of that."

Derrick gives me a lingering glance before jogging up the side staircase and, finally, I'm alone.

7 HUDSON

"Guess there's a reason they call this the dust bowl," my mother says, running her finger along the windowsill.

"It's probably from the renovations," I assure her. "Stuff like that settles."

"If they call these renovations, I shudder to think of what they looked like before," she says, plucking the bottle of wine from the welcome basket on the wooden countertop. She's only been here for fifteen minutes. Her list of complaints is lengthy.

The drive was too long. The cabins are too homely. The linens are too threadbare. The western air is too dry. And considering George went straight upstairs to bed, I have a feeling her nagging started a lot earlier.

Thank God the bottle in her hand is a twist top, because finding a corkscrew might throw her over the edge.

My mother, or "Susan," as she prefers to be called, has grown accustomed to a certain level of comfort, one that rivals the Kardashians', thanks to my stepfather's business acumen and position as one of the top financial advisors at his company. And even though they've been given the largest cabin on the property, it still isn't up to her standards. Just another thing to add to the ever-growing list of resentments towards her future daughter-in-law.

"I just don't understand why we had to fly across the country when we have a beautiful club back home?" she asks, pouring a generous helping of wine into her glass.

In her mind she expected Grant to get married in a bougie, black-tie event at the Grand Bohemian in Charlotte, with three hundred guests, lavish florals, a towering three-tier cake, and all her closest friends fawning over it in jealousy. Having to attend a forty-person affair in the middle of a national park, among the tourists, was never in her realm of possibilities.

"Because it's what they want, and it's their wedding?" I clarify.

"Grant only thinks this is what he wants because that woman's brainwashed him with her hippy-dippy nonsense," she argues.

For the record, *hippy-dippy nonsense* is socialite speak for Meredith being a massage therapist and holistic healer. Sure, she might pay attention to the phases of the moon a little too closely and try to explain our behaviors based on our birth charts, but my mother acts as if she's one step away from becoming a Manson Girl, convincing Grant to forfeit his inheritance to a mystical guru.

My mother takes a sip of her wine and grimaces, grabbing the bottle to inspect the label.

From the cheap graphics, I'm certain that this variety must be closer to Two-Buck Chuck than the aged merlot she's accustomed to, but it doesn't stop her from chugging half the glass.

"You know we offered to pay for the wedding? Unlimited budget. But no," she gripes. "She has to be one with nature, whatever the hell that means."

Thanks to the very long and very loud FaceTime sessions Katherine and Meredith shared, I already knew about my mother's offer. I also knew that Meredith turned her down, making me respect her even more. Coming from a single-income home, living with her aunt after her parents' deaths, Meredith doesn't care about money. She's never abused the lifestyle Grant has offered her and, if anything, being together has made Grant more aware of his privilege, forcing him to do something good with it. When I heard that she got him to donate to the Humane Society and help out at one of the local Food Not Bombs fundraisers, I was genuinely shocked.

My mother taps her long plastic nails against the counter, distraught. "I just want the best for my youngest boy. Is that so wrong?"

"I know," I say, gritting my teeth. Although Grant isn't hers, she's given him more care and compassion than she ever awarded me. At first, I thought her overly doting mother act was an attempt to fill the hole that was left after Grant's mom died of cancer when he was nine, but watching her flaunt him around the club as the perfect son, I realized he was just another symbol of her newfound status. And I was an outdated model she wanted to separate herself from.

"Just know when you and Katherine get married, we'll do it right," she states. "That girl, she'll love my ideas."

I stiffen at the thought.

Susan adored Katherine from the moment I introduced them, fawning over her as if she were the Duchess of Sussex. From brunching together to shopping sprees and monthly dinner invites at the lake house, my mother and Katherine became instant friends. To Susan, Katherine was everything that Susan would want in a daughter-in-law: natural beauty, an appreciation for designer goods, and a penchant for kiss-assery that I could never achieve even if my life depended on it. The only plus side to their close-knit relationship was the fact that my mother started to pay attention to me. She checked in more often, sent gifts I actually appreciated on my birthday, and started including us in family vacations.

I knew better than to start treating her like a real mom, but when we accompanied the family to Aspen for the holidays I started to believe that Susan had actually changed. Sitting around the fireplace, drinking whiskey, opening gifts, and eating cookies as a family was comforting in a way I'd never expected. And I found myself absorbing her adoration like a body with a vitamin deficiency. And I was certain that as soon as she found out Katherine and I were broken up, she'd revert back to the cold, distant mother of my youth.

"You two have been together, what, three years now?" she asks, taking another gulp of wine. "That's twice as long as I was with George."

I refrain from pointing out that she's omitting the two years of overlap between him and my father as I pour my own glass of wine. The taste is sour, and I swallow it back.

"I can block off a weekend in December at the club for an engagement party," she says, her expression giddy. "That would give us plenty of time to plan a fall wedding. Can you imagine the foliage up at the Biltmore?"

Clearing my throat, I try to think of anything to change the topic—the fall J.Crew catalog, George's new boat, how Martha's Vineyard is overrated, but before I can say anything, Adrian barges in, saving me.

"Sorry," he says, realizing he didn't knock. "Meredith told me you were in here."

"No worries, man," I say, out of my chair and across the room faster than he can blink. "Bring it back in one piece?"

"And with a full tank of gas," he states proudly, handing over the keys.

"Great. I've been itching to go to the park."

"Do you think that's wise?" my mother asks, her judgmental glare cutting me from across the room.

"There's plenty of time for me to go get a quick hike in," I lie, hoping to use the lack of service as an excuse to get out of this afternoon's activities.

"Hudson," she says, her voice dripping with condescension. "I'm not having you show up to dinner covered in dirt and wearing hiking boots. Especially after Meredith's been gushing about the new photographer she's flown in. Apparently, they're better than the original one they hired, which makes no sense because I don't know how one doesn't hire the best to begin with," she says, finishing off her glass. "Nevertheless, if these are the only family photos I will get before that woman takes Grant away from us, you will be in there."

"They're moving to Asheville, not Alaska," I argue, reiterating the fact that it's only a two-hour drive from Charlotte. But Susan has been sensitive about it since Grant made the announcement at our last family dinner.

"Just be at the boat at four o'clock sharp," she warns, as if I'm not the most punctual member of the family.

Accepting my fate of being stuck at the ranch, I turn to Adrian. "In that case, can I use your shower? My hot water is on the fritz."

"Please tell me you're joking?" my mother interjects, digging through her bag to retrieve her phone. "I'm calling my travel agent to move everyone over to a better facility. How are we expected to look our best if there's not even running water?"

"The water runs," I correct, silently praying that she finds new accommodation—far, far away.

"I got you, man," Adrian replies, giving me a sympathetic smile as I follow him out the door and into the blazing heat.

"Thank you for the save," I say, thankful to be out of that room. "I swear Susan has this uncanny ability to suck all the air out of a room. The joy too."

"My mom can be that way," Adrian says. "You should have seen her when I brought Vanessa home. A non-Catholic American girl. I thought she was going to have a heart attack."

"Unfortunately, my mom likes Katherine too much."

"Is that a bad thing?" he asks, seriously.

"In my case, yes."

8 MIRA

The lobby is thick with the scent of artificial pine as I roll my luggage across the birch-colored laminate. Rows of doors line the hallway, separated by well-worn couches and threadbare rugs that must have been purchased in the nineties from the looks of their outdated patterns. Muffled conversation permeates through the thin walls as I pick up my pace, in no mood for more unnecessary small talk.

Locating my room, I insert the key and turn it, only to be instantly assaulted by a pungent wave of floral perfume. The artificial, chemical stench is nauseating as I set my bag down to open a window. Besides the queen-size bed in the middle of the room, there are two end tables, a dresser, and a set of wooden bunk beds pressed against the far wall. If they added a handful of knick-knacks, this place would look more like an antique mall than a hotel.

Pushing back the green-and-gold dust-covered curtains, I unlatch the lock on the window and attempt to glide it open but the glass doesn't budge. I try again, moving the lock in the opposite direction. Still nothing. It isn't until I notice the white chips breaking off onto the windowsill that I understand the issue. The window is painted shut.

Great. Not only is my room slowly poisoning me to death, but it's also a fire hazard. Scooting around the bed, I unlock the patio door, throwing it open. Bears be damned. But I'm offered no relief, as the heat combines with the fumes, creating a tear-gas-like stench that ignites a coughing fit.

I bump a nightstand and send something crashing to the floor. From the clamor I expect a remote or cordless phone, but I find a toiletry bag lying open at my feet. Bending down to retrieve it, I'm overcome by the faint scent of rain, Hudson's scent, and I'm dizzy with raw emotion.

Bad clients, bad haircuts, I always let it go, I move on. I put it behind me, I buy a hat, but I'm still hung up on this. Maybe I just need to give it more time. Maybe it's because I'm so fresh off my fight with Phoebe. But a small part of me wonders if maybe I deserve this. Maybe this is punishment for getting too close. For letting my guard down. For not anticipating every outcome, even the ones I didn't know to look for.

Collecting the items from the floor, I place them back in the bag, setting them on the nightstand to bring to the Activity Center's lost and found later this afternoon. Eager to unpack, I lift my suitcase up onto the bed, and catch sight of a neon-pink garment bag hanging in the closet, a set of two purple suitcases resting underneath.

I navigate through the Tetris-like decor to inspect it. It's one thing to forget makeup, but there's no way anyone left their luggage here by accident. I go over to inspect them, seeing a name I don't recognize on the tags. Katherine Moore. And then it hits me. This isn't my room.

Of course the girl at the front desk gave me the wrong key.

How is she supposed to focus on her job in that overstimulation station?

Tamping down my irritation at making another trek across the property, I grab my luggage and reach for the door, but the handle twists underneath my fingers, giving me only a moment to move out of the way before Hudson Hayes pushes inside, almost falling on top of me.

The alliteration of his name is stuck in my brain in the same way I memorized the feeling of his mouth against mine, and I take another step back. The scruff against his cheeks I've come to love is gone, and his hair is wet and unruly, the soft curls that nestle at his nape starting to form as water droplets fall down his neck and freckle-covered shoulders. My eyeline trails down his torso to the towel around his waist and I realize he's practically naked. This is a scenario I've only conjured up alone, in my bed, with my favorite vibrator—definitely not one I imagined actually living through after our disastrous hookup—and the sight makes me unsteady.

"What are you doing here?" I ask, my voice dripping with disdain.

"I'm in the wedding party."

"If you're in the wedding party, shouldn't you be in one of the cabins up front and not skulking around the common areas half-naked?"

I'm used to the unexpected: a sudden rainstorm on a sunny day, a bridesmaid passing out in the middle of a wedding ceremony, but Hudson Hayes standing in front of me feels like a cosmic joke.

Hudson runs his hands through his hair, and in the daylight, I'm able to take in all the things I missed in the darkness. The broadness of his shoulders, the delicately placed freckles along his collarbone, the dusting of hair along his abdomen. There are also a few tattoos I had no idea were hiding underneath all those layers: a line of foreign script I can't quite make out on his chest, and a broken sword sitting on his ribs.

"My shower is broken and . . ." He trails off before focusing his attention on me. "Wait, what are *you* doing here?"

"I'm the photographer," I reply, unsure of it myself.

"*You're* the last-minute replacement?" he states, in a combination of bewilderment and delight.

"Is that an issue?"

He shakes his head. "No. I, uh . . . I just need to put some clothes on," he says, grabbing a few things from his bag on the bottom bunk. "Give me one sec, okay?"

I should bolt. I should run straight out of the door and up the hill and hitch a ride back to the airport because this is a sign. A glowing neon light in the darkness telling me that I should not be here. I should let my career die. I should sell my cameras and start a new life as a truck driver or lighthouse keeper. Something where I never have to deal with people ever again. But instead, I give him a nod, as he steps into the bathroom.

When he comes out, he's in a pair of forest-green shorts and a cream-colored tee.

"For the record, I didn't know you were in here. I think the girl at the front desk gave me the wrong key. Then again, they don't seem like the type that runs a tight ship?" I say, rechecking the plastic keyring in my hand to have something to concentrate on other than the fact that I've found myself in a fucked-up, parasocial episode of *The Twilight Zone*.

"I'm surprised they didn't give me the key to the equipment shed," he says, giving his hair a quick dry with a towel. His green eyes soften as they meet mine, and I'm right back where I was two nights ago, falling for him behind the bar.

"I was worried, you know, when you didn't answer my texts. I thought something might have happened. That you were hurt or I hurt you."

There's a gentleness to his voice that makes hope pool in my chest.

There's no way this man—the one who made me laugh at the bar, who sat next to me almost every night, who kissed me like I was the only girl in the world—there's no way he could be a cheater.

"I shouldn't have ignored you. I thought . . ."

"I know what you thought," he says, taking a step towards me, his thumb gliding against the inside of my wrist.

My eyes linger on a purplish bruise against his collarbone, and when Hudson catches me staring, a redness creeps up his neck towards his ears. Did I leave that there?

I'm not one to mark my conquests, but that is definitely a hickey. I feel self-conscious about it until my embarrassment quickly turns to panic. His girlfriend must have asked what happened, right? It's not like he could use the excuse that he burned himself on a hair straightener. And that's when I remember the bags in the closet, the ones with a woman's name on them. And my stomach lurches.

He's here with her.

As if I conjured her with my mind, the door bursts open, and Hudson catapults away from me faster than a cat in water, as the brunette from the photos breezes into the room. She's more beautiful in person. Her slim figure is accentuated by a purple sports bra and matching shorts that hug her sculpted curves. Her tan skin is flawless, not a pore in sight, and I wish I'd taken an inventory of the balms and lotions in her makeup bag to replicate the look.

"Who do we have here?" she asks, eyeing me skeptically.

"Katherine, this is Mira," Hudson says, introducing us. The words come out straightforward and monotone. Like he's answering a math problem instead of introducing the woman he cheated on to the one he cheated with, and I'm unsettled. How could he be calm in this situation? Does he have no shame? No remorse? Is he one of those emotionless sociopaths that I've read about who have multiple families without ever worrying that they'll find out?

I try to keep my face neutral, hoping she can't read the guilt that's etched across it. I'd take overbearing mothers, bitchy bridesmaids, and a frat house full of drunk groomsmen over dealing with this right now. But confronting this woman makes me panic, tying my stomach into tight knots, and I'm right back to Phoebe's wedding day.

"The photographer," Hudson clarifies.

"Oh," she says, assessing me as if I'm a pony on parade; one that's one bad day away from greener pastures. Although she must have spent the last few hours in the sun, there's a light floral scent on her skin and I wonder if it's a product of dry shampoo, sunscreen, or if she naturally expels scented sweat. I mean, she does seem like the kind of woman who would be on the ground floor of investing in that type of technology.

"I was explaining that they must have made a mistake at the front desk," I mumble, trying to shuffle around her to initiate a speedy exit. "I'm on my way to fix it now."

"Oh, no mistake," she chirps. "You're rooming with us."

Her words are muffled in my ears. Playing nice with guests when I'm on duty is one thing, but being forced to room with them, especially after I hooked up with one only a couple of days before, is another. The situation is so absurd I bet I could pitch it to the producers of *Survivor*. I'm sure by the end of the week, contestants would vote themselves off the island to get away from the awkwardness.

She beams with fake enthusiasm. "Hudson here volunteered you to stay in our room, isn't that right, sweetie?"

I glance at Hudson for confirmation, and his expression is just as pained as mine.

As an avid proponent of girl-on-girl loyalty, part of me wants to confess that her boyfriend is potentially a lying, cheating scumbag, but having a face-to-face confrontation, when we have to spend the weekend together, feels like an extreme sport I have no interest in playing. Perhaps I could slip a nicely worded, anonymous note into her luggage before we leave. That seems safe.

"Oh, um . . . I don't want to intrude." The words come out too quickly, and as I back away from them, my calf bumps against the dresser. Seriously, who designed this room?

"It's no problem, really," she assures me, nestling into Hudson's neck. "We'll make sure to keep the PDA at a minimum."

Hudson doesn't reciprocate her affection, stepping away from her as his eyes stay laser-focused on me. I'm sure he's trying to communicate with me telepathically, to plead not to rat him out. But I can't concentrate on him, or her, or anything but the floor, as a sudden wave of claustrophobia washes over me. The room's too small, the air too fragrant, and I'm back in that groomsmen suite all over again. The weight of the smooth metal cufflinks in my hand, the scent of Cliff's cologne, and the sound of Phoebe's voice reverberating off the marble walls. I must look as if I'm having a stroke, because when I come to, Katherine is staring at me and Hudson's hand is lightly pressed against my forearm.

The steady evergreen of his eyes finds mine, a color I could pick out of any palette, as he asks, "Are you okay?"

But I haven't been okay since Phoebe's wedding.

"I think I just need some air," I say, pushing past him.

"Feel free to take your gift bag on the way out," Katherine says, pointing to the blue bag resting on the desk. My name is written in silver lettering on the outside, and I snatch it up and head out the door.

9 HUDSON

Every muscle in my body wants to run after Mira. To scream, "*This isn't what it looks like.*" But I know better than to show my hand to Katherine. After last night's declaration, I'm certain that if she gets wind that something is going on between Mira and me, she'll do everything she can to ruin it. No, it's better to bide my time, approach Mira when we can be alone and talk this through. Because she's here, in Wyoming, staying in my room.

"Well, that was weird," Katherine says, opening the closet and laying out dresses on the bed.

"You're the one who made it weird with that PDA comment," I argue, trying to keep my voice steady. "Making it sound as if we have to restrain ourselves all weekend."

"I always have to restrain myself around you," she purrs, stripping off her top.

Instinctively, I turn my back to her. "Can you change in the bathroom please?"

"It's not like you haven't seen it before."

"But our guest hasn't. What if Mira walked back in here?" I say, in an attempt to utilize a few of the principles I read up on to prep for my upcoming position. *Be firm. Stay vigilant. Create boundaries.*

"Jeez. Lighten up." There's annoyance in her voice as she walks across the room, removing a garment bag out of the closet and tossing it onto the bed. "Your mom wants you to wear this tonight."

I keep my back to her as I unzip the bag. Inside is a long-sleeved shirt, brown suit jacket, and matching pants. It's exactly the type of outfit Susan used to put me in for grade school photos. While everyone else was wearing dinosaur t-shirts, I looked like a Baby Brooks Brothers campaign.

"I'm not wearing that," I argue.

Besides the fact that it's going to be over a hundred degrees, we're having dinner on a boat, not at a Michelin-star restaurant.

"I don't care what you wear," she sneers, "but do you really want Susan on your back?"

Considering my mother is one of the main reasons I agreed to this fake-dating ruse in the first place, not going along with her predetermined, color-coordinated outfits will only draw more attention to our lie. And then I remember that the only reason I am supposed to wear this stupid fucking outfit is so Susan can have family photos. Photos I'm going to have to smile and pose in, in front of Mira.

So much for waiting it out. I need to talk to her now. To explain the situation. But Katherine blocks my exit, her back exposed as a yellow dress hangs against her shoulders.

"Zip please," she orders, her sharp blue eyes piercing me as she glances over her shoulder. But serving Katherine isn't my job anymore.

"Do it yourself," I say, and open the door to go find Mira.

I do a full sweep of the Big Barn and the outdoor patios before making my way up to the main cabins, but there's no sight of her. I consider the real possibility that she left. That she went straight to Meredith and quit. That my inability to have hard conversations has not only fucked up my chance of happiness but made Mira lose out on a gig. I'm riddled with guilt as Meredith calls for me from her perch on the porch.

"Hey, stranger," she shouts, waving me over. "I'm still trying to get rid of some of this whiskey if you want a drink."

"I'm sticking to water today," I reply, my body still processing all the liquor from this week.

"Lightweight," she jabs as I crane my neck to survey the front lawn.

"You looking for someone?"

"Uh, Mira actually. You haven't seen her around, have you?"

Meredith shakes her head. "Why? Is everything okay?"

"Oh, yeah. Just wanted to let her know she left her key."

I hold up my own keychain, dangling it for effect.

"How did she take the room change? I meant to tell her, but with everything going on I got sidetracked."

"She's all settled in," I lie, guilt prickling against my skin.

This is all my fault. I should have told her about Katherine ages ago. And I should have never volunteered her to stay in my room.

Since my quick thinking got me into this mess, maybe it can get me out. "Do you think I could take a peek at your wedding binder?" I ask, hoping that there might be a willing party that would switch with Mira.

Meredith's eyebrows arch and she crosses her arms defensively. "If this request is coming from your mother, you can assure her that I have no intention of creating a seating chart, no matter how many times she insists that it helps the flow of the room or whatever."

"I'm here on my own accord. I swear." I hold up my hand against my chest as if taking an oath. Meredith stares at me quizzically, determining if I'm to be trusted. And I hate that after losing her parents, Susan is the mother-in-law she is inheriting.

"It's upstairs in our room, on the dresser."

"Thanks, Mere," I say, giving her shoulder a grateful squeeze as I pass by her and into the cabin.

I find the wedding binder exactly where she said. The contents are a disorganized mess. Illustrated drawings of bouquets are stuck between menu options and maps for hiking trails. Magazine clippings of dresses are glued onto cardstock and extra invitations are stuffed into a plastic sleeve.

I pass a section about the proper permits for the wedding ceremony at the Tetons and see that their application date is from two weeks ago. After working alongside the National Parks Service most of my life, I'm very aware that it can take months to get documents like this processed. Without a proper permit, they could be denied entry, fined, or face federal charges. Considering I do not see the actual permit number listed, I make a mental note to call in a favor to expedite the process.

Flipping to the next page I find the room assignments. Not only is every room accounted for, but every couch, futon, and cot is taken up by a cousin or a plus-one. There really is nowhere to move Mira. I've just set the binder down when Grant barges in, doing a double take when he finds me sitting at the vanity.

"Looking for makeup tips or considering a career in wedding planning?" he jabs, and I can't believe there was a time in my life when I actually wanted a brother.

"Trying to keep Susan off your back," I argue, knowing that is the one thing we can agree on.

"She's already pissed off the staff," Grant says, rummaging through the closet. "I swear if she racks up extra charges I'm sending her the bill."

"As if your dad wouldn't pay for it."

Unlike my own father, who made me work for everything, George has been using his Black Card to fix Grant's problems for as long as I can remember, facilitating his inability to grow up.

"Katherine said you were being an asshole lately, but I really see it now."

"Better than being one my whole life," I snipe back, irritated that Katherine would run off and complain about me, when she's the one who wants to pretend that everything is perfect between us.

I'm already plotting an over-the-top breakup scene on the boat when Meredith rushes into the room.

"Babe," she says, frazzled, "your mom is blowing up my phone."

She holds out the screen towards the both of us as paragraph-long messages come in one after the other.

"She's demanding to give a toast at the wedding, since she wasn't asked to do it at the rehearsal," Meredith sighs, taking a seat on the bed. "This is ridiculous. No one is speaking at the wedding. That's why we decided to do it at the rehearsal. I just wanted our day to be fun, no pressure. Now I don't even know what to say."

"It doesn't matter what you say," Grant says, slipping on a pair of leather loafers. "Susan's going to do what she wants either way; all you can do is go along with it." He hands her a bottle of huckleberry vodka from the dresser. "My advice, have a drink and try not to think about it."

I watch as she unscrews the cap and takes a swig directly from the bottle before handing it over to me.

If my problems could be dulled so easily, I'd drink the whole bottle, but blowing off steam for me involves disappearing into the wilderness for a few days with nothing but my backpack and a map. But even the best trails in the world can't assuage my fear that Mira may never speak to me again.

10 MIRA

In this job, I can grit my teeth and bear a lot of things: eating on the floor sans utensils, being asked to cut the cake for a hundred guests because they couldn't afford to hire a caterer, being treated like an errand girl as I rush tissues or ring boxes or double-sided tape from one side of a venue to another, but sleeping in the same room as Hudson and *his girlfriend* is where I draw the line.

There has to be an alternative option. A hammock, or a neighboring property with an Airstream? I'd even be willing to befriend the bears and spend the rest of the week eating porridge in the woods, if it meant I didn't have to go back to that room. But it's not like I can just leave. I don't have a car.

I could try rideshare again once I've found a new place to stay, but with spotty service and the height-of-tourist-season wait times, it'd be risky. But it has to be worth a try, right?

Digging out the brochure from my back pocket, I open the Wi-Fi network and type in the password, chuckling to myself. BESTVACATIONEVER! More like PAYINGFORMYTHERAPISTSSUMMERHOME123. I wait for several minutes, refreshing my browser until I determine that the network is non-functional.

That familiar ache pulses in my chest as I clutch my phone in my hand, ignoring the urge to call Phoebe. For the past seven years she's been my go-to person, my emergency contact, the one to talk me off more ledges than I care to count, and I know that with all her connections she would find a way to get me out of this mess, even if meant driving all the way from North Carolina to come save me. But now I can't even think about her without inducing a panic attack.

Staring up at the second-floor balcony I remember Derrick's open-door policy. I'm sure I wouldn't have to try too hard to persuade him to give up his bed for the evening. But before desperation can take hold, I hear Vanessa shouting my name.

She's leaning over the railing above, waving at me. "Help! I have a fashion emergency," she declares as I bound up the stairs, eager for something to do.

She's wearing a lilac romper, her hair pulled back to display long gold earrings that shimmer in the sunlight, as she turns her back to me.

"Do you see that eyelet at the top? Can you attach it to the hook? I asked Adrian to do it but he said he couldn't find it. Honestly, I doubt he knows what I'm even talking about," she explains, bouncing from one foot to the other with a frantic energy. "I wouldn't care so much but this zipper is notoriously slippery. And the last thing I want is to be topless in the middle of dinner."

"I got you," I say, hooking the little piece of metal over its delicate strap.

"Ahh! Thank you," she breathes, turning around to smooth out the fabric. With a low neckline and a cinched waist, the outfit flatters her tall frame. "Do you think it's too much?"

The self-conscious assessment makes me remember the Vanessa I knew in college, the one who only wore oversized t-shirts and biker shorts every day. I'm happy that she's let herself shine more as she's gotten older.

"It's chic and classy. I love it."

"And what about the shoes?" she says, showing off white Adidas. "I really wish Meredith would have sent clothing restrictions ahead of time. She's lucky I never travel with less than four pairs."

"There are clothing restrictions?"

"Did you not see the updated itinerary in your welcome bag?"

"I haven't looked," I reply honestly. Besides dealing with my uncomfortable roommate situation, I haven't had time to pay attention to anything else.

"Here," she says, handing me a folded piece of paper from her pocket.

> 4 p.m.: Board transport for the River Cruise, with a docked dinner to follow. All Guests Must Wear closed-toe shoes, in accordance with the captain's rules.

I knock together my chunky Doc Martens. "Good thing I packed my boots."

Vanessa stares at me with a look of concern and contemplation. "Don't take this the wrong way, but is that what you're wearing to dinner?"

I'm in the same clothes I wore on the plane: black jeans and a plain black shirt. My hair is in a sloppy bun on top of my head, and I'm makeup-less. Definitely not dinner-ready. But considering everything in my suitcase is a variation of this same outfit, my appearance isn't going to change much.

"What's wrong with it?"

"It's a hundred degrees outside. And you're wearing all black."

"It's standard photographer attire."

Although Phoebe tried to convince me to wear fancy dresses or pressed slacks to weddings, they were completely impractical for my style of photography. Between crawling on the ground, kneeling in the grass, and scooting around on dusty floors, I was spending an astronomical amount on dry cleaning. Switching to a more casual look allowed me to fit in with the other staff members and it was a hell of a lot cheaper.

"But are you working tonight?"

"Not technically, no."

"Then let's find you something else to wear," she says, grabbing my hand and pulling me down the veranda to her room. Adrian is sitting on one of the two twin-size mattresses watching an eighties movie on the TV.

"This is cozy," I say, considering what it would take to let me commandeer one of her mattresses.

"That's one word for it," Vanessa quips, scooping up a pile of clothes from the open suitcases on the floor and dumping them on the bed. "I've stayed in hostels bigger than this."

"It wouldn't be so bad if we didn't have to share with Angie and Jocelyn," Adrian says. I try to hide my disappointment. "And those two snore."

Well, there goes that idea.

"I got saddled with a bunk bed, if you want to trade." I try to make the option sound appealing, but as I hear it escape my lips, it comes out more like a timeshare opportunity.

"Vanessa doesn't do heights. Isn't that right?"

"I'm fine with heights. They don't like me," Vanessa counters.

"You can take the bottom bunk then," I say, crossing my fingers. She contemplates it for a moment, before shaking her head.

"It would take me forever to repack, plus Adrian shouldn't really be climbing up and down stairs to go to bed. He has a bad back."

"It's a rugby injury," he clarifies. "Stop making me sound like I'm an eighty-year-old man with sciatica."

"You're the one who brings it up."

"I complained about it one time. When you made me sleep on the floor, which was completely made of rock, I'd like to add."

Vanessa waves her hand, dismissing him, and I can't help but find it cute, the way they bicker like an old married couple.

"Here, try this on," Vanessa orders, shoving an outfit into my arms. There's a silky green top and a pair of khaki dress shorts—definitely not my vibe or color palette but I can tell they're expensive by the feel of the fabric.

"I couldn't," I argue.

"Please. I'm a notorious over-packer."

"It's true," Adrian adds. "I don't think we've gone anywhere without her bringing multiple bags even for overnight trips."

"It's called having options," Vanessa clarifies.

"I'm glad you don't have that outlook on boyfriends."

"Luckily you never go out of season," she replies, ushering me towards their bathroom. "Go try it on. I want to see."

"I'm pretty gross right now," I say, not wanting to soil her clothes if they don't fit. "I should probably shower first."

"Use ours," she offers. "Everyone else seems to be."

Not having to go back to my room feels like a gift from the universe, but I also don't want to overstep. "You sure that's not weird?"

"How many times did I vomit in your trash can in college?"

"A few," I chuckle, thinking back to those college nights.

"Exactly, so I think it's totally fair for you to use my shower. Just be sure you're wearing that outfit when you come out."

Giving in, I go inside and take a minute to appreciate how easy it is to pick up where we left off.

I spend seven glorious minutes ridding myself of the grime, sweat, and emotional damage with Vanessa's travel-sized gels and conditioners. Freshly scrubbed and scented and wearing her clothes, I step out of the bathroom feeling like a completely new woman.

The silky top is cool against my skin and the shorts are breezy and lightweight. I want to live in this outfit for the rest of the week.

"It's perfect," Vanessa coos, giving me a once-over.

"You were right. This is so much better than jeans."

"And that's why I packed you a few other things too," she says, handing me a tote bag full of clothes. "This should get you through the rest of the week."

"This is too much."

"It's nothing," Vanessa says, coming over to pull the tag off the top. "Perks of having two sisters. Anything they forget to return they pass along to me. I'm glad to see it get worn."

"Well, I appreciate it."

"No worries. Now, let's go eat."

11 MIRA

The Activity Center is bustling with people. Wedding guests and tourists mill about, creating a hodgepodge of dry-clean-only attire and neon-colored nylon. Most of Meredith and Grant's guests are taking refuge under the café awning, antsy to get to our destination.

Vanessa and Adrian are finishing up the story of how they met in Ireland. Their comments are perfectly timed as they recount their adorable meet-cute, before they turn their attention to me.

"Are you dating anyone?"

"Uh," I stutter. "The dating pool is pretty shallow right now," I say, hoping that will shut down this line of questioning. Besides the Hudson fiasco, the last few dates I've been on crashed and burned—yet another reminder that I need to get my own life together before I bring anyone else into it.

"At least you have this amazing career, though," Vanessa says, trying to lift my spirits. "I can't believe the last time we saw each other, you were prepping for a gallery opening, and now you're this big-time photographer, traveling the world, capturing love stories."

Instead of enlightening them on how it's also working on demand, surviving eight-hour workdays on a slice of cake, and staring at the computer so long you develop an astigmatism, I just nod politely.

“I get that safety is important, but these shoes do not go with my ensemble,” Katherine gripes to Hudson as she stomps down the stairs. The shoes in question are two-hundred-dollar Golden Gooses that still give her a chic New York commuter look. They’re paired with a marigold sundress that clings to her hips and accentuates her long legs and toned arms. Two yellow bows are attached to the shoulders and cascade down her body. She looks like she’s in one of those over-the-top perfume commercials.

Hudson trails a few paces behind her, looking uncomfortable in a white button-down shirt and brown slacks, a matching jacket hung over his arm. The perpetual smile I’ve grown accustomed to has been replaced by a tight, hard line.

I’ve seen Hudson calm down heated arguments, charm tears away from emotional drinkers, and put himself in the line of fire of many a birthday boy or girl who wanted to do a belly shot. But I’ve never seen him this reserved.

I try to hide behind Vanessa and Adrian, but Katherine beelines for our group. She gives Vanessa a few air kisses and doles out compliments.

“You look amazing.”

“Thank you,” Vanessa beams. “You do too. That dress looks like it was made for you.”

“It was actually,” Katherine whispers, as if it’s a secret. “Susan got me a few custom pieces. Just wait ’til you see the dress I got for the rehearsal.”

After a beat her eyes find me. Glancing down at my outfit, I realize that my mud-covered Docs paired with my khaki shorts are giving off *Jungle Cruise* vibes.

“I hope I didn’t scare you off earlier,” she says.

“Do you two know each other?” Vanessa asks.

“She’s my new roomie,” Katherine explains, an artificial sweetness to her voice. As an antisocial introvert I get not wanting to befriend the girl who infiltrated your room. "Meredith has nothing but nice things to say about you."

At least I have that going for me. At the mention of her name, cheers erupt from the crowd as the couple of honor descend the stairs towards the group. They're swept into hugs and handshakes before Meredith sneaks past gushing guests to come over to me.

"Mira," she says, giving me another hug. She's wearing a matching white linen set, the subtle crop top showing off a hint of skin, and her hair is parted into two braids pinned to the top of her head. Her naturally golden skin glows, and besides a bit of mascara to make her hazel eyes pop, she isn't wearing any other makeup.

"You look wonderful," I say, giving her a squeeze.

"Thanks." The smile on her face doesn't reach her eyes and I can tell something is wrong.

My pulse quickens as she reaches for my hand.

"I hate to ask this, but is there any way you could take a few photos tonight and at the rehearsal dinner? I know I said you wouldn't have to work, but Grant's stepmother would love it, and I'll do anything to get her off my back," she says, scoping out the crowd. "That's her over there."

She points towards an older woman in a red wrap dress with gold accessories and shoes that definitely don't adhere to the closed-toe dress code. She's talking with Hudson, his arms crossed in annoyance as she punches her eyebrows together in a disapproving line.

"Not a problem," I say, forcing a smile.

I'm not one to give myself additional work, but having a task to focus on would be a way to distract myself from being trapped on a boat with Hudson. Not to mention, late-night editing sessions will give me an excuse to sleep out in one of the chairs in the sitting area, a fate I've already decided for myself.

"I just gotta run back to the room and get my gear."

"Thank you." Meredith beams, grasping my hands. "And I'm sorry again about the room mix-up. This week's been a bit chaotic."

"It's not a problem really. But if anything frees up, let me know. I don't want to cramp their style, since I know many couples view destination weddings as romantic getaways."

"Oh, please," Meredith says, waving me off. "Those two have been together for three years. I'm sure they can keep it in their pants for a weekend."

Three years! They have been together for THREE FREAKING YEARS.

The whole time he was texting me, he was probably sitting on the couch with Katherine, cooking dinner, or picking out baby names. The thought makes me want to run over and punch him. To call him out in front of everyone. But I know better.

Clenching my jaw, I shoot a death stare in Hudson's direction before I stomp back to the room to get my camera.

By the time I make it back, a stocky, baby-faced adventure guide is addressing the group. "Welcome, guests of Meredith and Grant. Are we ready to have a good time this weekend?"

"Hell, yeah!" Derrick cheers, his giant bodybuilder frame wobbly from an afternoon of day drinking.

"My name is Bo, and this is Tonya," the guide says, nodding towards his mousy-haired counterpart, dressed in a matching blue-and-red Majestic Ranch t-shirt. "And we will be your river guides and co-captains this evening. But before we head to the gorgeous Snake River, I need each of you to sign a waiver." He holds up a clipboard and passes it to Adrian.

"Do you think I should be worried that this clearly states that they aren't responsible for death, drowning, *or* dismemberment?" Adrian asks, scanning the one-page document.

"Considering that the word 'liability' is misspelled, definitely," I joke. "On the other hand, it also means this document probably won't hold up in a court of law, so you'd still get a good payout if something happened."

"You hear that, babe? If I lose an arm, we could be rich," Adrian says, passing the clipboard to Vanessa.

"I think I'd rather have you in one piece than buy myself a Rivian," she counters, jotting her own name down as the rumble of heavy machinery grabs our attention.

I've seen plush, overpriced vehicles, luxury party buses, and vintage cars driven by professionals, but the worn-down school bus that heads towards us is a first. The words "MAJESTIC RANCH AND RESORT" are hand-painted on the side. Water cascades from the emergency exit door as it brakes in front of our group.

"Who's ready to go to the river?" Bo shouts, as the door to the bus opens.

The wide-eyed onlookers quickly turn their horrified stares from Bo and the bus to Meredith's soon-to-be mother-in-law, who is throwing a fit worthy of a suburban mom who has just been handed the wrong Starbucks order.

"Twenty bucks says she doesn't get on the bus," Adrian says, holding out his hand towards Vanessa.

"Forty," she replies, and they shake on it.

I've seen Momzillas throw fits, shed tears, and completely obliterate staff, but no matter what chaos they cause, they always put on a smile and power through the evening for the sake of the couple.

"You really think she won't come with us?"

"Susan's not a fan of Meredith to begin with, this is just fuel for the fire," Vanessa explains.

"But Meredith's great."

"I know, but to Susan she's a witch who has hypnotized Grant with her mystical voodoo."

"Mystical voodoo?" I laugh. "You can't be serious."

"Deadly," Vanessa sighs. "She went so far as to hire a PI to follow Meredith around for a month, totally convinced that her reiki business was a front for drugs."

"I thought it was because she believed Meredith was running a cult," Adrian adds.

"Either way, that's intense."

Adrian smugly nudges me as Susan moves up the stairs towards the cabins, Grant chasing after her. He's already holding out his hand for his prize when Katherine links arms with the woman, talking to her calmly until she walks back down towards the group.

"Damnit. I didn't account for the Katherine factor," Adrian says, shaking his head.

"The Katherine factor?"

"She's like the Susan-whisperer," Vanessa explains, as we move in line to board the bus. "They're practically glued at the hip. Every time she picks a fight with Meredith over the proper time to arrive at a function or making reservations at a vegetarian-only restaurant, Katherine is always there to smooth it over. We're convinced that's why Hudson stays with her."

"Why would that matter?" I ask, confused.

"Because Susan is Hudson's mom."

Staring at the woman now, I can't believe I missed the resemblance. From the wrinkle they share between their brows to the same piercing green eyes. Even the roots of her blonde hair shine with a hint of red. I add her to the list of people to avoid this weekend as I find a seat behind Vanessa and Adrian.

The window is caked in dirt and there's a weird film on the back of the seat that sticks to my arm when I accidently graze against it. Removing my backpack, I locate my hand sanitizer inside my emergency kit. It's nestled between gum, wet wipes, eye drops, a sewing kit, Band-Aids, and various creams, lotions, stain kits, and hairsprays. I squeeze a dollop onto my hand and offer some to Vanessa and Adrian.

"Do you always bring so much stuff with you?" Vanessa asks, examining my bag. It's fully stocked with everything one might need to ensure a successful wedding day.

"I've learned it's best to be prepared for any situation. I can't tell you how many broken straps I've repaired, or blisters I've bandaged, or stray hairs I've smoothed down. I've used almost everything in here at least twice."

"Is that really part of your job description, though? I'd assume that'd be more of the planner's forte."

"There's more crossover than you think," I explain, echoing the words Phoebe told me when I first started in this business. "It never hurts to be remembered as the one who averted the crisis. Sometimes the memory of being the one with double-sided tape or stain remover outweighs bad weather or imperfect lighting."

"As someone who is notoriously overpacked but perpetually underprepared, I'm going to need you to stay by my side all weekend."

"I can definitely do that," I assure her.

The vinyl sticks to the backs of my thighs as I settle into my seat, and find Hudson standing in front of me, his arms resting over the top of the seat. The scent of his cologne is a reprieve from the odorous bus, the earthy fragrance familiar and comforting. I pinch the skin on my thigh in an attempt to write over this positive association.

"Do you mind if I sit?" he asks, his evergreen eyes alight with the afternoon sun. I consider whether to be impressed by his audacity or concerned by his lack of survival instinct.

I move my bag into the empty space beside me. "I'm not big on sharing."

I swear I see a flash of hurt on his face before he moves further down the aisle. I wait until he finds a seat in the back of the bus and let out the breath I'm holding.

"That was interesting," Vanessa says, her eyebrow raised in a sharp arch.

"What?"

Her eyes dart from me and my backpack. "You don't like sharing?"

"I just don't like that guy," I blurt out, the professional filter I try maintaining when I'm working all but abandoned.

"Hudson?" she asks, her jaw dropping in disbelief. "Really? I don't know a single person who dislikes him."

"Now you do," I reply, crossing my arms in defiance.

"But he's like a golden retriever, if golden retrievers looked like a ginger Paul Mescal. If I didn't have this one," she says, clapping her hand against Adrian's shoulder, "he'd be a top contender."

"Wow, babe. Good thing I'm not insecure," Adrian scoffs.

"You know I prefer my men foreign and brooding," she replies, returning her attention to me.

"How long have you known him?" I pry, hoping to fill in some of the blanks.

"A year or so now. But Adrian's known him longer," Vanessa says.

"I worked with him at Elite Elevation before I snagged my job at Duke. But I was only in the customer service department. It wasn't like I was hanging out with the top brass."

"Top brass?"

They both stare at me wildly as if I said I have no idea who Britney Spears is.

"His dad owns the company," Vanessa whispers, inflicting another gut punch.

Over the last few months I thought that Hudson and I were in the getting-to-know-each-other stage of our relationship, sharing all the minute details that make up our lives. Even though he told me how he saw Future Islands at a house party in college, and they subsequently became his favorite band, and he spent a summer working for a brewery in Asheville, learning how to make beer, and that he only wears his Grateful Dead shirt he inherited from his uncle when he's having a bad day, there's so much he's kept hidden. Like there's always a hint of honeydew underneath his earthy scent. And that he makes the softest, lowest moan when I pull at the hair at the nape of his neck.

"He was head of research and development for new products when I started. But he's stepping in as CEO next week," Adrian explains, the words processing slower than normal.

"It's not nepotism, I swear," he continues. "He's crazy talented. Always coming up with the coolest shit and letting anyone in the company try the products. I must have taken home four of those hammock hooks he came up with. Freaking genius."

"I had no idea," I mumble.

If Hudson is the heir to a giant corporation like Elite, what was he doing working at Finn's? Maybe being a barback was his alter ego? Or more likely it was a side hustle to pick up chicks he could cheat on his girlfriend with. The thought makes me gag.

Vanessa rubs her chin in contemplation. "I just can't believe you don't like him. Did he say something? Do something? I need to know everything so we can get to the bottom of this. It has to be a misunderstanding of some kind. I swear, Hudson has no enemies."

"It's just a vibe," I reply, not wanting to involve anyone else in my fucked-up interpersonal relations. If he's as beloved as they claim, I won't be the one to sour their opinion of him. I learned the hard way that exposing someone's true nature to those who don't want to see it is a fruitless endeavor. It's easier to let people go on believing what they want to believe.

"Remind me not to be around you when I'm PMSing. I'm nothing but bad vibes," Vanessa jokes, and takes a seat as the bus moves forward.

I spend the drive staring out the window, cursing myself for pretending that everything was fine between us. Pretending is part of my job description. Pretending that a bad haircut can be disguised with the right veil, or that the roadside flower bouquet the bride's sister has put together is elegant, not kinda sad. Pretending a timeline is fixable after the day has fallen so far off course that we lose all the daylight before they say "I do." And most importantly, pretending that I am happy to do it.

I should have said that I was saving the seat for someone or made up an excuse that we'd found ourselves in an in-depth conversation about cameras and I didn't fancy picking it up. Anything but my actual opinion of him. An opinion I'll have to spend the rest of the day backpedaling on so as not to cause any unwanted drama. Not that it stops me from turning in my seat and sneaking a glance behind me. I expect to see Hudson and Katherine canoodling like popular kids in the back of the bus, but instead I see Vivianne reading Katherine's palm as Hudson sits alone, eyes focused on me.

The bus takes a sharp turn onto an embankment and I barrel forward in my seat. We all bounce up and down on the uneven terrain as I keep a tight grip on my camera bag. A few guests gasp, bracing themselves for impact. Thankfully the tires lock against the gravel, stopping right before we careen into the river. The driver gives us a lackadaisical thumbs up as we all anxiously disembark.

"Nothing like a little crash landing to remind you you're alive, right?" Tonya, our guide, is unfazed by this descent, opening the doors with the same enthusiasm as a cast member at Disney World. And I have a new understanding of why the bus was leaking upon its arrival.

"Why do I have bad feelings about this?" Vanessa asks, still gripping onto the seat as if we survived a plane crash.

"Because it's giving murder camp vibes," Adrian replies, getting up with shaky legs.

I breathe a sigh of relief when I spot a quaint forty-person river cruiser with a blue-and-white awning waiting for us.

Bo stands on top of a boulder to assert his authority and addresses the group. "First things first, we gotta get you all squared away with some life vests."

"Wish we would have had those on the bus," Adrian pipes up.

Tonya opens the door to a metal shed to our left. A slew of life jackets plop onto the ground with a thud. Their absorbent material already weighed down by a day's worth of water.

"Alright now. Don't rush all at once," Bo jokes as no one moves.

"Do we really have to wear these?" Katherine asks.

"Unfortunately I cannot allow anyone on board without one," Tonya says sternly, and it's apparent she's the one really running this operation.

Willing to take the lead, Meredith and Grant are the first to toss the puffy polyester over their heads, which forces everyone else to fall in line behind them. Vanessa shrieks as cold water drips down her arms.

"Ew. Ew. Ew," she whines as Adrian follows suit, clipping the protective strap around her chest.

Removing my backpack, I toss mine over my head and do my best to hold in the retch that wants to escape. If the suffocating, fishy odor weren't enough of an omen, the residual river water instantly seeps into the silk shirt I've borrowed from Vanessa, exposing my black lace bra.

"You've got to be fucking kidding me," I mumble to myself, crossing my arms over my chest. Even though the buoyant material covers most of me, it does nothing to hide the side view.

"At least it's a cute bra," Vanessa says, and I'm thankful she's not mad I've completely ruined her shirt.

12 HUDSON

“Ma’am I can’t let you on without a life vest,” Bo argues, as Susan tries to push past him. Although she might look like a brittle woman, I know that those forearms are built from three Pilates classes a week and the weight of countless shopping bags.

“We own a boat twice this size and I’m on it every other weekend. I know how to stay aboard,” she replies, tone sharp.

“It’s the liability issue,” Bo continues, his eyes darting towards Tonya, who is ushering on guests on the other side.

Between Mira giving me the cold shoulder, Katherine’s incessant flirting, and my mother’s inability to go with the flow, I’m overcome with a queasy seasickness and I haven’t even stepped onto the boat.

“Isn’t that what I signed that waiver for? To remove your liability?” she retorts. As someone who’s watched my mother chew out countless hotel managers, I know Bo won’t be winning this fight.

“I’m CPR and swiftwater certified,” I say, trying to de-escalate the situation. “I’m more than happy to take responsibility for her.”

As someone who deals with liability insurance claims at work, I know it doesn’t really work that way, but Bo must decide it’s not worth the headache and nods his head in affirmation.

"If she goes in, you're going after her," he warns as I lead my mother onto the vessel.

"This is definitely not the *Carolina Dreaming*," Susan says, referencing the two-story yacht George purchased last year.

"That's for sure," Katherine says, slipping her arm through my mother's. "But think of the story you'll be able to tell at the club when you get back home. It'll put Cheryl's debacle of having to fly commercial to St. Barts to shame."

"Where are the welcome drinks?" George scoffs, his gruff voice booming behind me. I turn and find that he too is not wearing a life jacket. Great. Another person I'm going to have to take care of.

"Food and drinks are going to be provided after we reach our destination," Meredith explains, but her sweet smile isn't enough to placate my mother.

"And who is going to be providing the food?" Susan retorts. "A private chef, I hope."

"Don't worry, ma'am. Tonya and I got a load of great grub in the cooler," Bo chimes in, not helping the situation.

My mother's eyes widen. "You're going to be the one cooking?"

"I'm more of a sous chef, but Tonya's been called a grill master a time or two," he says, clasping his hands together, a joyful smile on his face as if he's given us a gift.

George crosses his arms over his linen suit, a scowl on his face. Unlike my mother, who voices her opinions loudly and often, George is more of the stoic silent type. But when he has something to say, everyone knows it.

My mother is already digging into her purse to pop a Xanax as George's voice cuts across the crowded boat. "Grant, can I have a word?"

There's a coldness in his tone that sends shivers down my spine, and for a second, I actually feel bad for my stepbrother. Grant straightens his shoulders in an effort to hide his inebriation as I slink off and away from the inevitable confrontation.

Like its namesake, the Snake River curves through the landscape, each curve leading its visitors to golden rock formations and dusty clifftops. While the guests stare out into the distance, appreciating all the river has to offer, my attention is focused on Mira. She's standing at the stern, peeling bangs off her sweaty forehead, her lips pressed together in a thin line. Even though she's captured weddings across the world, I know being here, with me and my family, is a little outside of her element. I know I should look away, to give her space, but this is the woman I woke up every morning excited to text, who made my six-hour shifts fly by, that I shared almost everything with, and now she's standing a few feet away and I can't even talk to her.

I try to ignore her, to focus on making sure my mother doesn't go overboard, but as guests shuffle about the vessel, eager to catch the breeze or take in the picturesque scenery, I find myself migrating towards her.

I don't know if it's because her presence here has taken me by surprise, or if it's because I'm used to seeing her in jeans, but my eyes trail over her legs, the shorts she's wearing making them look endless as she stands against the bow of the boat. Leaning forward, her hands against the railing, she holds up her phone to take a photo, and I catch a glimpse of her black lace bra underneath her shirt thanks to the sodden life jacket that's made the silk garment completely see-through. My brain oscillates between offering her my jacket to cover up and remembering what that lace felt like underneath my fingertips.

Closing my eyes, I let the breeze brush against my face and calm my thoughts, but all it does is waft the scent of her hair towards me, a concoction of orange and honey that makes me grip the railing even harder.

"Excuse me," Meredith's great-aunt says, coming up beside me holding a pair of binoculars. "Would you mind scooting over? I'm trying to see if I can spot any black-billed magpies."

She doesn't wait for me to slide down before she pushes in, and I find myself elbow to elbow with Mira.

She glares at me, unyielding, and I understand this is yet another one of my many missteps.

"Mira," I say, a hitch in my voice, but she holds up a hand to stop me.

"We don't have to have this conversation right now. Honestly, we don't ever have to speak again." She crosses her arms over her chest, turning her back to me.

"Please, I owe you an explanation."

Her eyes are dark, tactile, ready to destroy me with a laser beam of loathing.

"You should save whatever energy you're going to use on this excuse and channel it into an apology to your girlfriend, who seems lovely and beautiful and who has no reason to be with a lying cheater such as yourself." Her voice drips with animosity. "And I want you to know if we weren't stuck in a room together, I would tell her what happened. So I'm giving you a choice. Confess that you're a scumbag."

"You don't understand."

"Oh, I do though," she whispers, her tone still razor-sharp. "You flirted with me for months, waited for your girlfriend to be out of town to get into my pants, and I fell for it. All I can hope is that it was the best sex of your life and that it haunts you until the day you die, because I promise you will never, ever be experiencing it again."

“Mira, you have this all wrong. We didn’t—” I say, my mind trying to determine which misunderstanding to clear up first. “Katherine and I . . . we aren’t—”

But before I can finish my sentence, the boat jolts forward, and she stumbles into my arms.

13 MIRA

I lunge forward, gripping onto Hudson's shoulders, as he stares down at me in concern, his hands pressing against my back to keep my steady. For a moment we stay there, his face mere inches away from mine.

Falling into his arms is an involuntary response to almost going overboard, but enjoying the way his fingers move against my spine, sending goosebumps down my arms, is just the universe's way of punishing me for my sins. I shouldn't have these feelings. I shouldn't want to move the stray hair from his forehead, or breathe in the scent of rain against his skin. But it's not like I knew he had a girlfriend. If I had, I never would have entertained the idea of us. I would have gotten my drink, read my book, shot the shit with Lilah, and gone home. I would have never texted him, or flirted, or stayed late at the bar. And I definitely wouldn't have daydreamed about us going to farmers' markets or whiling away rainy afternoons on the couch in each other's arms. If anything, these lingering feelings are his fault. He wormed his way into my psyche, into my life, into my heart, and for what? A one-night stand?

I knew men would go to great lengths for sex but this felt too much.

"Do these people know how to arrive anywhere without causing an accident?" Vanessa snaps, as I push myself out of Hudson's grasp. I wipe at a few stray water droplets on my face as I follow her through the crowd and onto dry land.

Our destination is a bit more barren than I expected. With only a few picnic tables, overgrown grasses, and no shade coverage, getting the photos Meredith wanted is going to be tricky, but on the bright side there is enough space here that Hudson and I can always stay at least a hundred feet away from each other.

"At least now I can take this fucking thing off," Vanessa says, removing her life vest and throwing it to the ground with a heavy sigh.

I go to remove my own, realizing that my bra is completely visible through my shirt. Great. Guess I'll be wearing this for the rest of the day.

"Ah. Now that I don't feel like I'm being waterboarded, why don't you tell me what's really going on between you and Hudson?"

"There's nothing going on," I say, moving to take a seat at one of the picnic tables.

"Girl, y'all just had a moment."

"That wasn't a moment," I argue.

"Really? Because from where I was standing it seemed like you two *didn't* hate each other."

Panic radiates through my body. The last thing I need is for Vanessa to think that I'm sneaking off with Hudson for a romantic rendezvous with his girlfriend just feet away, so I pivot.

"I'm just really clumsy."

Vanessa holds her hand to her chin in mock contemplation. "Mmhmm."

"Seriously. The boat hit something and I slipped. He just happened to catch me. It's not a big deal."

Vanessa is readying another question when Derrick breaks the tension.

"Anyone up for a dip?" he asks, stripping off his shirt like he's posing for the fireman-of-the-year calendar.

"Ugh, put your clothes back on," Vanessa scolds. "There are elderly people here."

"Everyone needs something to live for. Even the elderly," he says, sprinting towards the river and hopping in with a splash.

"Guys, life jackets please," Bo says, running towards the shore and tossing Derrick his jacket.

"Sorry, bro," Derrick replies, strapping himself in. I watch as he bobs along the river, climbing into one of the inner tubes Tonya's hooked onto the side of the boat.

"Mind if I hide out with you guys?" Meredith says, joining us at the picnic table.

"Not much of a hiding spot, considering we're out in the open," I reply.

"Susan doesn't do direct sunlight. For me this is a safe zone."

"Here, you can take my spot," Vanessa says. "I'm going to go see what the food situation is."

Meredith sits down beside me, her arms falling to the side with a heavy thump as if she's just run a marathon. Her usual sunny disposition is gone, replaced by an air of defeat.

"Rough day already?"

"You can say that," she says, giving me a half-smile. "It's just, when I thought about my wedding day, I imagined all my closest friends and family having fun together. Doing all the things I never got to do as a kid. I never thought I'd be bowing down to the whims of a woman determined to make my life hell."

"If it makes you feel better, I've seen worse."

She eyes me skeptically.

"I'm serious. Until she actually burns down the wedding venue with a stress cigarette, you're golden."

My anecdote earns me a smile.

"At least you're off the hook," she says as we watch Jocelyn and Angie jump into the river.

"What do you mean?"

"Susan couldn't care less about photos right now," Meredith replies, glancing over her shoulder at her mother-in-law, who is currently hiding under an umbrella, dark sunglasses covering her face as she gesticulates towards Meredith's aunt, Vivianne, who looks like she's being tortured.

"I wouldn't be surprised if she calls a search and rescue team to evacuate her out of here."

"Those are like eighty thousand dollars."

"I'm sure it'd be worth it for her," Meredith replies, taking another sip of her drink, and I hate that she has to deal with this. "I really tried to like her but that woman gets under my skin. And I work in customer service."

"Some people are so unhappy in their own lives, they can't allow others to be happy either."

"I really thought this was my chance to make a new family. To finally feel like a daughter again . . ." She trails off, her eyes cutting towards Susan. "I didn't realize there was something worse than being an orphan."

"At least complaining about in-laws is a pretty universal experience."

"You're right," Meredith chuckles. "And I won't have to deal with her for much longer anyways."

"Oh? Did you put out a hit? I won't tell," I reply, holding up three fingers. "But I will be taking notes for the future podcast special."

"We're moving actually," Meredith explains. "Grant took a job at a startup firm in Asheville. He'll be managing their financials and investments and I can expand my holistic healing business. It's not like we're cutting her out, but a two-hour distance means no more casual pop-ins."

"I can totally see you living there. Between the tourists and the locals, I'm sure it's the perfect market for you."

"It really is," she gushes. "And it's better for our lifestyle."

With Meredith's penchant for home-brewed kombucha and hand-dyeing her own clothes, I know she'll thrive there.

"You'll have to come visit," she says, nudging me on the shoulder. "I'm sure you shoot weddings there all the time, right?"

"Not so much anymore," I reply, since the few I had scheduled just canceled.

"For a girls' weekend then," she says, before Grant calls over to her and I'm left alone with nothing but my growling stomach.

14 HUDSON

All I had to say was one more word.

Together.

We aren't together.

But I choked.

And of course, to make matters worse, Mira thinks she and I slept together—another clarification I'll have to make if she ever lets me get a word in. Until then I get to sit here and watch Derrick parade his half-naked body in front of Mira like he's in a goddamn bodybuilding competition.

"Come on in, the water's fine," he shouts as Mira takes a seat on the edge of the riverbank. She's applying sunscreen to her arms and legs, leaving a radiant sheen over her pale skin that sparkles in the sunlight. Her life vest is still strapped around her as if she's afraid of falling in. But after the verbal beatdown she gave me, I'm the one who feels like I've drowned.

"Enjoying the view?" Vanessa asks, coming up from behind me.

"God," I say, jumping, "it's dangerous to sneak up on people like that!"

"I think you should be more concerned with Derrick trying to steal your girl than what's lurking in the woods," she replies playfully, her gaze following mine towards Mira.

"She's not . . ." I stammer.

"Oh my God. I was right," she coos, smacking me in the chest. "You do like her."

"Shhh," I hiss, gently placing my hands on her shoulders and moving her further away from the group to avoid any wandering ears.

If Vanessa, a woman I've only met a handful of times, can tell that I am a lovesick wreck, Katherine's going to catch on. I consider doing damage control, lying my way out of the situation, but if Finn has taught me anything about his sister it's that she is loyal, trustworthy, and gifted with a surprising ability to hold her liquor.

"I met her at Finn's. And we've been friendly," I confess.

"Friendly?" Her question is a challenge I instantly fail.

"We may have fooled around a bit on Monday."

"You little slut!" Vanessa squeals, placing a hand over her mouth.

"It's not like that. Katherine and I . . ."

"Are broken up?" she says, finishing my thought.

"Did she tell you?" I ask, unbelieving.

With how tightly Katherine's been holding onto the threads of our relationship, I have a hard time believing she would let anyone know that we're not together—even someone like Vanessa.

"Katherine is not hard to read," she replies. "She hasn't posted a single photo of you guys together on her story or feed in weeks. And my brother might have mentioned you do more flirting than working. And since I know you're not the type of guy who would cheat, I put the pieces together."

"That gossip," I squawk, pretending to be appalled.

"Finn looks like a hard-ass, but he loves the drama," Vanessa laughs.

"So, I'm assuming Adrian knows?"

"Not yet. I wanted to confirm my hypothesis first, but we've had a bet going and I can't wait to gloat."

"What was the bet?"

"The usual. Back rubs and pick of the TV selection for the week. It's going to be *Gilmore Girls* all day every day."

"Do me a favor and keep it between the two of you," I say nervously.

She holds up her hands innocently. "I'm not one to blast other people's personal drama, but why would it matter?"

"I don't think Katherine would take it too well."

"Oh, so are you and Mira sneaking off in secret? Hot."

"Not exactly."

Vanessa crosses her arms over her chest. "What does that mean?"

I drag my hand through my hair, regretfully. I've had a million chances to tell Mira the truth. The night she casually asked me if I'd ever be a participant on *The Bachelor*, I could have made a joke that the reason my relationship ended was because my ex thought it would be a good idea to bring strangers into our relationship. Or when she asked if I ever took a night off after seeing me four in a row, I could have told her that being at Finn's and serving college students was better than a second spent in my apartment with Katherine.

"I may have omitted a few of the messier details of my life."

"Wait. So what? Mira thinks you're with Katherine?"

I nod my head.

"This explains the bus."

"The bus?"

"Mira said she disliked you, which I found weird, because you're great."

"Thanks," I reply, happy to have an ally.

"But she didn't know you worked for Elite. Or anything about you. I couldn't figure out how you two knew each other. And then I saw you being all gooey-eyed on the boat. I thought maybe the whole rooming situation put her off—" She stops mid-thought.

The pieces fall into place. "HOLY SHIT, Hudson. You're sharing a room with both of them!"

"I know," I say. "It's an actual nightmare. If Dante ever wanted inspiration for an additional circle, he need look no further."

"Fuck," Vanessa says, drawing out the word. "You have to tell her."

"Who?"

"Mira. Duh," she says, smacking my forehead.

"I'm pretty sure I fucked that up already," I say solemnly. "She hates me."

Vanessa shakes her head. "I very much doubt that. No one gets that defensive over someone they don't care about. Trust me. You can still salvage this."

"I just want her to talk to me. She's freezing me out."

"Wait until she comes to you. Or better yet, do something nice for her. A girl always loves a grand romantic gesture."

"Like what?"

"I'm sure you'll figure something out," she winks, finding Adrian and wrapping an arm around him and whispering in his ear. I'm not even mad that she's gossiping about me. Because it means I still have a chance.

Before I can brainstorm my options, my mother appears at my side, digging her sharp nails into my arm, making me jump. "Can you do something about this sun? I'm sweltering out here."

I have to control my response. It's not like I can change the rotation of the Earth on her whim.

"There's not really much I can do," I reply.

"Maybe hurry this along then? I'd really love to get back to civilization in this lifetime."

"Let me check out what's going on," I say, just as eager to get out of here as she is.

I find the adventure guides congregating around the far end of the boat. Bo is setting out aluminum trays of premade food on foldout tables. The baked beans look burnt, the potato salad is an artificial yellow, the coleslaw is watery, and a tray of congealed Mac and cheese is reheating in the sun. When he unveils a tray of pre-formed burgers, I can still see the freezer burn along the edges.

"I think that meat's gone bad," I say, noting the discoloration.

"Someone put all the ice in the beer coolers," Tonya says, aiming the blame at Bo, as she strikes a match and lights the grill. The grates are covered in a thick layer of blackened char and I can't imagine they've been cleaned in a decade.

"Hudson here teaching you the proper way to make a fire?" Grant says, taking a swig of his beer.

"Just trying to ensure none of the guests get food poisoning."

"Don't let this one give you a hard time. We can't all be purebred wilderness leaders."

"Wilderness leader, eh? Are you in the forest service?" Bo asks with genuine interest. Uttering the words "Elite Elevation" to a guy like this is like feeding a gremlin after midnight, but it doesn't stop Grant from doing it anyways.

"Hudson works for Elite Elevation," he says with a shit-eating grin, and I regret not going through with putting Nair in his shampoo when he was sixteen. "His dad is the owner. Elder Elite if you will. And little Hayes here is going to be taking over next week."

Bo stares at me as if I'm the messiah about to guide him to the promised land. "Working there is like my dream, man," he says shakily. "Do you have any openings? I'd be happy to email my resumé."

I consider letting him down gently until I realize I might be able to use this to my advantage.

"One of the things we admire at Elite is ingenuity and problem-solving, especially on location. I'd love to get your insight on a solution to our problem here."

"Our problem?" Bo asks, confused.

"Well, the food doesn't look very appetizing, if I'm being honest. This is a wedding party, as you know, and there's a certain level of expectation. Don't you think it might be best to head back to the resort? Where there is an actual café with food that hasn't been sitting in the hot weather for hours without ice?"

Bo contemplates this for a moment, and I think he's coming around to the idea of returning right up to the moment Tonya tosses the burgers on the metal rack, causing flames to flare up around them.

"I'll cook 'em for longer. They'll be fine," she says, as Bo gives us a sympathetic smile. And we both know it's too late. There's nothing to do now but endure.

Twenty minutes later an eager line forms in front of the tables as ravenous hands reach for paper plates. Little do they know that there is nothing very tasty waiting for them. I wait for Mira to get in line, before jumping in myself. If she doesn't want to talk to me, fine, but the least I can do is save her from an evening of food poisoning.

Adrian is ahead of her, placing a blackened burger on his plate. "Maybe I could salvage it with ketchup."

"I don't see any condiments," Vanessa adds, not even bothering to pick up a plate.

"I might have some," Mira announces, reaching into the side pocket of her backpack, pulling out packets of hot sauce and honey mustard.

"Do wedding clients typically need sauces?" Adrian asks.

"Not yet, but they've come in handy for me a time or two when all there is to eat is a plain turkey sandwich," she replies, as Adrian takes the assortment from her.

"I doubt drenching it in sauce is going to be enough to save this meal," I say, causing Mira's eyes to dart towards me.

"Maybe I'll just stick to the sides," Adrian says. "There's no way to fuck up baked beans, right?" he says, shoveling a forkful of gelatinous brown sludge into his mouth with a disgusted grimace before putting it back onto his plate. "Oof. I was wrong."

"Are you not eating?" Tonya asks, as Mira grabs a lonely hamburger bun and nothing else.

"I'm a vegan," Mira says, taking a bite of her bun and adding another to her plate. Considering I've seen her take down many *carne asada* tacos at the bar, I know that this is her way of being polite.

Growing up, my dad always taught me that what makes a great leader is the ability to anticipate others' needs. And through our many conversations Mira told me all the horror stories about eating at work: the plates of green beans she consumed even though she hated them, eating from the dregs of the buffet bowls, or having her plate get thrown in the trash before she had a chance to take a single bite. It was one of the reasons I always ordered takeout to the bar on days she had a photoshoot, ensuring she didn't go to bed hungry, and I want to be that guy again.

"Me too," Adrian says, dumping his plate into the plastic trash bag.

"What about you?" Tonya asks, eyeing me suspiciously. "You a friend of PETA too?"

But my mind is spinning too quickly to answer her, as I figure out a way not only to save this disaster of a dinner but to make a grand gesture to Mira.

I've not been confident in many things in my life, but living off the land is one area where I've earned my fair share of gold stars from an early age. Foraging, hunting, and cooking meals in the wild is my specialty. Right now, my best option is to fish. Making my way into the tree line, I scout for the perfect limbs to use for my makeshift rod.

"If you're planning on beating us out of our misery, I'll volunteer as tribute," Adrian replies, chewing on a piece of bread.

"As much as I appreciate your sacrifice, I'm trying to find us some real food," I say, bending a branch against my knee to check for flexibility.

"Thank God," he breathes. "I've eaten a lot of sketchy things in my life, but this might be hitting my threshold."

The branch is too dry, snapping easily. I move into the small patch of forest.

"So, are we like foraging for mushrooms? Or . . ."

"I'm trying to catch us some fish," I explain, and snap another stick.

"Are you going to spear them like the guys on *Naked and Afraid*?" Adrian asks excitedly.

"Unlike Derrick, I'll be keeping my clothes on," I reply, peeking over my shoulder to see if Mira is still paying attention to his antics. Thankfully, she's lying with her head on her backpack, eyes closed, ignoring him entirely. "If you really want to know, I'm making sure that the branch I choose has enough flexibility to withstand the weight of the fish and the tension of the string," I explain, as I find a branch that passes my test.

"But, like, it takes more than a stick, right?"

Adrian's correct. It does take more than a stick. And it's then that I remember my wilderness bag, with all the items I need to finish my project, is sitting in the back of the Jeep. I left it there in hopes of going to the park. But from our many talks at the bar, I know that the only other person who would have the items I need is . . . Mira.

A part of me considers asking Adrian to relay my message, but if I'm going to prove myself to her, I have to step up.

She's relaxed, laughing at something Vanessa has said as she bathes in the sun. She's still in her life jacket, a godsend considering I can see the bra she's wearing peeking through the side of the waterlogged fabric. If she took it off now, my thoughts would practically be broadcasted to the entire group in these shorts.

Get it together, man, I argue with myself, as I make my way towards her.

"Finally going to join the party, Hayes?" Derrick shouts up to me from the river, causing Mira to whip her head back to find me. Her entire body stiffens in annoyance as she quickly turns her gaze back towards the river.

I ignore Derrick, my heart already pounding in my ears with nervousness.

"Do you have your emergency kit with you?" I ask Mira, hoping she can't see through my false confidence.

"Why?" Her mouth hardens into a thin line as she clutches her camera bag tighter, as if I might take it by force.

"I'm trying to find some fresh food and I'm ninety-nine percent sure your kit has what I need."

Studying me, she turns her attention towards Vanessa, who gives her an enthusiastic nod of approval, and she relents.

"I will be doing inventory after," she says, handing me her bag, "so go ahead and expect an invoice for any items missing."

"Understood," I say, unzipping it. She told me once that her bag rivaled Mary Poppins's and I have to admit I'm impressed. Although it lacks collapsible cutting boards or foldable silicone measuring cups like mine, it is stocked with everything I need to finish my project.

Mira watches me bend a safety pin back quizzically.

"You really think that's going to work?" she asks as I wrap the thread from her sewing kit around the metal until it attaches, creating a makeshift fishing lure. "My father's been taking me on fishing trips since I could walk. One time I accidentally threw all our lures off the side of the boat and we all had to learn a valuable lesson in improvisation," I say, slipping into the confident man she's accustomed to. "And considering I saw a school of trout on the way down, I'm not too worried about coming up empty-handed."

Mira raises her eyebrows, impressed, and the fact she's even looking at me is enough to boost my ego. Taking a sturdy stance next to her, I cast my line into the water and wait for the familiar tug on the other end.

God, I need this to work.

The water is flowing steadily, and I spot a school of trout traveling in our direction up ahead. I only have a small window of opportunity to catch as many as I can. Unlike professional rods, where I can slowly reel them in, I have to be quick about it, yanking the fish out of the water the second I feel tension. Unwilling to fuck this up, I prepare a backup rod just in case. I say a silent prayer to the water gods, as I wait for a bite on the line. It only takes a few minutes before the rod closest to me goes tense and I jerk it up, displaying a pink-and-blue striped fish attached to the end. I let out a breath, detaching the rainbow trout from the line. It wobbles on the shore, as Vanessa, Adrian, and a few of the other party members clap in appraisal behind me. But Mira's slow clap is the only sound I pay attention to.

"Impressed?" I ask, wiping my hands on my pants, my palms scratched from the wooden rod.

"Depends," she replies, peering down to inspect my catch. "Are you really going to be able to cook that?"

"Oh yeah. All I need is some tinfoil and a little salt and pepper."

She raises her eyebrow skeptically. I can feel the ice between us defrosting as I push her goodwill a little further.

"Want to help?"

I know she's about to refuse my offer, but Vanessa comes to my aide.

"Go," Vanessa says, pushing Mira towards me. "He might need to use some of those condiments you have left in your bag."

"Fine," she caves and my heart flutters. "But if you call yourself a grill master, I'm out."

"Totally fair," I reason, holding my hands up.

"Can you grab me one of those aluminum trays?" I ask, sending her away for long enough for me to handle the more gruesome details of the process, offering the animal a swift death.

There's a faint smile on her face when she returns, carrying several empty containers.

"I didn't know how many you'd need," she offers, handing them over.

"One will be fine," I say, putting the fish inside and making my way over to the grill.

"I heard you were over here showing off your skills," Katherine says, inspecting my bounty, and I know whatever ground I've recovered with Mira has just been swept away. "Isn't he just so talented?" she continues, her hand giving me an almost territorial squeeze. "My little mountain man."

She says the last phrase in a mock baby voice and Mira's eyes roll so far back, I barely see the hazel of her irises.

"Oh yeah, he's a real Christopher McCandless," Mira replies through gritted teeth, referencing the nomadic college student from *Into the Wild*. "Make sure he forages dessert too. I think I saw some nice berry bushes over by the tree line."

"Really?" Katherine asks, not getting the reference. Her idea of casual reading is scrolling TikTok before bed.

"She's kidding," I say, having to stop her from running over and ingesting something toxic, the exact scenario that led to Christopher's death.

I place the fish over the hot coals, as Mira retreats back to the group. "Did you need something?"

"No, I just saw you over here and thought I'd check in."

"Really? Or did you see me paying attention to someone else?" I ask, irritation prickling up my spine. Before our split Katherine always left me alone at social functions, but now that I want space from her, she's sticking to me like static cling.

"What is up with you? You're being overly assholish this weekend."

Smoke billows up from the pan, flames charring underneath as I cover it with foil.

"All I'm asking is for a little distance. Can you give me that for once?"

The words come out sharper than I intended, but since Katherine is accustomed to me rolling over she might need a little scratch to get my point.

"Fine. I'll leave you alone," she says, irritated, and skulks off. On any other day, I'd apologize, but today I couldn't care less about her bruised ego.

"Damn, that smells delicious," George says, giving the fish a big sniff. "Guess all that time with your dad really paid off."

Unlike my mother, who only mentions my father with disdain, George's words radiate respect. Topping out at six-four, he's an older, more rugged version of Grant, with toned arms and a lean frame from his years of sailing around the Atlantic.

"He's definitely taught me a thing or two."

George nods knowingly, as if he too has bestowed fatherly wisdom upon his own son. Unlike my dad, who made me work for everything I earned, Grant was rewarded for doing the bare minimum. When he barely graduated high school, they bought him a Toyota 4Runner. And after he got kicked off the UNC lacrosse team for partying, they funded an all-expenses-paid trip for him and his buddies to blow off steam in Miami.

"I always told Grant never to settle down until he was sure," George says, taking a step closer to the grill, "and yet here we are, in the middle of nowhere, to celebrate a relationship that probably won't last the year."

As much as I don't care for my stepbrother, I can admit that what he has with Meredith is genuine. "They seem pretty solid."

George glares at me, like I'm an idealistic grad student asking him if he wants to help save the environment.

"She signed the prenup without even having a lawyer look at it," he scoffs. "I wonder how long until she figures out that she gets nothing if they divorce."

From the fair amount of time I've spent with Meredith, I know that money is very low on her list of priorities.

"I don't think Meredith is in it for the money."

"That's what they all say," George scoffs, and I can't help but wonder if this sentiment might be aimed at my mother more than Meredith.

"Nevertheless, I already had a word with Grant about putting his foot down with her. I know pussy can make men do some stupid things, but letting her embarrass our family like this," he says, motioning towards the boat, "it's deplorable."

I know that my mother isn't fond of Meredith, but hearing George talk about her makes me even more defensive.

"Have you even gotten to know her? She's a really lovely person," I say, hoping Grant has stood up for her as well.

"I saw her credit score and her background check. That's all I need," George replies, eyeing my fish. The trout is royally burnt, the skin bubbling off as I remove it from the heat and dig my knife into the center, portioning a helping onto a plate to give to Mira.

"Make sure to save some of that for your mother," George says, taking the plate from my hand, sinking his fingers into it to take a bite. As if Susan has consumed food in front of anyone since 2003.

I plate another portion, this time guarding it from prying hands as I bring it over to Mira. She's sitting by the riverbank, and from the way her eyes are fixed onto a single point, I know she's crashing, her body savoring the last of its nutrients.

"This is for you," I say, offering her a plate.

She doesn't even fight me on it as she places it in her lap.

"It's not my best work," I say, handing her a fork, "but it's better than anything over there."

I watch the way her lips part as she takes a bite and listen for the familiar hum of satisfaction that rumbles low within her chest.

"Mmm," she says, going in for seconds.

"Good?"

"It's better than your drinks." There's snark to her tone, but I'll take it if it means she's speaking to me again.

"You love my drinks."

"Lilah remade every one."

I study her face, unsure if she's just trying to get a rise out of me, but then she continues. "But hey, that's why you have your day job to fall back on, right?"

The hint of disdain in her voice is unmistakable.

"I should have told you about Elite," I say, hating that I held back so much of myself from her. "But I try not to tell people about my dad right away."

"Apparently you keep a lot of secrets," she retorts, the energy shifting around us.

"I know, I fucked up. I should have been honest with you about so many things, but I promise, I'll tell you everything if you let me."

Even after three years with Katherine there were parts of myself I kept hidden, knowing she wouldn't accept them, but with Mira I want to open myself up to her, let her flip through my pages, to learn all the best and worst parts of me.

She runs her teeth over her bottom lip in contemplation, and I'm certain she's about to give in, to nod her head and allow me to unburden myself, but her decision is stifled by the sound of a bullhorn blasting through the air.

"BEARS! We have bears!" Bo shouts, pointing towards the valley in the distance. And I spot two burly black bears wobbling back and forth, their heads up in the air. They are a reasonable distance away, another hundred yards or so, but I'm well aware that they could catch up to us with the right motivation, and by the way their noses sniff up in the air, I think they found it.

"Grab your life jackets and calmly retreat to the boat," Tonya orders, ushering guests down the riverbank.

Being trained for these situations, I know that my first priority should be helping Bo extinguish the fire and locate any guests who may have wandered off, but I bypass my responsibilities and focus on Mira.

"We have to go," I say, as she slips her feet back into her boots.

I know that I should let her finish tying her shoes, that proper boot safety is as important as wearing a life jacket, but as I watch the bears get closer all I care about is getting her on the boat and down the river to safety.

"This is all your fault," she spits, hobbling behind me. "You just had to show off your gourmet cooking skills."

"Gourmet? I put unseasoned trout on a grill."

"The bears wouldn't have cared about those burgers. No one wanted them. But the second you start grilling their favorite meal, they appear," she argues, walking ahead of me.

The embankment to reach the boat is steep, built by soft dirt and rocks, with an incline perfect for spraining ankles. With Mira's untied shoe, I want to keep a steady hand out for her, but she keeps her distance, refusing it.

"At least let me take your bag," I offer, watching her unbalanced steps carefully.

"Shouldn't you be helping your girlfriend?" she snaps back.

"Goddammit, Mira, she's not my—" I shout as Bo lets off another round of the bullhorn, and it all happens so fast. One second Mira's beside me, and the next, the loose dirt slips underneath her feet, the riverbank sliding away like an avalanche. And the last thing I see is the look of shock on her face as she careens straight into the river.

15 MIRA

I hold it together until we make it back to the lodge before I promptly vomit in the first bush I see. Between my anxiety, the embarrassment, and the stench of the river, my stomach is wrecked.

In a feat of what I can only call heroic stupidity, Hudson decided to jump into the river after me, throwing a life preserver over my head, a completely unnecessary act considering I was still wearing one. Although the flotation device might have saved me, it did nothing to protect my camera bag.

On the ride home I assessed the damage to my equipment: my cameras, my batteries, and my flashes, all waterlogged. Fifteen thousand dollars' worth of gear ruined in a single moment. But the worst part isn't the insurance claim, or the fact that I let Hudson make an ass of me yet again, it's that I'm going to have to tell Meredith that I won't be able to shoot her wedding after all.

Discarding my camera bag in the trash barrel outside the Activity Center, I can't help but wonder if this is all Phoebe's doing. If ruining my business wasn't enough for her and she hired Hudson to ruin my life.

I'm still dripping when I make it back to the Big Barn. My boots are covered in mud and I'm pretty sure there's an allogenous plant congealed in my curls. I must look like the Creature from the Black Lagoon as I stomp around to our patio to discard my soiled shoes.

I wish I had somewhere to go to be alone, to lock myself away and hide from this shitty day, from my shitty circumstances, but as I turn the doorknob, I know that I'll never find peace here, or at least not with Hudson always circling me.

My footprints stain the linoleum floor as I make my way to the bathroom, eager to remove the stench of river water from my skin. Turning on the shower, water gushes out, the pressure excellent as I stick my hand underneath to wait for it to get warm, but it never gets above freezing. After a minute I twist the nozzle in the opposite direction, but somehow it only gets colder.

"It doesn't work," Hudson says, his voice startling me.

"I'm sure you don't know how to turn it on correctly," I argue, trying again. I've visited enough hotels and Airbnbs to know that hot and cold nozzles aren't always labeled correctly. And sometimes all it takes is a little finagling to get it going.

"I promise you, there's no hot water," he assures me, running a hand through his auburn hair. He's being his usual approachable, attractive self, the same guy who encouraged me to let my guard down the first time. Men like this should be marked to show they're in long-term committed relationships. Perhaps they could grow a unibrow or expel a foul body odor that can be detected only by those they're planning on cheating with.

"Why do you think I came in here with a towel earlier?" he asks, and I'm reminded that thanks to the silk shirt Vanessa loaned me I'm equally exposed.

"Hooking up with one of the party posse?" I reply, holding one arm over my chest.

"Mira," he says. He's very close to me all of a sudden. His earthy scent is deceptively comforting, like freshly cut grass after a shower of summer rain. He stares down at me, the green of his irises flickering like gemstones in the river.

"Cold water is good for you," I reason, moving away from him so quickly I slam my back against the sink. "It resets the nervous system."

And since I am still lusting after a liar with a girlfriend, mine definitely needs another reset.

"Now if you wouldn't mind giving me some privacy."

"Wait," he says, palming the door I'm about to shut in his face, "I need to tell you something."

"What? That you're riddled with STIs? Don't worry, I already made an appointment to—"

"Mira, we didn't sleep together."

The admission knocks me back as I take a beat.

"But I remember . . ."

"We fooled around a little, but you fell asleep when I went to the bathroom. I woke you up and gave you one of my shirts, which you mocked mercilessly for a few minutes"—he laughs in reminiscence—"but nothing happened besides that, I swear."

"Thanks for letting me know," I say, closing the door.

Stripping down, I step into the shower, allowing the cold water to rattle my bones and bring me some much-needed clarity. As grateful as I am that we didn't cross that line, it didn't change anything. Because no matter how I feel about him, or how I thought that we could be something, or how deep down I want to know why he's still bothering to make it up to me, there's one undeniable fact I can't ignore. Hudson has a girlfriend.

16 HUDSON

"Guess you didn't smooth things over then?" Adrian asks, taking up space beside me on the second-floor balcony. The peaks of the Tetons glow a majestic purple as the day blends into night, and as much as I'm grateful for the extra hours that come with western summers, I'm thankful that this one is ending because I'm not sure how much more I can take.

I wish I could go in there and scream that this is all a misunderstanding. That over the course of our friendship, I meant every word, every laugh, every well-timed innuendo. That I could take her in my arms and press my mouth in the space right under her ear and have her melt into me again. That she'd look at me the same way she did outside Finn's. But more than any of it, I just want her to trust me again.

"I think she hates me more than before," I sigh, gripping the railing, the soft wood splintering into my skin.

"Take this from a guy who doesn't make friends easily—you're hard to hate," Adrian says, pulling out a cigarette and handing the pack to me.

The first and last time I smoked a cigarette was when Grant and his friends invited me to party with them on George's sailboat one summer. And just like the cigarette, the experience left a bitter taste in my mouth.

"I'm good," I say, waving them off.

Adrian slips the pack into his pocket, and pulls out a lighter.

"Good on you, mate," he says, lighting up and taking a drag. "I've tried to quit, but occasions like this, with all these people, and the drama, it's good to have an excuse to go outside for a few minutes."

He leans his back against the railing, facing me as he takes another drag. "Vanessa told me not to say anything, but I have to ask, man, why are you and Katherine even faking this thing in the first place?"

"The truth?"

Adrian nods.

"I thought it would make things easier," I reply, chuckling at the irony. "I didn't want to deal with my mother asking a million questions or playing matchmaker, or worse, trying to get us back together. But I never considered that Mira would be here, or that she'd be sleeping in our fucking room."

"Oof. That's a tough break," Adrian says, stamping out his cigarette. "But if you like this girl you have to consider her feelings too. I mean, if Vanessa was here with another guy, pretend or not, I'd be losing my shit."

I drag my hand down my face. "I want to tell her. Hell, I've tried to tell her. But at this point I doubt she'd believe anything I said."

"If it helps, Vanessa and I will back you up," Adrian assures me.

"I appreciate that," I say, watching as the purples and golds fade into an inky darkness over the mountaintops. It's beautiful and I wish I could be sharing this moment with Mira, moving that stubborn curl behind her ear before I kiss her goodnight.

"Before you talk to anyone though, you should use our shower. You smell like a river."

"You sure?"

"Everyone else is at the party," Adrian assures me, opening the door to his room. "And it might be good for you. Clear your head a bit."

"Thanks, man."

"Don't mention it."

I set a reminder on my phone to send him and Vanessa a thank you for their generosity as I make my way into their bathroom once again.

Stripping down, my suit is wrecked, the fabric damp and the fibers discolored, but I don't care.

Going in after her had been instinctive, a deep-rooted impulse to keep her safe at all costs. A gesture that only made matters worse as she swam away from me, more irritated than before. In my life I've always been the one to think things through, to slow down and make rational decisions, but with Mira I seem to be always jumping first.

Once I'm clean, I borrow a pair of Adrian's shorts and a tee, and towel-dry my hair. My body might feel refreshed but the tension is still heavy across my shoulders as I make my way outside.

"Hudson," Tonya says, flagging me down outside the entrance and handing me a sheet of paper. "I'm sure you don't need one of these, but we wanted to make sure everyone is prepared in case any of our furry friends make another appearance this week."

I stare down at the infographic on bear safety.

"There's a twenty-percent-off coupon for bear spray in there too."

When it comes to black bears I know it's safer to scare them away using a bear bell or raising your arms and making loud noises than it is to try to Mace them in the face, but I nod just the same.

"Make sure to spread the word," she says cheerfully, making her way inside, tacking a sheet on every door.

Folding the paper, I place it in my pocket as I follow the gravel path to the cabins. I'm only halfway up the drive when I hear Grant shouting.

"You can't be serious?" he says to George, who is lugging a pair of suitcases down the stairs.

"That cabin isn't suitable," George states, stopping in front of the black SUV, the headlights lighting the scene ahead.

"For Susan?" Grant argues, placing his hand on the door before his father can open it.

George puffs out his chest, making him appear taller. "Do you really think we would stick around after that disaster this afternoon?"

"We didn't know it was going to be like that. The brochure said—" Grant claims, but George cuts him off.

"The brochure? Are you kidding me? We offered you all the money in the world to have a proper wedding and you chose a venue out of a roadside brochure. I swear, Grant, it's as if you brought us out here just to humiliate us."

"Dad," Grant sighs, his voice soft, his shoulders slumped in defeat. And for a moment I glimpse the nine-year-old kid I first met, begging his father to stay home for the weekend instead of going to another golf tournament. The one I'd hear crying alone in his room, aching with grief for his mother. I can't help but wonder if he might have had a bit more compassion for others growing up if anyone had taken the time to give him some proper loving attention back when he was a boy.

I don't realize that I'm walking towards them until George turns to me.

"Ah, Hudson, can you go inside and help your mother? I think she has a few more bags to bring down."

Grant's eyes flash at my presence. I can tell he didn't expect to have an audience for this exchange. I give him a sympathetic nod, an olive branch, but he retreats to his cabin, slamming the door.

Inside my mother's cabin, the energy is just as toxic.

"You wouldn't believe it," Susan roars into the phone. "That girl drags us all the way to the middle of nowhere, shoves us in this tenement housing for the week, and then proceeds to torture us for an entire afternoon." She acknowledges my presence by holding up a finger, as I lean against the kitchen counter. "Yes. I need your help. Any connections you have out here I'll take them. Doesn't matter the cost."

My mother moves her conversation upstairs, as George steps back into the cabin. Since we have almost nothing in common, our relationship consists mostly of long stretches of silence.

We both stand there, waiting for Susan to finish up.

"So," George says, pouring himself a glass of wine, "you're going to take Elite public when you take over? Finally bring that company to the next level?"

I'm not sure if he's asking because he wants to be first on the jump or if he's planning on offering actual financial advice, but I mimic the same answer my father has been shelling out for years.

"We aren't considering it at this time."

Although opening Elite to the public market would increase our profit margins, my father has never wanted the core values of the company to get lost in corporate greed. From the beginning he has always paid a living wage, offered health and dental packages, and given each employee a two-week travel opportunity on top of their vacation days.

"If you change your mind, you know where to find me," George says, pouring the remaining wine down the sink.

"Let's go," my mother says, carrying a Louis Vuitton duffel down the stairs. "I can't be in this place another minute. Hudson, can you bring the rest of my luggage?"

"Are you coming back tomorrow?" I ask, grabbing two heavy suitcases and wondering if they are forgoing the wedding entirely.

"I have a meeting with a wedding planner in an hour," my mother says, checking her watch. The fact that it's already nine o'clock makes me wonder how much money they're shelling out for this last-minute addition. "Please tell your brother to answer his phone when I call in the morning. We have some things to discuss."

I give her a reassuring nod as I follow her out. After loading her cases into the trunk, I watch them drive away and I swear I can hear celebratory applause coming from the cabins as their taillights disappear into the darkness.

17 MIRA

By the time I make it out onto the lawn, the party posse have fallen into a Shakespearean-level ruckus. I see Angie and Jocelyn roasting marshmallows and Meredith squealing while Derrick chases her playfully across the lawn. And as much as I'm not in the mood to partake in a party, going back to the room, to Hudson, isn't an option.

Thankfully I spot Vanessa and Adrian hanging at a picnic table away from the group.

"You feeling better?" Vanessa asks sympathetically. On the bus ride home she tried her best to console me, but I sat in stoic silence, disassociating for the entire ride, unwilling to break down in front of everyone.

"A bit," I reply, knowing that the mental toll of this week is going to last a lifetime.

Digging through a plastic bag, she hands me a granola bar. "You should eat something."

I open the wrapper and take a bite. It's the first real food I've had since I left this morning, and I relish the crumbly, dry bar as if it's a steak. A number of other snacks sit on the table: Pop-Tarts, individual cereal containers, protein bars, and bags of beef jerky.

"Where did all this come from?"

"Grant hit up the convenience store down the road."

"He didn't rob it, did he?" I ask, watching as Grant pours an entire bottle of liquor into a dual-slot slushie machine.

"Believe it or not, that was already on the property," Vanessa explains, offering me a plastic glass of blue liquid. "Want one?"

"Depends. What is it?" I ask, staring down into the cup.

"Sloshies," she explains. "They're a Wyoming staple apparently."

I gasp hoarsely after taking a sip, the alcohol going straight to my head. "They're aptly named."

"No kidding," Adrian says, as Vanessa sucks down the remaining liquid in her glass.

"I wonder if I can convince Finn to get one of these for the bar?"

My ears perk up at the mention of my favorite dive. "Finn? Like from Finn's bar."

"That's the one."

Invisible strings start threading together in my mind.

"How do you two know each other?"

"He's my brother." Vanessa flashes me a giddy smile. "We don't get to see each other as often as I'd like, living in Charlotte and all, but I've been thinking about moving closer."

"You should," I say, trying to tamp down the hope building in my chest that this rekindled friendship might last longer than the weekend. "Who wouldn't want to live near a bar where you're related to the proprietor?"

"Psh," she scoffs. "Finn'll probably charge us double after the damage Adrian did at the soft opening."

"I can't help that I'm genetically bred to metabolize alcohol like water," Adrian adds, finishing his own drink. "Bring it up with my ancestors."

I chuckle, reaching for a bag of chips, when I spot Hudson walking across the lawn. He's dressed down in a pair of black drawstring shorts that hit above his knee and a pale green tee. I wait for him to greet his friends, say hello to the bride and groom, or kiss his girlfriend, but he saunters over to a chair directly across the lawn from me. His gaze is like fire, igniting a heat deep inside my belly as I gulp down half of my drink to try to numb the flames.

"That's how you two know each other," Vanessa pries, following my gaze. "From the bar?"

"Mmmhmm." I nod, lips pursed, protecting myself from saying anything else that would elicit more unwanted questions. Sharing personal information about my life is hard enough, but revealing the truth about Hudson and me is akin to standing in front of the class naked.

"I have to admit it was pretty badass how he jumped in the river to save you earlier," Vanessa says, scooting closer to me.

Except he's the reason I fell in the first place, I think to myself.

"It was just a reflex," I reason. "Part of those safety seminars companies like his are always boasting about."

Adrian shakes his head. "As a former employee I can attest that while we learned how to save someone choking on a peanut, or to properly team-lift an object over seventy-five pounds, I never saw a training video about jumping into a raging river to save anyone from drowning."

I wish I could explain that his actions were only in penance for the guilt of his indiscretions. But if I cheated on my partner, I would want to stay as far away from the person I cheated with as possible. And yet Hudson continually forces himself into my orbit. Everywhere I turn, he's there. I can't tell if it's because he's trying to keep an eye on me or if he's truly a glutton for punishment. I consider the latter as Angie approaches.

"Anyone tried the beef jerky yet?" she asks, reaching for the bag of petrified meat, ripping open the bag, and taking a whiff. "I swear if I don't get some protein soon I'm going to pass out."

"Can't be as bad as those hamburgers," Adrian says as she pops a piece in her mouth and begins chewing.

"Where'd Jocelyn run off to?" Vanessa asks.

Angie motions across the lawn. "Throwing axes with Derrick."

We all turn our heads, catching sight of a steel blade flying through the air.

"Who gave that man a weapon?" I ask, as the axe lodges itself in the dilapidated barn.

"He stole it from the woodpile," Angie explains as she watches her girlfriend take her turn with the axe. "I'm pretty sure they're doing structural damage to the barn, but none of the staff have tried to stop them."

"I mean, would you?" Vanessa shrugs. "The staff are like lanky babies, and Derrick is like The Rock."

We all watch as Derrick throws again, this time making the entire building shake.

"Want me to get you a refill?" Adrian offers, looking into my empty cup.

"I need to get up anyway," I say, moving towards the Sloshie machine. I need all the liquid courage I can stomach if I'm going to break the news to Meredith that I won't be able to shoot her wedding after all. Sure, it might lead to another bad review but maybe she'll send me back home. At least I'll be free of Hudson and the lingering feelings I still have for him.

Before I can refill my cup, Derrick falls to his knees beside me, opening his mouth beneath one of the nozzles and taking a giant gulp of vibrant red slush as if it's a water fountain.

"These are so great, right?" he says, wiping his mouth with the back of his hand, giving me a playful pat on the back and running back to his game. I stand there for a moment, dazed, as Meredith sneaks up behind me.

"Mira," she squeals, draping her arms around me and giving me a kiss on the cheek. "I'm so glad you're here."

I can tell from her red-stained lips that she's had a Sloshie or two, as I turn to face her.

"How are you enjoying Wyoming so far?"

"It's a beautiful state," I reply genuinely. "And it's been so nice catching up with Vanessa. I haven't seen her since college."

"I know! It's great, right? The Bishop Hall girls are reunited again," Meredith says, her arm wrapping through mine as she guides me to sit down next to her. "We should all meet in my cabin tonight and have a sleepover like the old days."

"For that we'd need a janky laptop, a DVD collection of *New Girl*, and really cheap vodka."

"I can definitely provide the vodka," she jokes, taking another sip of her drink.

"These are good, but I can only have a couple. I swear my tolerance isn't what it used to be."

"That's because we're getting old," she whines dramatically. "I swear it was just yesterday we were playing seven minutes in heaven at the freshman orientation party, and now I'm getting married."

I shake my head, the memory so far away. "Oh God. Please don't remind me of that."

"Why? I remember you having a great time with . . . What was his name . . . ? Callum?"

"Cameron," I correct.

"Man, he was pretty," Meredith says, reminiscing.

"But very dumb," I remind her.

"You always did like the nerdy ones," she jokes, and I'm instantly reminded of Hudson. How he's always armed with a fun fact about plants or animals. How he'd always pull out his well-worn copy of *The Hobbit* on breaks. How he can quote from *The Princess Bride*. Although I shouldn't look for him, I locate him across the lawn. He's sitting with Vivianne, listening intently as she talks, and I know that he's processing every word. I love the way

Hudson would never interrupt a train of thought to interject with his own, giving space for people to be truly heard. I considered it one of his most endearing qualities. And now I wonder if it's a tactic to make people trust him.

"I swear you made all those guys look fuckable after you took their photos for the 'GET TO KNOW ME' wall."

"I did not," I argue, taking a sip of my drink.

"*Catfish* could have done an entire special on that wall, because you made everyone look like supermodels."

"Shut up," I say, swatting her away, my professional plaster chipping off as I revel in the comfortable camaraderie. With Phoebe, I always held back little parts of myself, the messy bits that didn't fit in her perfectly curated world, but Meredith saw the real me—the girl who likes watching scary movies before bed and who screams Midwest emo songs in her car, and who doesn't care about matching her socks or wearing makeup anytime she leaves the house—and she became my friend because of it.

"I would have asked you first," Meredith says, breaking me from my thoughts. "To be my photographer. But I didn't want that to be the first time I'd seen you in years because I needed something."

I swallow hard, not ready to end our friendship just as it's begun again.

"I've always loved your photos, though," she continues, giving my hand a squeeze. "And more than anyone you know how important they are to me."

Unlike other college freshmen who arrived with their entire wardrobe and posters of their favorite bands to tack on the wall, I brought boxes of photographs: years of memories with my friends and family to look back through anytime I wanted to feel close to them. But at least my parents and siblings could share the stories within the pictures, recounting the hidden meaning within each frame. But Meredith would never get that context. She'd never be able to ask them what flavor her birthday cake was, or how long it took to get the crayon off the wall, or what made her parents so happy on that particular day.

"I think it was those nights sitting on the floor, going through those photo albums, that convinced me that I could be a wedding photographer," I admit.

"Really?"

I nod. "I think I wanted people to have a chance to keep as many memories as they could. Those hugs, those secret smiles. They are all a part of someone's story, their life. They're important."

I catch Meredith wiping at the corner of her eye.

"I'm thankful you're here, Mira. That you get to experience this with me."

"Me too," I say, genuinely.

She gives my hand another squeeze, sunshine and adoration glowing behind her eyes. "Let's not go so long without seeing each other again, promise?"

After that heart-wrenching conversation I can't give up now, not when I've got another day to figure something out. Statistically there has to be at least one hobbyist photographer on the property. All I have to do is meet every guest until I suss out which one is secretly harboring a DSLR in their bag. It shouldn't be too hard, since the second those types know I'm the photographer they immediately bombard me with technical questions.

I nod in agreement, as Grant runs over, throwing his arms around his fiancée. She squeals in delight as he leans down to kiss her neck, before scooping her up into his arms and over his shoulder.

"This woman is about to be my wife!" he shouts as he carries her across the lawn towards their cabin. Her laughter echoes through the air as the rest of the party posse couple up, winding down to spend the rest of the evening snuggled up together, but I'm in no hurry to go back to my room.

Sneaking off, I look for a quiet place to wait it out for Hudson and Katherine to fall asleep, or hook up, or whatever it is they do together, but I barely make it halfway across the lawn before the ground spins beneath me.

"Fuck," I say, overcome by the urge to lie down. The grass is cool against my skin, a fine layer of dew forming against the blades as I let the moisture cool me down. All I need to do is let the alcohol work its way through my system. Hiding away in the darkness, I stare up at the sky. It's so luminous, thousands of stars sparkling like pinpricks in fabric as I begin mapping out the constellations: Cassiopeia, Gemini, the Little Dipper.

The last time I stared up at the stars like this was with Phoebe. It was after our final wedding of the season and we'd rented a cabin in Asheville to spend the night drinking red wine and daydreaming about the next chapter in our lives. It was only a few weeks after Phoebe got engaged but I was already thinking about the speech I'd give at her reception, the babies I'd be an eccentric aunt to, and the double dates we'd have once I found the right guy. I could see it so perfectly, growing old beside her.

"I can't imagine doing this without you," she said, clinking our glasses together underneath the stars.

People can understand romantic breakups, the soul-crushing depths of losing a person you thought you'd be with forever. But losing a friend could feel the same way. The only difference is that a partner could be replaced as easily as swiping right on an app, but replacing a best friend, especially as a woman pushing thirty, feels like an impossibility.

A prickle of tears builds behind my eyes, the salt stinging against my cheeks and I know I'm on the verge of an emotional breakdown. The ugly-tears, don't-care-if-snot-runs-down-your-nose kind of breakdown. So when I feel someone sit down beside me, I can't help but look over and want it to be Hudson. To have his calming presence here, even now, after everything. But it's not him. It's Derrick. And I can't hide the disappointment that washes over me.

"Why is there no fucking service out here?" he asks, holding his phone up in the air. "I could kill for some pizza right about now."

"I doubt this place is in anyone's delivery zone," I reason, subtly wiping at my eyes.

"Who the hell can live out here like this?" he groans.

"Cowboys," I reply, chuckling at the inside joke. The only thing I knew about Wyoming came from a casual viewing of *Yellowstone* at Finn's bar. The remote had been lost years ago, so the screen was always on mute with no subtitles, leaving Hudson and me to make up dialogue.

"Fancy seeing you here, partner," he'd say with a thick drawl.

"Yes, well, I came to see some cattle."

"You mean buy cattle?" he'd correct.

"No, see 'em. I got a thing for counting spots."

I stifle a snicker as the memory fades.

"You know, I haven't stopped thinking about you all day," Derrick says, his voice low and rough as he lies down next to me in the grass.

"Embarrassing yourself in front of an entire wedding party does leave a lingering impression," I reply, the sting of humiliation still raw on my skin.

"No. I mean, thinking about you and me." He scoots closer, an arm propped up behind him to lean over me, staring at my lips. I know what he wants and a part of me considers giving in to him, to end the evening in his room just to have a place to sleep away from Hudson and my many mistakes. But before I can decide what *I* want, Derrick's mouth is against mine, his tongue making its way inside my mouth, like an overeager puppy.

His technique is sloppy, and there's a sour acidity under the sickly sweet Sloshie on his breath as his hands paw at me.

I hoped that this might make me feel better. That it might erase the memory of my last kiss, the one with Hudson that set my entire body alight. But there's no passion here. No ache in my chest. Regret pools over me, the sensation akin to bile churning in my stomach. I'm certain that I'm on my way to another mistake, but then Derrick pulls away the second I hear someone scream "FIRE!"

18 HUDSON

The principles of "leave no trace" are ingrained in me the same way I know to look both ways before crossing the street, but watching Derrick kiss Mira, his big hands clumsily reaching for her, I forget everything I've ever learned about fire safety as I drop my flaming marshmallow onto the dry grass. Although I know a hundred different ways to stifle the flames beneath my feet, I allow them to consume the stalks beside me until a wave of glowing sparks shoots into the sky and I yell the word "FIRE!" as loud as I can.

Derrick's instincts kick in immediately as he pushes himself off the lawn to come sprinting towards me. My sigh of relief that he's away from her is cut short as he rips off his shirt. He falls to the ground, pumping his arms back and forth to smother the flames in front of me until he's covered in a thin sheen of sweat, and I worry that I might have just turned him into a fucking Harlequin romance hero.

I glance back to where Mira was sitting, in the hope that she too isn't gazing at Derrick in awe, but she's not there.

"You really need to be more careful," Derrick scolds me, as I spot Mira stumbling down the gravel path.

I leave him to bask in his glory as everyone gives him congratulatory pats on the back, while I catch up to Mira.

"Wait up," I call. "You're going the wrong way."

"I don't need your help, Hudson," she barks angrily, and stops to gain her bearings. She corrects her direction, changing course from the adventure guide camp to the Big Barn.

"I know that," I assure her, taking no offense at her outburst. Unlike Katherine, who needs assistance with almost every task—doing her taxes, opening jam jars—Mira is fiercely independent. Running her own business, living alone, and shutting down assholes at the bar. I've never doubted that she can do anything.

She assesses her surroundings before reorienting herself, a task easier now my phone flashlight is illuminating the path.

"I'm not drunk," Mira argues.

"I didn't say you were."

"But I know you're thinking it," she replies, pressing her finger to her temple.

"Actually, I was thinking about what you had to eat today."

Since the bears disrupted her meal earlier, I'm certain most of her daily calories today have come from sugar and alcohol.

"Vanessa gave me a granola bar," she announces, and my heart sinks. I have a car, I could have gone out and got her something instead of sulking upstairs. I've been so wrapped up in my own feelings, I haven't done the one thing I want to do—take care of her.

I consider asking her to go with me to find a late-night taco stand or twenty-four-hour diner, but I doubt a place exists here.

"Come on," I say, guiding her towards the Big Barn. "I think I saw a vending machine earlier."

"Tried it already," she says, threading her arm through mine. "All I found was a can of Surge and a bag of 3D Doritos."

My pulse quickens as she leans into me, her body warm against mine. I keep my voice steady. "I thought they discontinued those in the early 2000s."

"They call them preservatives for a reason," she says, her voice reverberating through the thin walls. I usher her towards our room.

"I bet we could sell them on eBay," she states, holding up a finger in a eureka moment. "There are collectors out there who will buy anything."

"Is there really a market for moldy chips?"

"If they're shaped like Jesus," she laughs as I unlock the door.

Even though everything is still a mess between us, returning to our typical banter gives me a glimmer of hope that I might be able to salvage this.

"I think I get it now," she says, kicking off one of her shoes.

"Get what?" I ask, keeping a watchful eye on her as she balances on one foot to remove her other shoe.

"Why they call them Sloshies."

"And why is that?"

"Because I am sloshed," she giggles, bumping into the dresser with a clang, and placing her hands on the frame of the bunk bed to steady herself.

"How about we get you to bed?" I say, leading her towards the bottom bunk.

"I'm not tired," Mira protests, like a child, her arms across her chest. Even angry at me I can't help but think how adorable she is.

"If you get into bed, I'll tell you a secret."

It's a long shot. A game we played on particularly boring nights at Finn's. An elevated version of twenty questions that allows the secret-sharer to decide what they are ready to disclose without having to evade unwanted questions. It's how I found out that she never learned how to ride a bike after falling off one when she was five and spraining her ankle. And that her secret comfort show is *Hannah Montana*.

"You do have a lot of those," she scoffs, as a heavy creak rings out through the silent room. I expected her to roll onto the bottom bunk, or stake her claim to the queen bed, both of which I'd award her gladly, but I turn and see her climbing the rungs of the ladder towards the top bunk.

Standing behind her, I keep my arm below her back, at the ready to catch her in case she falls. With each step, her toned legs move upward, until her perfect ass is in my face. I turn away, silently praising the inventor of spandex, and wait for her to get settled.

Once she's completely horizontal, I take my place underneath her in the lower bunk. I stare up at the graffiti scribbles on the slats above me. Typical teenage vandalism. A graphic doodle of a penis. An assortment of rainbow stickers. And a heart with the words "Heather and Ashton 4EVER." I consider if Ashton and Heather are still together when the bed creaks above me.

"Hudson?"

"Yeah?" I ask, desperate for her words.

"Everything is falling apart."

There's a crack in the usual hard cadence of her tone and the softness rips me in two. I hate that I've put her in this situation. I hate that I've caused her pain. And more than that I hate that I can't be the one to take it away.

She takes a breath, readying her words, and I wait for retribution.

"I let someone else drag me into this career because I thought they cared about me, that they wanted what was best for me, that they'd be my support system. And now, I'm stuck fighting for a reputation I don't know if I even want. And I really thought this week could fix everything. And now . . . I feel like I should give up."

As I've gotten to know her, Mira has confessed minor irritations about her job, but I had no idea that she was struggling. This omission makes me want to stand up, crawl into her bunk, slip my arms around her, and assure her that everything will be okay. But I keep my hands at my sides, gripping the fabric underneath me.

“Think of all the great moments you’ve immortalized with your art. Those memories matter to people.”

I think back to her page. The way her photos inspire emotion in anyone who views them, whether they know the subjects or not. As someone who’s seen a lot of flat images in his life, I know how special Mira’s gift is.

“That’s the thing . . . without my camera, I’m nothing to these people. And now that it’s gone, what use am I now?”

“Mira. Don’t say that,” I whisper, hating that she’s been silently battling these feelings. That I might have exacerbated her anxiety.

“I’m going to have to tell Meredith I can’t shoot her wedding.” She’s crying now, her voice breaking into fragmented pieces, and I can’t let her suffer alone. Scooting out of the bunk, I step on the bedframe, resting my arms against the guardrail so that we’re eye-level. She’s cradling her pillow, her mascara-streaked tears leaving a black mark on the pillowcase as I reach over and smooth down her hair.

I expect her to pull away from me, to smack my hand, but she grips her pillow tighter, burying her face. “You’re going to make it through this okay,” I say, rubbing my hand over her back.

“I’m going to have to refund her money. And admit that I’m a sham. I’m going to have to get a job as a barista or a bartender. There’s still an opening at Finn’s, right?”

Her sobs grow louder, as she uses her shirt to wipe her nose.

Dismounting from my perch, I grab a pack of tissues from my welcome bag and hand them to her.

“Take these too,” I offer, giving her an aspirin and water bottle.

Her fingers graze against mine as she takes the pills, popping them between her teeth and swallowing them with a gulp of water. I wait for a moment to see if she needs anything else.

She lies back onto her pillow, but when I go to move I feel her grab my hand. I relinquish it freely, willing to give her anything she needs from me.

"I really, really liked you," she says, her hazel eyes hazy through tears, and the squeeze of her fingers is like a vise grip around my heart.

"I really, really like you too," I admit as I watch her eyelids close, exhaustion taking hold. I continue to stroke her back, moving in little circles, and I realize it's the same technique my mother used on nights I couldn't sleep, standing in the doorway until she led me back to my room. I'd forgotten that she did that. The memory opening a long-sealed door inside of me.

I wait a few minutes, repeating the gesture until Mira's breath falls into a steady rhythm. I wish that I could crawl in beside her, hold her against me, breathe her in and let her know she's safe here, with me, but instead I take my place underneath her.

"Hudson," she says again, her voice just above a whisper.

"Yeah?"

"I want my secret now."

"I'm afraid to start my new job on Monday," I confess, the weight of my insecurities pressing against my chest. "I'm afraid that I'm going to let my dad down or ruin the company he's built. But more than that I'm afraid that no one is going to take me seriously. That I won't be respected. What if I don't have the confidence it takes to actually be a CEO and that I'm only meant for the sidelines?"

The words release like a waterfall, falling in rapid succession.

"That's why I'm in such awe of you, Mira. You're so much like him, my dad. You turned something you love into a business, and you made this amazing career for yourself. You trust yourself enough to know that you can do it on your own. What I wouldn't give for an ounce of that confidence," I say. "But I'll never know what that's like. To be my own person. To create something of my own. I'll always be the boy with his dad's hand-me-down."

I wait for her response, but after a minute, when all I hear is the soft, low hum of her snoring, I know she's asleep. I should follow in her footsteps, close my eyes, and rid myself of the day, but I'm wired, my brain buzzing. I knew that Mira took her job seriously, but I had no idea how much of her self-worth was directly correlated to it, that she thought her ability to take photos was the only reason people wanted to be around her. As if that's all she offers the world.

I want to tell her that it's bullshit. That she's so much more than her job, her camera. To understand that her ability to see the world with a keen intuitiveness, to make magic out of mundane moments, to see the best of everything, is a gift ingrained in her psyche. Her camera is just the conduit. But if she needs it to feel whole, then the least I can do is get her a new one.

Quietly, I sneak out of bed, hoping to locate her ruined equipment, when Katherine barges in through the patio. The door slams behind her and she stumbles in, drunk.

"Can you be any louder?" I ask, my voice a stern whisper as she tosses her bag onto the dresser with a heavy thunk. "Mira's asleep."

"My bad," she says, removing her earrings and bracelets, setting them on the bedside table.

"I'm assuming the party is over then?"

She nods, distracted, and I make a mental note to ensure no one left the fire burning, Derrick's safety speech notwithstanding.

She plops down onto the mattress, patting the space beside her. "Do you want to come to bed?"

I ignore her advances as I grab my keys and wallet from the table. "I have something I gotta take care of."

"At this hour?" she asks, pushing herself off the bed. "I thought we might be able to talk a bit."

"There's nothing to talk about," I assure her for the millionth time.

Rolling her eyes, she makes her way into the bathroom, turning on the faucet. Closing the door, I leave her to complete her thirty-minute nighttime skincare routine as I sneak up to the second floor.

I knock on Vanessa's door twice before she opens it.

"Hudson?" she asks, wiping her sleepy eyes as she greets me in a pink pajama set. Behind her I can see Jocelyn scrolling on her Kindle and Angie asleep on the floor cuddling a pillow. Adrian gives me a wave, eating from a bag of potato chips.

"Sorry, I know it's late but I need your help."

"What's up?" she asks, yawning.

"I was wondering if you knew where Mira left her camera bag?"

"Umm. I think she tossed it in one of the trash cans by the Activity Center."

"Thank you," I reply, retreating to let her go back to sleep.

She gives me a soft smile and goes into her room, while I head straight towards the Activity Center. Mira's bag is exactly where she left it. Except now it's covered in blue Sloshie and discarded baked beans. Pulling it out, I unzip it and begin cataloging the items inside. Once I have all the information I need, I pull out my phone. Two glorious bars greet me as I type into the search.

There's a store four hours away with everything I need in stock. It'll take all night, but if I stop at a gas station and load up on energy drinks I can make it. Pulling out the company credit card, I place the order for next-day pickup and start driving.

19 MIRA

"Ahhhh," I groan, rolling over and removing the water bottle digging into my back. Light streaks across the room through the blindless windows as I reach for my phone to check the time. It's almost noon. Whatever sleep I was able to manage through the drunken night was dreamless, leaving me with the sensation of having just closed my eyes.

I open the bottle and take a swig, trying to wash away the rancid aftertaste that's lingering in my mouth. The memory of Derrick's tongue against mine immediately inspires an urge to brush my teeth. But then another memory comes into focus. Hudson's face illuminated by firelight. Of him getting me into bed safely. And the words that echo in my mind.

"I really, really like you too."

Present tense.

How could he say that to me, and then go to sleep next to his girlfriend?

I tell myself not to rationalize his actions. Because if this year has taught me anything, it's that some people have no shame. Peeking over the edge of the guardrail, I expect to find them cuddled up together, but the bed is empty, the sheets crumpled and mussed, and I wonder if they spent the evening tangled up in them.

I push the image from my mind as I lie down and pretend to be asleep when the door opens.

I can tell it's Hudson by the scent of his shampoo, the earthy aroma soothing my nervous system as he passes by. I hear the rustling of a paper cup being placed on the windowsill beside my bunk, the smell of fresh coffee wafting through the air, and I open an eye and see my name scribbled along the side.

"Thought you might need that," Hudson says, standing a few steps away from me. He's dressed more like himself this morning, in burnt-orange shorts and a boxy white t-shirt with the Great Smoky Mountains screen-printed on it. There's stubble on his face, having forgone his morning shave, and I'm reminded of the man I knew at Finn's. Who exuded confidence even when he had no idea what he was doing. Who always made me a priority no matter how busy it was. Who I couldn't imagine going a day without seeing.

I grab the cup, bringing the warm, aromatic liquid to my lips. The simple, sweet cinnamon balances the robust richness as I moan into the cup before realizing it's my exact order.

"How did you know?"

"You told me," he explains. "The day we were complaining about Starbucks."

It was a blip of a conversation, a side note on how corporations like to rip people off with overly sweet drinks that are excessively complicated. I can't believe he remembered; then again, I knew what would be in his cup as well.

"Earl Grey or peppermint?" He kept both on his person at all times, explaining how no matter where he went he could always find hot water. The quirk came in handy a few times I complained of a sore throat at Finn's, as he offered up his selection for me to choose from.

"Earl Grey," he clarifies, taking a sip.

I watch as he cradles his cup close to his chest.

"I thought you might be hungry, so I left a few things down here for you," he says, taking a step back. The thought of food immediately makes my stomach rumble as I try to remember the last time I ate a proper meal.

I wait for him to leave before I climb down, ecstatic to find a pastry box waiting for me on the desk. Inside is a smorgasbord of sweet treats: croissants, scones, muffins, Danishes, and even a chicken biscuit. I've devoured half the biscuit when I see a large bag, plain tissue paper tucked around the edges, sitting on the bottom bunk. I pluck the note attached.

> *I know this doesn't make it up to you, but I hope it earns me a fraction of your forgiveness. If you're willing to give me a few minutes of your time, I'd love for us to be able to talk. Meet me outside by the main cabins? Hudson*

I peek inside and see a beautiful leather camera bag, a replacement for the one I destroyed yesterday. The gesture, while sweet, still stings, adding proverbial salt to the wound as I'm reminded of everything I lost. But when I lift it out of its wrapping I'm taken aback by its weight.

With shaky hands, I unzip the main compartment and find an arsenal of items inside. Three camera bodies, multiple lenses, two flashes, and even a matching leather hand strap. Hudson hasn't just replaced my gear; he's upgraded it.

I reach for the camera body, removing the protective cap and attaching my go-to lens, a prime thirty-five millimeter. It snaps into place beautifully as I power on the camera, glancing through the viewfinder, snapping a sample photo. The shutter is quick, the focus sharp, and the image on the LCD is crisp and vibrant.

I'll be able to give Meredith the photos she deserves. I'll be able to save my business.

Elation courses through me, until I do a mental calculation of how much this must have cost him. Feeling guilty is one thing, but thirty thousand dollars' worth of gear doesn't feel like an apology, it feels like a bribe.

I can't use it, can I?

I don't want Hudson to think I can be bought, but I have to admit I'm curious as to what he wants to say to me. It's not as if he can lie about having a girlfriend at this point. And after all the trouble he must have gone through to get this for me, a simple conversation doesn't seem like that unreasonable of a request.

Throwing on one of Vanessa's athleisure outfits that make my boobs look amazingly perky, I make my way outside to find him.

"Glad to see you survived last night," Vanessa says when I step out of the door, her eyes hidden behind dark sunglasses as she sits at one of the picnic tables outside the barn, her head resting in her hand. She takes a giant gulp from the pink plastic water bottle she's holding, the color matching her activewear set. "I, on the other hand, am struggling."

"It's the sugar," Adrian groans, taking a seat beside her, looking a little less worse for wear. "You Americans have to put sugar in everything. Alcohol should be simple. Beer or whiskey."

Vanessa swats at a mosquito on her arm, grabbing a bottle of bug spray from the table and spraying it all over her body.

"Good call," I say, noticing the bites on my own arms. "I got eaten up last night."

"Considering we're about to spend the rest of the day outside, I need to be proactive."

"What are you doing?" I ask, curious if Meredith's scheduled one of those group-building exercises like capture the flag or a human relay.

"We are sourcing wildflowers for the bouquets and floral arrangements on our nature walk," she explains, just as Angie, Jocelyn, and Katherine file out of the lobby carrying plastic buckets.

The statement takes me off guard. "Meredith didn't hire a florist?"

"She said she wanted the entire event to be authentic to the land," Jocelyn explains, pulling her hair back into a ponytail.

Vanessa's eyes find mine, and I know we are thinking the same thing. On nights out in college, Meredith would always forget something: her keys, her phone, where she parked her car. So it's entirely possible that she would forget something as pivotal as a florist.

"Are you going to be joining us?" Katherine asks.

It's the first time we've really spoken since I arrived, and although her words sound friendly enough, her body language is anything but.

"I was actually going to do some recon at the park. Find the best spots for photos for tomorrow," I lie, avoiding the fact that I came out here to find her boyfriend. But now that I've said it aloud, it would be a way to get me out of any group activities for the rest of the day. "Adrian, do you think I could borrow your Jeep? I can show proof of insurance and gas it up and everything."

"As much as I'd love to let you have it, it's not mine."

"Whose is it?"

Hudson clears his throat, coming up from behind me. "It's mine."

His green eyes are warm and inviting in the sunlight, the freckles along his cheekbones more prominent, matching the faint dots that coat the rest of his body.

"I can give you a ride if you want," he offers, but before I can respond, loud honking rips through the air, as Grant's green Subaru makes its way down the path.

"Aye," Grant says through the open driver-side window as he parks in a space right in front of us. Getting out, he shares a half-hug, half-handshake with Derrick. "You ready to go fuck up these rocks, bro?"

"Hundred percent," Derrick replies, jumping in the air and grabbing one of the beams overhead, hoisting himself up with one arm.

"Get down from there before you break your leg," Meredith says, exiting the passenger seat. At her request, his feet return to the pavement as he throws a playful arm around her shoulders. "What the bride wants, she gets."

"Rocks?" I ask Vanessa, confused. "I thought you were wildflower-picking?"

"A few of us are going to go rock climbing at Blackrock Ridge," Derrick explains, running his hands through his dark hair suggestively. "You should come."

"You a climber?" Grant asks, showing his first real interest in me since my arrival.

"No. Not at all. Weddings are the only physical exertion I need," I joke.

"What about you?" Grant nods towards Adrian. "You in?"

"Hard pass, mate," Adrian says, setting down his book. "Can't be breaking a bone in these parts. Your American medical rates are astronomical."

"That means you can come flower-picking with us," Vanessa says, patting his knee and handing him a pair of shears and gloves from the pile.

The groups begin splitting off—Derrick, Grant, and Jocelyn towards the Subaru for rock climbing, and Vanessa, Adrian, Meredith, and Katherine towards the flower field.

Hudson hangs back, waiting for me. "You ready to go?"

I nod, eagerly, as Katherine doubles back.

"Hey, Mere. Weren't you just saying that Grant was a bit camera-shy?" she asks, her voice sharp. "Maybe Mira should tag along with them, give them a chance to get to know each other before the big day tomorrow."

"Oh, that's a wonderful idea," Meredith beams. "Mira, what do you think?"

Given that I've barely spoken a handful of words to Grant since my arrival, the request makes sense, but my stomach feels queasy. Phoebe made the same suggestion when she started dating Cliff, but no matter how many times we tried to bond I never warmed up to him. I put on my best friend hat and faked it. I laughed at his jokes and asked about his life anytime we were together. I should have told him to fuck off. That he'd never be good enough for my best friend.

But Grant isn't Cliff. And Meredith isn't Phoebe. So I reply through gritted teeth. "That sounds great."

"Hell yeah," Derrick says, slinging an arm over my shoulder, the unexpected intrusion into my personal space causing me to bump into Hudson until my back is pressed against his chest. I swear he keeps a protective arm by my side as he moves me out of the way.

"You guys got room for one more?" Hudson asks, and I can't help but notice the visible shock on Grant's face.

"You want to come with us?"

"Yeah. It's a beautiful day, why not."

"Oh no you don't," Katherine says, shoving a bucket into Hudson's hands. "Meredith needs your botanist skills. I can't have anyone infect my guests with poison sumac or flesh-eating spores."

Hudson gives me a sympathetic stare that makes me wish I'd gotten up five minutes earlier, as we head in different directions.

20 HUDSON

"Thanks so much for tagging along," Meredith says, walking beside me as the rest of the group moves slowly through the field. I can smell the faint scent of alcohol permeating through everyone's sweat as they power through their hangovers.

"It's no problem," I lie, kicking my bucket like a child who just got told they have to do their chores before they can go play with their friends.

I should be driving Mira to the park right now, or catching up on sleep since I watched the sunrise from the highway this morning as I made my way to the camera store. But thanks to Katherine butting in, I'm here, losing the headway I gained last night while Mira spends her afternoon with Grant and his lackeys.

"Are you two doing okay?" Meredith asks, pulling me from my thoughts.

"Who?"

"You and Katherine."

"Oh yeah. We're fine," I reply half-heartedly.

"Does she know that?" she asks sweetly.

"Did she say something?"

"No," Meredith says, shaking her head. "But she's been moping around ever since you got here. I know weddings can be stressful, especially with Susan. I know she's been putting stress on you to propose but I'd love it if you could try to put whatever's going on between you two aside, just until tomorrow. I don't want to have my best friend sulking on my wedding day."

I give Meredith my best smile, trying to hide my annoyance. "I'll see what I can do."

"Thanks, Hudson," she says, giving my arm a squeeze and venturing into the field.

I easily catch up with Katherine. She swats at a honeybee flying above her, and when it lands on her shoulder, I watch her pull out a travel-size can of bug spray from her fanny pack.

"Don't," I say, taking the can from her.

"Right, because the bees are your priority," she says, picking up her bucket and moving towards the field.

"Considering a third of our crops rely on them, they should be everyone's priority."

"Meredith is deathly allergic so I'm just trying to be prepared," she says, taking the can from me and putting it back in her pack before bending down and aggressively cutting a flower at its stem.

In front of us the field is covered in native flowers, the orange Indian blanket flowers, blue Rocky Mountain columbine, and purple daisies blending together harmoniously among the tall grass.

"Why did you volunteer me for this?" I ask, following behind her.

"I thought I was saving you," Katherine argues. "You never want to spend time with Grant."

"Maybe I'm trying to make an effort."

"That's funny," she scoffs. "You never wanted to do anything with anyone when we were together and the second we break up you've become an extrovert, saying yes to hangs with the guys?"

"And I think it's funny that for someone who wants to pretend we're still together, you told Meredith that we're fighting."

"I needed some excuse to explain why you've been hanging out with everyone but me since you got here."

"Some of these people are my friends too," I argue back.

"Like the photographer?" Katherine shouts, then lowers her voice. "I swear every time I turn around you're talking to her. You know how that looks, right?"

"Like I'm trying to be friendly to the person who's staying in our room."

Katherine huffs, her stare as sharp as the shears in her hand.

"What do you want from me?"

"I want you to do what you said and pretend that you still like me. I mean, fuck, Hudson, I haven't seen you in weeks."

"We live together, Katherine. You've seen me."

"No. I haven't. You took a second job just to get away from me. You sneak in when I'm asleep and sneak out before I wake up. It's like you can't even look at me anymore."

I pull at the neckline of my shirt, sweat dripping down my sides.

"I'm not stupid. I know that we aren't together, but I didn't realize that we couldn't even be friends."

"We are friends."

"No. We aren't. We used to talk about our days. Check in with one another. Let each other know when the milk was empty. But you've completely shut me out."

There's pain behind her eyes, the sting of rejection a foreign notion to her. And it's not fair.

"I guess I thought this trip might give us a chance to reconnect."

I reach for her bucket, knowing that we need to have a serious conversation, one away from the prying ears and eyes of the party posse.

"Katherine, I think we need to talk," I say, as Meredith screams from across the field.

"I lost my ring!" she shouts, holding her hand up, her ring finger bare. "I told Grant we should get it resized but we both kept forgetting, and now . . ."

"We'll find it," Katherine assures her, bending down to start searching. "Which direction were you coming from?"

Meredith points to the section of stomped-down grass behind her.

"I bet they have a metal detector back at the Activity Center," Adrian says. "I can run down and check."

"Does that work on white gold?" Meredith asks, her face pale.

"That's still a metal," Vanessa quips, setting down her own bucket with a heavy sigh, bending down to aid in the search.

"It has to be in this area," Meredith explains, extending her arm to indicate the search ratio.

"And you checked the bucket?" I ask.

Meredith peeks inside, handing the flowers to Katherine as she dumps out a smattering of leaves from the bottom. "It's not there."

"Let's divide into sections," Katherine says, instructing Angie. "We'll each go to our left, and then after five minutes we'll switch. Sound good?"

Angie nods, before they slink through the tall grass on their hands and knees, almost indistinguishable beside the movement of the stalks.

"Are you going in?" I ask Vanessa, who's standing next to me, sans bucket.

"What's the expression about too many cooks . . ." she replies. "I'm sure it's like right under their feet."

"That's what I'm worried about. They're probably digging it further into the dirt."

The grass sways frantically as they crawl through.

"You should wait for the metal detector," I call out, but they ignore me.

"Oh my God!" Meredith shrieks, jumping up and down. "I FOUND IT!"

Meredith and Angie both stand, their brows sweat-stained as Katherine places the ring back on her finger, clutching her hand to her chest.

"Mere," Katherine says, her voice panicked. "I need you to stay still, okay."

"Why?" Meredith asks, her eyes wide.

"There's a bee."

"Get rid of it," Meredith shouts, freaking out.

"I'm going to," her friend assures her, digging in her fanny pack.

"Kat, for real, I can't find my EpiPen, I thought I packed it. You have to do something."

Pressing down on the nozzle, the aerosol shoots out. But when Meredith lets out a blood-curdling scream, I know something is very wrong. I'm certain she's been stung, that she's going into anaphylaxis, until Katherine falls to the ground behind her, dry-heaving.

"What's happening?" Vanessa asks as Meredith runs in circles, her hands over her eyes. It isn't until the wind blows the faintest scent of pepper and toxins towards me that I understand what's happened.

"Bear spray," I say, running over to help them.

Vanessa and Angie follow behind me as we rush to help them up, only to be intercepted by Tonya and Adrian.

"What the hell is going on here?" Tonya asks, dropping the metal detector.

I hand Tonya the bottle, and her eyes go wide. We both know that between the bear sighting yesterday and her informational pamphlets, this mishap is partly her fault. But neither of us mention it as we move the girls down the path towards the Activity Center.

"There's an eye-washing station over here," she instructs, as we guide Meredith towards the industrial spray unit.

"What about me?" Katherine wails, her eyes inflamed and puffy from the blowback as she cries.

"We only have one station," Tonya says as she helps Meredith wash out her eyes.

"I got you," Adrian says, running into the café. I expect him to come back with a bottle of water but instead he holds out a pint of vanilla ice cream. Scooping it out with his hands, he slathers it on Katherine's eyes.

"Better?"

"No," she cries, kneeling over and retching on the lawn, as milky liquid pools down her face.

"She needs to get in the shower, to get the oil off her skin," I explain to Vanessa, hoping she can take her off my hands.

"Can you take me?" Katherine cries. And as much as I don't want to see her in pain, I know that taking care of her like this will only blur the lines further.

"I've got her," Vanessa offers, taking pity on me.

"Make sure to use cold water," I say, remembering that's all there is in our cabin. "If things don't improve in an hour, then it might be a good idea to head to Urgent Care."

Katherine wails again as Vanessa guides her down the path towards the Big Barn.

I consider going with them, but worry gnaws in my stomach. If wildflower-picking could go so haywire, could something worse be happening to Mira at rock climbing?

Grabbing my keys, I head to my Jeep and speed off the property.

21 MIRA

It isn't until I'm staring up Blackrock Ridge, with its sharp edges and towering peaks, that I realize I've made another error in judgment by agreeing to this excursion. It's hard to say no when people are paying you to be agreeable, to provide a service, to smile and say "Of course, I'd love to," even if that means riding in a tiny airplane piloted by the groom or taking photos in the middle of a three-day bluegrass festival or climbing a cliffside.

"Ready to saddle up?" Bo asks, handing me a helmet.

"I should probably stay on solid ground today," I reason.

Although this trip might not reflect it, I do learn from my mistakes, and after yesterday's fiasco, bringing my camera into another danger zone isn't something I'm comfortable with.

"It'll be fine," Derrick says, strapping into his harness. "You came all the way out here, you might as well experience what Wyoming has to offer."

"I can't really climb with my camera bag," I say, hoping the excuse will be enough to placate him. But Derrick seems to have an answer for that as well.

"Bo will look after it for you, right, man?"

"Yes, ma'am. It won't leave my sight." Bo holds out his arms as if he's about to cradle a newborn baby. Even though I don't have much faith in the man, I take off my bag and hand it over. It's a caramel-honey color, the leather conditioned and smooth. With thick stitching and precise craftmanship, the piece should last a lifetime, or at least longer than the cheap bags I'm accustomed to.

Hudson always suggested that I invest in a better bag, one that didn't have plastic buckles that would break off and scratch my skin, or zippers that would stick. I'm sure he picked this bag carefully, with its brass hardware and suede detailing just for me. That he put thought into choosing a bag that would serve me just as well as I served it.

I can't deny that my mind ruminated on what he might have to say to me the entire ride here. If he'd shower me with excuses or find words that would make me consider forgiveness. The scenarios linger in my mind as I move forward in line.

Grant is standing in front of me, shifting his weight from side to side.

Before Phoebe's wedding, getting grooms to open up to me was one of my crowning achievements. I'd gone so far as reading up on a handful of topics to connect with them: from NCAA basketball to top-charting video games, Marvel movies, and even the future of crypto. And it worked. After a few carefully timed comments I'd have them relaxed enough to crack jokes and enjoy their time in front of the camera. But now, since Phoebe's wedding, a layer of fear hangs over every interaction.

"All that energy for the cliff or for the wedding tomorrow?" I ask, doing my best to honor the assignment I was sent here to do.

"The wedding for sure." Grant stares down at me, stretching his arm over his head, completely unfazed by the bodies scaling the cliffside.

"I don't know, that's pretty high off the ground there," I say, watching the climbers scale up ahead of us.

"Yeah, but once I get to the top, it'll be over. I'll know the course. It'll never change. But with Meredith, I'm going to spend the rest of my life getting to know her. We're going to keep evolving and changing, becoming new people, and I'm ready for that. Of continuously getting to fall in love with her."

The sentiment is endearing but after enduring so much change these last few months, I want something permanent. A dedicated partner to drink coffee and watch bad TV with, someone who will always laugh at my jokes, and who knows when I need a hug at the end of the day. A person I can depend on. A person who won't change their mind about me.

"I don't think Meredith told me the story of how you two met," I say as we watch the next group begin their ascent up the mountain.

Typically, this was the first thing I learned about a couple. The first question on my contact form. But since Meredith called me directly, I'm clueless as to the specifics. Just another reminder of how far I've let our friendship slide these past few years.

"Labor Day party at my dad's house," he states. "Hudson brought Katherine, and she brought Meredith."

"You're stepbrothers, right?" I ask, piecing the family tree together.

"Yeah, my dad married his mom when I was nine."

"You must be close then?"

"Not really," Grant mumbles, running a hand through his hair. "He stayed with us a few summers, but then he went off and did camps with his dad. I don't blame him really. I'd choose travel over being stuck at our house."

I can hear the pain behind his words, and I can't determine if it's jealousy or anger seeping through.

"But Meredith and Katherine are best friends?"

"Yeah. They try to get us to double date but it's more awkward than fun. I'm not saying I hate the guy or anything, but Hudson and I, we're just different. And you know how sibling relationships can be. You act like dicks to each other and then you move on. But I think I took it too far a few times, and Hudson never got over it."

I can't imagine anyone being mean to Hudson without cause. Hell, even I'm struggling to keep up my own cold shoulder and I have a valid reason. I want to ask about their relationship, to gain more insight into who Hudson really is as a person, but Bo interrupts our conversation.

"Alright, Majestic group, you're up!" he says, instructing us to gather at the base of the cliff.

"Think fast," Derrick says, tossing me a small bag that covers me in a white powder.

"What the—?" I ask, dropping it onto the ground, and clapping my hands together to expel the residue.

"Chalk," he explains, picking up the bag. "It helps with grip."

"Cool," I reply, as if grip is going to be my biggest problem.

"I've done this hundreds of times," Jocelyn assures me, sensing my hesitation. "You go up, you come down. Easy peasy."

"I think we have different definitions of easy," I say, readjusting my helmet. I've never been one to shy away from new experiences, but lately I'm more hesitant of my decision-making abilities.

"Make sure these are tight," Derrick says, helping me adjust the straps of my harness. His hands linger a second longer than necessary as he tightens them around my waist and thighs. "I'm part of a rock-climbing gym back in Charlotte and this is nothing. And I'll be behind you the whole way."

I bet you will, I think to myself as I watch him check out my ass for the umpteenth time this afternoon.

"You just gotta find your footing," Derrick explains, effortlessly leaping into the air and grabbing hold of the first rock he touches.

"Footing. Sure," I mumble, moving my boot up off the ground and against the coarse rock, kicking myself for agreeing to this.

Luckily, the course is color-coded. Little green-and-blue markings symbolize easy-access areas, yellow and purple are intermediate, and red and orange are hard. Jocelyn is already a quarter way up the ridge, as I attempt to move towards the first green rock. I barely make it to the second marker before my foot slips, and I slide down to the ground, skinning my knee.

The rock is rough against my skin as I use my limited upper-body strength to try again. I assumed that carrying all that camera equipment on my shoulders would have made me stronger, but all it seems to have given me is lower back pain. Harnessing the power of my legs, I push myself to the next marker, and then the next, until I'm a quarter of the way up.

"See, you got this," Derrick cheers from above, as I slowly continue climbing.

My muscles are on fire, and my skin is peeling off every time my shin collides with rock, but I keep going, determined to make it to the top. I'm just passing the three-quarter marker when I feel my boot slip.

I try to hold on, but my grip is weak, and I free-fall downwards. The harness prevents me from careening into the ground below, but the force of it takes my breath away. I don't even notice that I'm swinging back towards the cliff face until my knee smacks against it, ripping the already thin skin to shreds.

"Fuck. Fuck. Fuck," I hiss, trying to steady my breathing back into a normal rhythm, as blood streams down my leg.

Shock and calm fight one another as I glance down and see Hudson bypassing the line to secure himself to the rope.

"Mira, hold on, okay? I'm going to come and get you."

I wish I could tell him to fuck off, but it seems that my mouth is incapable of making any sound other than a frightened whimper as I watch him climb up to me with the speed and agility of an Olympic athlete.

"Are you okay?" he asks, once he reaches me, worry etched across his face.

"My knee is fucked," I say, exposing the trail of blood running down my leg.

"I'm going to get you down from here, but to do that I have to attach your clip to mine," he assures me, as a protective hand makes its way to the small of my back. His green eyes find mine, tranquil like a Pacific Northwest forest, and staring into them I forget that I'm dangling from the side of a cliff as he reaches for my rope.

"Are you sure you know what you're doing?" I ask, watching him clip his carabiner to mine. His fingers trail down my spine, firm yet gentle, and my heart starts pounding for another reason besides fear. He must feel it, the rapid thumping against his chest, because he moves a hand to my face.

"You can trust me," he says, his tone reassuring. And yet the word presses the bruise in my heart.

"You've proven the opposite, actually."

"I know," he breathes, regret softening his features. "But no matter how you feel about me right now, I need you to know that I've done this hundreds of times. And I promise I will get you to the bottom safely."

I know that everyone is watching us, and a part of me is afraid that if I let Hudson help me, they might see how much I want to hold onto him, that they might intuit what transpired between us, and it'll earn me another strike against my already tarnished reputation. But the other part of me, the one that wants to be rid of this mountain, slowly moves towards him.

"Put your arms around my neck," he instructs, the words an order, as I try not to breathe in the earthy scent of him. Instinctively I cling to him, and I'm hyper-aware of the tightness in his shoulders, the muscles flexed against his abs, the pressure of his hands. Regret tightens in my chest as I remember the way those hands rubbed my back last night. Of how I wished he'd crawl into bed with me and use those hands to hold me; to brush them against my lips and kiss me like he had the other night.

I worry he might be able to read my thoughts when I notice a bashful shade of pink flush against his cheeks.

"Hold on tight, okay," he says as I bury my head in his neck, breathing him in. God, he smells good, like rain and honey. Subtle and inviting. And I take another deep breath before we're in free-fall, triggering a stomach-dropping sensation that makes me grip onto him even tighter.

"I thought you said you were going to get me down safely," I scold, clinging to him like a small child.

"We have to release the tension from the line," he explains, tugging on the rope. His feet press up against the mountainside as he takes another step back and we move down another few feet. I don't realize that we've hit solid ground until I hear the clapping from the onlookers beside us.

Hudson's hand is still pressed against the small of my back, holding me close. I want to sink into him, to press my lips to his, to let go, but I can't. Pulling back, I unbuckle my helmet, toss my harness to the ground, and walk away.

I need a minute to think, to get away from the smell of him. To remind myself that no matter how badly I want him, he belongs to Katherine and that's a line I'll never cross.

"Mira, wait up," Hudson says, chasing after me, but I'm using every speed-walking technique I can remember from freshman gym class. I heel, ball, and toe it towards the desert, tricking myself into believing I have some semblance of control over my life, before Hudson grabs my arm. The gentle tug is enough to get my attention.

"What do you want from me, Hudson?" I snap, spinning around and ripping the delicate seams of my emotions. "At first, I thought you were trying to cover your ass. Then, I considered that the fish, the coffee, the camera, that it was guilt. But having you perpetually show up and come to my rescue, to act like you care about me, it feels like torture, okay? You're torturing me. So please, just leave me alone."

The words hang in the air between us, a tension building like a summer thunderstorm as I wait for him to respond. Finally, after what feels like a lifetime, he speaks. "Katherine and I aren't together."

"As of what? Two seconds ago?" I scoff, the words hollow in my ear.

"We haven't been together for months," he clarifies, but I'm wary.

"Does she know that?"

Hudson nods, dragging a hand down his face. "We thought it would be easier to keep up the pretense of a relationship until the wedding was over and we could move on. We didn't want to put more stress on Meredith's plate."

No matter how badly I want this to be real, I'm skeptical. I've seen first-hand how easily men can lie to get what they want, and I refuse to get caught up in another man's mess.

"And so that's why you still have photos of you together in your apartment? For Meredith's benefit?"

"Katherine didn't have enough money to get her own place so I told her she could take a few months, save up. She was waiting for this big sale at work, and then she started dragging her feet. I couldn't kick her out but I couldn't be there either," he explains. "I took that job at Finn's to put distance between us. Then, when I met you, I signed up for as many shifts as possible in the hope that you'd be there. I even started coming in on days I wasn't scheduled. I told Lilah I'd give her all my tips so she wouldn't tell me to go home."

I stifle a chuckle, realizing why Lilah was so distraught to lose him.

"Why didn't you tell me?"

"I was scared," he admits, shifting his weight, rubbing his hands against his neck nervously. "The situation isn't exactly normal, and I thought you might not believe me, or be comfortable with it. So I thought I'd wait it out until Katherine moved out. You have to admit, it's a bit crazy."

"I'd say pretending to still be together is a little crazier, but I get your point."

"I need you to know I was going to ask you out for real. I had it all planned. I was going to take you to dinner and share a bottle of wine, and tell you everything. But when you kissed me, all logic went out the window. I'm so sorry, Mira."

The admission makes my skin tingle like the breaking of a spell, as I see him in a new light.

"It was stupid and—"

Before he can say another word, I grab the fabric of his shirt, bring his mouth to mine.

22 HUDSON

How is this happening again? I think to myself, as I allow Mira's tongue to slip into my mouth. Her lips are salt, and fire, and sweetness all wrapped in one as I thread my hand through her hair and pull her closer to me.

"Wait," I say, resting my forehead against hers, trying to catch my breath.

"What?" Mira asks as her hand rests against my chest, my heart pounding underneath her fingers, mine atop hers.

"I think I just need a minute to process," I say, taking her in. The usual heavy makeup she wears is gone, showcasing a dizzying array of freckles that dance along her nose and cheeks. I thought she was beautiful before, but seeing her like this—unfiltered and bare-faced—takes my breath away.

"I'm the one who just got info-dumped," she replies, a smirk growing across her lips.

"I know. I'm sorry. I just can't believe this."

"That I forgave you or that we're kissing?"

"Both," I chuckle, insecurity washing over me. "I guess there was a part of me that worried when you snuck out of my apartment that you regretted coming home with me, or had a bad time, or weren't that into me."

"Hudson," Mira says, tilting her chin so her lips are a whisper away from mine, "I've been into you since the first time we met."

"I'm pretty sure I spilled PBR on you that night."

"It was endearing," she replies as she lingers in my arms, her hazel eyes staring at me with the same warmth and trust she had for me at Finn's.

Now that there are no more secrets between us, I'm ready to give her all of me. But before I can, I glance down and catch the sight of the blood caked on the side of her leg.

"Fuck," I breathe. "We need to get you bandaged."

"It's just a flesh wound," she laughs. And even though I find her quoting *Monty Python* to me utterly endearing, I find it impossible to find humor in her being in pain.

"Come on, I have a first-aid kit in the Jeep." Reaching for her hand, I'm overcome by the sensation of her fingers slipping into my hand as we walk across the parking lot together.

"I've hurt myself on the job a lot worse than this," she assures me, as I help her into the front seat.

"Are weddings that dangerous?"

"You have no idea," she says, pointing towards a long thin line down her shin. "See this scar? The maid of honor pushed me into a door because she wanted to be the one to hold the bride's train even though I assured her I got it. Had to have six stitches. But I didn't get a drop of blood on the wedding dress."

"Jesus," I say, popping open the top of the first-aid kit and extracting the necessary items.

"That's not even the worst one." She tosses her hair to the side, exposing a slew of discolored marks along the side of her neck.

"Burn marks, from a Fourth of July wedding, where the groomsmen bought bottle rockets instead of sparklers. Luckily the groom was in the Army, so he jumped on top of the bride before she could get hurt. I wasn't as lucky."

"I'd hate to be your insurance provider," I jest.

"My premiums are pretty high."

Delicately, I wipe away as much of the blood on her knee as I can before ripping open an alcohol wipe.

"This might sting," I warn.

"I can handle it," she says, wincing.

My hands work slowly, relishing the feeling of her skin against mine as I make sure there aren't any deeper lacerations hiding underneath the blood. But when all I see are surface scratches, I slather on disinfecting ointment and wrap it in gauze.

"Why are you smiling like that?" I ask, securing my work with a piece of surgical tape.

"I'm just thinking about how you're so good at so many things, but you can't make a whiskey sour to save your life."

"You really don't like my drinks?" I'd thought her earlier comments were a dig to cut me down. But they couldn't be that bad, could they?

Mira bites at her lip, holding back a smile as she tries to gently let me down. "No one wants to tell the sweet, attractive bartender that they wasted twelve dollars. But, Hudson, your drinks suck."

I mockingly place a hand over my chest. "Damn. Even hearing you say I'm attractive doesn't ease the hurt."

"Oh my God. Shut up." She blushes bashfully, and I have to admit every time it happens it's like I've completed a quest.

"How about I make it up to you by taking you out for a real cocktail when we get home. At one of those fancy bars where they have the mood lighting and overpriced olive bowls," I offer, ready to put a real date in the calendar.

"Or you could buy me one now?"

23 MIRA

"I thought we were getting a drink," I say as Hudson pulls the Jeep off the side of the road, parking in an unmarked spot in front of a trailhead.

"I want to show you something first," he says, letting his fingers linger against the bare skin of my thigh before unbuckling his seatbelt. He didn't stop touching me the entire ride. While one hand stayed on the steering wheel, the other stretched over to play with my hair, or dance along my shoulder, or hold my hand.

Walking around the car, Hudson opens my door for me. He extends his hand, and I use it to support my weight as I drop the two feet down onto the ground.

"God, I hate being short," I say, regaining my balance.

"I know what you mean," Hudson replies, dragging a hand down his face, an insecurity tic I've grown to notice.

"What, you're five ten? Five eleven."

"Five nine according to my last physical."

"That's tall," I argue.

"Is it?"

"Please," I scoff. "I hate this idea that men have to be six feet tall to be attractive. Not that you're short," I ramble. "All I'm saying is, I bet you've never had to ask for help to reach the yogurt on the top shelf of the grocery store."

"You got me there," he laughs. It's a genuine smile, and I want to capture it, print it out, and keep it in my wallet to look at whenever I need a pick-me-up.

Standing on my tiptoes, I reach into the backseat to grab my camera bag. I made Hudson double back for it before we left, and I'm aching to test it out.

"I got it," Hudson says, grabbing the strap and hoisting it over his shoulders. "My dad told me about this place just below this ridge. It has breathtaking views if you're up for a hike."

"This isn't going to be one of those nine-mile hikes, right? Because I would like to point out that I am injured and definitely not wearing the right shoes and . . ."

"It's not," Hudson replies, intertwining his fingers with mine, the motion distracting me from the fact he's leading me to a trail. "But we can take breaks if you need."

"If it's so short, why would we need to take breaks?" I counter.

He flashes me a devious smile and I know that this is going to be the longest hike of my life.

"I promise it'll be worth it."

And because I've no reason to doubt him anymore, I follow him into the forest.

Hudson stays one step ahead of me, pointing out obstacles on the path. We bypass a fallen tree, a handful of boulders, and with each one, he ensures I make it through safely, holding my hand and helping me over each one. Through the woods, the shade of the treetops provides pockets of cooler air that offer a little refuge from the blistering heat of the day. We take it slow, no rush to get anywhere, and I have to admit that it's nice being away from the hustle and bustle of the ranch. Here I don't have to smile or entertain conversation. I don't have to worry about what I'm wearing or how I'm perceived. I can just be.

Hudson must feel that way too because he stops along the path several times to point out native plants and insects, or to admire a cluster of mushrooms growing on a mossy tree. He's smiling from ear to ear, teaching me about things I would have never thought to look up. And I can tell that here, in nature, is where he truly thrives.

"If you love this stuff so much, why are you afraid to take over Elite?" I ask, recalling his words from last night.

Hudson sighs, the tension in his shoulders returning. "You remember that?"

I nod, recalling the words he spoke to me, the vulnerability behind them. "You've worked for your dad for what, a decade at least, right? I'm sure you're more than qualified to run his company."

"On paper, technically. But it's a lot of pressure. My dad has this presence, you know. And I don't think I can ever garner that level of respect, or if I even deserve it."

"Think of it like Excalibur. You wouldn't be able to wield the sword if you weren't worthy of it," I say, excited to see the reference light up his face.

"You watched *Merlin*?"

"I couldn't sleep and you wouldn't shut up about it," I explain. "If I'm going to mock you I need the evidence to back it up."

"Still. I'm no King Arthur," he replies, sullen, and I hate that he thinks so low of himself.

"You're ready for this," I state, matter-of-factly.

"Tell that to my anxiety nightmares," he jokes, extending a hand to help me over a tree stump. His grip is gentle as he guides me, keeping a steady hand on my waist.

"Think of this as an opportunity to make Elite your own. Sure, it was your father's, but he's passed it on to you. Is there anything you'd want to change about the company?"

Hudson stops in his tracks, as if he needs to use his entire concentration on the answer.

"I want to do more community engagement. Weekend programs and summer camps to teach about native plants and animals, all while creating space to inspire people to take on similar work in the future."

"That sounds totally doable."

"And I want to start a scholarship-based education camp for kids, to bolster interest in environmental studies and parks and recreation programs."

"I'm surprised you don't have one already."

"My dad was more focused on expanding the brand, getting us in a good financial position," Hudson explains. "We have programs that work with already established camps, but I'd love to create my own. The Elite Elevation Experience."

"That sounds cool as hell. I only lasted two days at summer camp before I was calling my mom to come pick me up," I admit, recalling my brief stint in Girl Scouts. "I don't last long without my creature comforts."

"I'll remember that," he says, as he guides us towards a clearing. A glistening body of water lies ahead of us. It's crystal clear with colorful rocks embedded beneath the surface. It feels as if we've traveled to another dimension. The Tetons are reflected across the surface of the water, which glows a jade green—the same color as Hudson's eyes.

"Why do I feel like I just stepped inside a Bob Ross painting?" I ask, hypnotized by its beauty.

"It's gorgeous, right?" he says, taking a deep breath, letting the mountain air fill his lungs. "I've wanted to come here since I landed."

"You had a car. You could have left anytime."

"Yeah, but once I saw you, I knew I didn't want to come here alone," he says, taking my hand and leading me down to the lake. We find a spot along the water's edge, and Hudson sets my camera bag down and takes a seat beside it. I follow suit, staring into the distance with awe.

I focus my attention on the landscape. The towering evergreens and the yellow-and-gold flowers growing between. The lake holds a perfect reflection of the blue sky. The sound of sloshing water mingles with birdsong and the chittering of insects to create a soothing song. For the first time since I arrived, I'm thankful I said yes to Meredith. To Hudson. To going outside my comfort zone. And although I gravitate towards photos with moving subjects, I want to take this memory home.

Opening my camera bag, I click my lens into place and set up my shot, waiting for the clouds to cross along the skyline before I click the shutter.

"Can I see?" he asks. I hand him my camera.

He takes a moment to study the image. "This is amazing."

"It's just this place. I didn't do anything."

"Mira. I have to sort through photos from my colleagues all the time and this is better than anything we've ever done."

I try not to let his words go to my head.

"Thank you, by the way. For the camera. I know it must have cost a fortune and I'm going to pay you back. My insurance should cover the old one and then—"

"Don't worry about it," he says, cutting me off.

"Hudson, I can't accept thirty thousand dollars' worth of camera equipment."

"It's a write-off."

I stare at him incredulously. "I do taxes too you know, and I can't let you start off your CEO career with embezzlement."

"Trust me. No one will bat an eye about it, especially if you take a few photos we can use for socials."

"A few photos is not worth that much."

"We pay a thousand dollars an image for licensing rights. So, by my count you just need to take thirty photos."

"That's outrageous. I could never charge that."

Asking clients to spend five to seven grand on their wedding already felt exorbitant, but paying that much for a single image, I couldn't imagine it.

"You're worth that," he replies, his words ripe with affection, "if not more."

The heat of the day is nothing compared to the way his eyes burn against me as I melt beneath his gaze. Sliding off my socks and shoes, I slip my feet into the chilly water to cool off.

"We're actually looking for an in-house photographer," he says, following suit, "someone to make our content more cohesive. We've hired a few different contractors over the years, but the quality is so inconsistent. I'd really love to have someone full-time, that I trust."

"Why does this sound like a pitch?" I ask, wondering if this is an actual invitation or him just talking aloud.

"Do you want it to be?" he asks, with genuine interest.

I consider the offer. The idea of traveling the world. Of working together, of capturing images of beautiful places.

"As much as I'd love to have you on my team, I'd never want to take you away from weddings."

"What if I want to get away from weddings," I reply, saying the words I've yet to speak aloud.

Hudson raises an eyebrow. "Do you?"

"I've thought about doing something different for a while. Getting a real job. Finding stability. But who wants to hire a girl with no college degree whose only relevant job experience is wrangling drunken bridesmaids?"

"That's bullshit," Hudson scoffs. "You started a company from scratch. You had to market and manage events. Hell, in the last two days, I've watched you navigate impossible situations, problem-solve, and manage different personalities gracefully. If you can handle a high-stress event like a wedding, I'm sure you could handle a team in corporate America."

"I don't need you to get me a job," I argue, shutting him down. The last thing I want is for Hudson to see me as some charity case. Or worse, to find myself in the same position I was in with Phoebe, where I was just a tool in her work kit. She never really understood me. She always wanted me to be someone else, to censor myself, to tone down my artistic expression to meet the desires of the masses. And, over time, I adhered to her demands until the personality I displayed in my photos started to vanish and my work looked like everyone else's.

"I know," Hudson replies genuinely, "but I think you could do it, if you wanted to. Honestly, I think you'd be perfect for it."

"Because my portfolio of taffeta gowns and three-tiered chocolate cakes really makes people want to buy hiking boots and plan a trip to the Alps."

"No, but your documentary work does. I loved that photo of the man at the park, feeding the ducks. It reminded me of days I spent at the lake with my grandfather."

I stare at him, incredulous. "You scrolled that far back?"

This time Hudson's cheeks are the ones to flush. "To the beginning."

"There's like seven years of work on there."

"And every single image captivated me."

I roll my eyes.

"I mean it. There's life within every frame. Like there was one shot, this pair of shoes that'd been discarded on the floor. You could see a part of the table, a half-eaten piece of cake, an opened bag, and a glass with lipstick on the rim. What other people might think of as a throwaway image made me feel as if I was there. I could hear the music in the reception hall. Feel the vibration of wood against bare feet. Feel the joy of living in the moment. That kind of talent is rare."

"I didn't know you were such a fanboy," I quip.

"Only for you," he says, holding the camera up to snap a photo of me, catching me off guard.

"Delete that," I command, certain that it caught me at my worst angle.

"Never," he boasts, flipping the camera to show me the image. I usually dislike photos of myself, but seeing my reflection through his eyes makes me feel beautiful.

"It's . . . amazing," I say, meaning it. The composition could use some work, but seeing the emotion within the frame, the genuine smile streaked across my lips, one inspired by him, makes me grateful to have it immortalized on my screen.

"I think so too," he replies, staring at me as if he's talking about more than the photo.

Snatching the camera back, I tuck it away in my bag. His job offer bubbles away in my mind. I've always assumed that I'd have to find a normal job, an office job. And I have to admit that kind of soul-sucking corporate environment kept the fire for self-employment burning. But I didn't realize that there might be another option.

When I turn around, I find Hudson is removing his shirt, exposing the freckles that cover his torso. I can't help but stare at his toned arms, the whisper of abs beneath his lanky frame, the trail of red hair that starts above his belly button and travels down into his shorts.

"What are you doing?"

"Going for a swim," he says, stripping down to his black boxer briefs and extending a hand towards me. "You want to come?"

I divert my gaze from the bulge protruding through the thin fabric.

"I think we discovered yesterday that me and water don't mix well."

"There are no rapids here. No danger," he assures me, wading into the water. And although I should have an aversion to all water-based activities, I find myself removing my clothes. His gaze lingers on my body, and I've never been more grateful to have put on matching underwear.

"I'm only doing this because it's blistering out here," I explain, as sweat drips down my back.

"Whatever you have to tell yourself," he says, diving underneath the surface.

I go to follow him in and stop short when the water hits my knees.

"It's freezing," I shout, as he swims further away from the shore.

"You just have to go for it," Hudson explains, dunking his head and popping back up like a mythical creature. Desperate to be near him, I close my eyes and jump.

"This is worse than the shower," I say, wading through the icy waters.

"Give it a second," he says, swimming over to me, his body warm as it presses against mine. "See? Not so bad, right?" he asks. I wrap my arm around his neck, keeping him close to me. The sun sparkles against the water, as Hudson points out schools of whitefish underneath our feet.

"I like this," I say, tracing the illustration etched onto his ribcage with my fingers.

"It's Narsil," he explains, "the sword Aragorn is awarded to signify his birthright to the throne."

"Of course it is," I tease, knowing that his Lord of the Rings obsession runs deep.

"Did you know that Aragorn reforged the sword to defeat Sauron in the final battle?"

"Is that why you got it?"

"Partly, but I think for me it's a representation of inner strength. A reminder that, no matter how broken we become, we can always reshape and reforge to become the ruler of our own destiny."

"That's beautiful," I say, before focusing my attention on the words written against his chest, but the script is in a language I don't understand.

"It says '*Mor Boe Vanya*,'" Hudson says, running my thumb over the tattoo. "It's Elvish for 'even darkness must pass.'"

"Wow. So it really is an obsession then," I say, picking at his fandom.

"More of a comfort thing," he explains, floating beside me. "My dad wanted me to see the adventure in everything, or at least that's what he said when he gifted me his copy of *The Hobbit* on my eighth birthday."

"Those are impressive reading skills."

"It took me a few years to actually understand it, but it's my favorite of the series."

"Oh, I know."

He raises an eyebrow towards me. "Do you?"

"Everyone always thinks that my job is just capturing the big moments, but I pay attention to the little details too," I say, floating alongside him.

"And what have you noticed?"

"Besides the fact that you have an indention in almost every pair of your jeans from where you carry it around in your back pocket. I also saw you reading it in the room earlier."

"Mira, are you admitting to checking out my ass?" he asks, in mock scandal.

"As if you haven't checked out mine," I retort, giving his butt a squeeze.

He returns the gesture, resting his lips against my neck. His breath is warm against my skin and he kisses down my shoulder, gently biting against me.

"I also have a confession," I say, pulling away from him.

"What's that?" he asks, his voice playful as he moves my hair behind my ear.

"Be warned, it might change everything between us, but *Fellowship of the Ring* is my go-to nap movie."

"No!" he scoffs, slamming his hands against the water in mock devastation.

"Orlando Bloom doesn't appear until an hour and a half in. And by then I'm already asleep."

"You have to watch the extended cuts. That's where the stories shine."

"You really think if I can't get through the standard edition, that those stand a chance?"

"What if we made a date out of it?" he says, as we float further toward the lake's center.

"We can try but I'll just end up falling asleep on your shoulder."

His eyes study me, as the gentle sway of the water rocks us against one another, and I'm greedy for his attention. "I'm sure I could find ways to keep you awake."

There's a challenge in his words that makes my entire body shiver, and I want him to show me now. To take those hands and explore my body. To make every nerve ending alight with sensation. I hook my legs around his torso, making me weightless as he holds me up in the water.

"I've dreamed about this for so long," he says, his fingers trailing up my spine. "About me and you, together."

"Is it as good as you imagined?" I ask, his eyes lingering on my lips.

"It's better," he says, raking a hand through my hair, guiding my mouth to his. Eager to make up for lost time, to thaw the cold shoulder I've been giving him, I squeeze my legs around him until I'm flush against his chest. I can feel the heat against his skin as my lips move to his neck, and up towards his ear, gently biting against it.

"Mmm," he moans as I run my nails along the back of his neck, nibbling at the bruise I left there. He sighs into my touch and I bite down harder.

The last time we were together like this I rushed through it, letting adrenaline take over, but today I can take my time. I pull at the back of his hair and am thrilled when he moans the same way he had outside of Finn's.

"That's not fair," he says, his cheeks flushed so vibrantly I wish I could bottle the color and paint my ceiling with it.

With no space between us, I can feel him harden against me as I slide my hand below his waistband, moving to stroke the length of him. He breathes my name and I grind against him, using the water's buoyancy to our advantage.

"Mira," he pleads, as I continue working him over.

I know we should stop, that we we're exposed out in the open like this, but with nothing between us, I want all of him.

24 HUDSON

"Fuck," I breathe, holding her steady against me. In all my life, of all the years I've spent outdoors, I've never been one for exhibitionism, but at this moment, I don't care who sees—all I want is to have her, right here right now.

Threading my hand through her hair, I keep her steady against me, my fingers placed against the nape of her neck. She's holding onto me tightly with one arm locked behind me, while the other moves over me in a heady rhythm that makes me dizzy.

Her skin is warm against the chill water as I explore her body like uncharted topography. From the valley of her spine to the flowing river of her hips and the worlds held within her hazel eyes, I want to map every line and curve of her.

I shift our weight, I slide her body up my thigh, giving myself a moment of reprieve. The moment is short-lived when I feel the warmth radiating between her thighs, my hand moving between them to rub my palm against the thin cotton of her underwear. I try to contain myself, to not go too far, especially because I'm well aware of the legal ramifications of getting caught in such a state in a national park, but when Mira moves my hand underneath the fabric, her teeth grazing against my lip, I forget propriety.

All I want is to stay in this moment as long as we can. We can forget about my shitshow of a family, the wedding, and make camp here. Spend these next two days exploring one another.

Mira must want it too, because she reaches for my waistband, pulling me free, just as a voice shouts at us from the shore.

"Hey, you guys can't do that here!"

We both turn to see a disgruntled park ranger glaring at us, his arms crossed against his chest in stern disappointment.

Mira breaks apart from me, giving me a moment to put everything back in place as she swims towards him. "Apologies," she calls back, "the beauty of the day just got to us."

"Just get yourselves together and get out of there," he warns, waving us out.

I remind myself that the last thing I need to start my first week as CEO is a sex scandal. I focus on the cold of the water as I swim back to shore. The ranger gives us enough space to save our dignity as we gather our things.

Mira shakes excess water out of her hair. Droplets fall onto her shoulders, glistening in the sunlight. I wish I could stay here and watch as they evaporate one by one, but the ranger lingers, making sure we actually vacate the premises.

"Have a great day," Mira waves to the ranger, and I can see the crimson on his cheeks from here.

My heart pounds as we race back to the Jeep in our underwear, laughing.

"I haven't had that much excitement in God knows how long," I say, unlatching the trunk and digging through my travel bag.

"I can't say I have either," she says as I hand her a dehydrated towel from my pack. She stares at it quizzically.

"What's this?" she asks, examining the compressed fabric.

"A towel."

"For dolls?" she says, holding up the tiny sponge-like wedge skeptically.

"It expands as it absorbs the water," I explain, rubbing it along the water droplets against her skin until the towel starts to grow.

"Whoa!" she says, eyes alight. "It's like those hand towels you could buy at the dollar store when we were kids."

"Exactly. That's where I got the idea from," I say, helping her pull the fibers apart until it's big enough to wrap around her. "It's also microfiber, so it doesn't mildew. And all you have to do is leave it out in the sun, and it'll shrink back up."

"And you developed this?"

"Yeah. I loved being in research and development. Figuring out new products that would make camping easier for our customers. It was like playing imagination every day."

"And you got to keep all the prototypes?" she asks, digging through my bag.

"Perks of the job."

Wiping herself off, she wraps the towel around herself before getting into the front seat.

"Of course, you opted for a vehicle with no doors or windows," she says, maneuvering her towel so that she can unhook her bra.

"If I knew that there was a possibility that this would be happening," I say, motioning towards her, "I would have asked for the full secret service package—tinted windows, soundproof glass, the works."

"Don't make me laugh. This is difficult enough as it is."

Her body stretches across the passenger seat as she shimmies off her underwear, and I try to focus on anything other than how I want to pull her into my lap and have her right there. But with the ranger's truck parked beside us, I know better.

"Can you hand me my clothes please," she asks, with a coy smile.

Collecting the items from the trunk, I pass them to her, watching as she throws on her shirt over the towel, and then her shorts.

I follow suit, throwing my shorts on over my wet boxer briefs, settling into the driver's seat and turning the ignition.

On the way back to the ranch my hand rests against the bare skin of her knee as I admire the lightness in her shoulders as she lets her arm dance along the wind. I'm already thinking about how it'll feel to hold her hand down the street, walk her to her apartment, make her a grilled cheese in bed, please her every night until she makes that sound that won't stop echoing in my ears.

The words stick at the back of my throat. The *I love you* itching to break free like a butterfly from its chrysalis. The last time I said it, it was a reaction, an involuntary response. And now that I'm certain I actually feel it, I don't know how I ever gave it away so freely.

"I think we're going to miss the shuttle," Mira says, pointing towards a black van parked in front of the main cabins, guests already climbing aboard.

"I'll drive us there," I assure her. Now that we've come this far, being separated from her is unfathomable. I want to soak up every minute together, savor every time she smiles at me.

After I park the car, we sneak into the room like teenagers who can't get caught coming home past curfew. I shut the blinds and lock the door behind us before I pull her back into me. The fact that I can do this now, without hesitation, without worry, is invigorating. My lips move along her sun-coated skin, making their way up her collarbone towards her neck as she relaxes into me. Pushing back her hair, I move my hand against her stomach, and up her torso until my thumb falls below her chin, holding her in place. Her breath is heavy and I know she can feel how badly I want her by the way she moves her ass against my erection.

"We have to get ready," she reasons, and yet doesn't move from my grasp.

"You can take the first shower," I offer.

"Or we could share?" she says, and I practically salivate at the suggestion. "Mitigate the cold water with a little body heat?"

"That would definitely make it more enjoyable," I agree, moving my hands to her perfect ass, turning her around to face me. Thanks to our dip in the lake earlier, Mira's dark hair is extra bouncy, an explosion of curls framing her pink cheeks. And I'm dying to know all the ways I can make her flush. "But first, we got to get you out of these clothes."

The thin fabric of her activewear gives me a perfect view of her nipples as I move my mouth over one, biting hard enough that her breath catches. Glancing up at her, I watch as she lifts her arms for me, allowing me to guide the fabric up over her head. Her body is all curves and valleys, her skin velvety soft as I slide my palms up her sides and over her breasts, watching her body tremble in anticipation.

"You're so beautiful," I say, tilting her mouth up to mine. Her lips part for me as I slide my tongue into her mouth, guiding her forward until her back meets the wall. She kisses me harder, rougher, messier, until my body buzzes from the pressure of her against me. In one movement, my hands reach underneath her ass, lifting her off the ground and onto the dresser, and she gives me another one of those giggles that make me weak.

"Let's skip dinner," she suggests, "say we came down with a bout of heat exhaustion."

"I do think you're feeling quite flushed," I say, sliding my hand between her legs, rubbing the silky fabric of her shorts. The warmth of her pools against my fingers, and when I remember that her panties are in the backseat of my Jeep, I press harder.

"Hudson," she breathes, writhing underneath me, my thumb rubbing circles around the hot core of her until she lets out a velvety moan against my earlobe, biting down against me so hard I have to clench my fist to keep from coming undone right there.

"Fuck me," she whispers, her voice pleading. But I shake my head no. I don't want our first time to be a quickie before dinner with my family and ex. I want to enjoy her far away from here, where we aren't rushed, where I can savor her.

"Please," she begs, with a pout on her lips. Bringing them to mine, I kiss her gently, moving to her collarbone, her breasts, her stomach, until I sink to my knees in front of her.

If I can't fuck her yet, I can at least give her this.

"Are you sure?" she asks, as I pull her shorts down, slipping them off.

"I've never been more sure about anything in my life." I toss one leg over my shoulder, leaning in. She arches her back against the wall, her other hand digging into my hair, as I lick against the sensitive bud of her.

She breathes my name, keeping her voice low, and I take a moment to glance up at her. She's so beautiful like this, undone and unencumbered. I can tell I found the perfect spot by the whimpered moan that escapes her lips. The sound is ethereal, akin to a nightingale's song, and I'm determined to hear it again.

"You taste so fucking good," I murmur, letting my words tickle against the sensitive core of her. She writhes against me as I slip a finger inside her easily.

"Fuck," she breathes, as I add another. I can tell she's close by the way her breath quickens, her eyes close and she throws her head back, and I keep going until she unravels. And as soon as she comes down, I do it again.

25 MIRA

"That was . . ." I gasp while I try to process the orgasms that erupted throughout my nervous system.

"Everything," he finishes, as he rests his head against me, and I'm well aware that his arms are the only thing keeping me from becoming a puddle on the ground. My muscles tremble and my skin tingles as Hudson crawls his way up my torso, kissing every part of me he passes.

My breath is erratic when I try to steady it, an impossible task now that he's standing again, and I can feel the hard length of him, firm against my thigh. I've wanted him for ages, and now that he's here, the taste of me on his lips, I can't wait any longer.

"Take off your clothes," I order, as Hudson lifts his shirt over his shoulders, tossing it onto the floor.

I've already memorized my favorite pieces of him—the sword on his side and the mole below his collarbone—but I still want to explore more of him. To know him completely.

"All of them," I command, my gaze lingering on the erection visible underneath his shorts.

He's wild-eyed and ravenous at the suggestion as he slips them off. Even though I had an idea of what was hiding underneath there, seeing it in front of me is more than I expected.

"That'll do," I joke, pushing him on the bed just as there's a knock at the door.

"Ignore it," Hudson says, before Vanessa's voice pierces through the particleboard.

"Hudson, you need to open the door!"

"Fuck," he mutters, his face flushed, and I'm sure I look twice as red when I see the door handle jiggle. As happy as I am that Vanessa and I have rekindled our friendship, this situation is messy, even for me.

"One sec," Hudson says, standing to find his shorts.

"I'm trying to save you here," Vanessa shouts, as I slip back on my clothes.

"Go ahead," I say, motioning him to get the door.

"I might need a minute," he replies, glancing down. His erection is clearly visible through his shorts. The disappointment of not being able to take advantage of that is not lost on me, but I have to focus on my current problem before I can tackle that one.

"Fuck it, I'm coming in," Vanessa says, bursting through the door, a bent Sephora card in her hand.

"What the hell?" she asks. Her eyes dart between me and Hudson.

"This isn't what it looks like," I say to her, trying to figure out how to explain the situation without sounding like a lunatic.

"Really?" she replies, glancing towards Hudson, who is clutching a pillow over his crotch. "Because it looks like Hudson finally told you the truth about Katherine."

I look back to Hudson for confirmation. "She knows?"

He gives me an embarrassed nod, clutching the pillow harder.

"I had suspected for a while," Vanessa interjects, "but Hudson confirmed everything yesterday when I caught you two canoodling on the boat."

"We were not canoodling," I argue.

"Okay, exhibiting signs of sexual tension," she counters. "Either way, it was obvious you two had a thing."

"And now we've cleared that up," Hudson says, shifting his weight from side to side. If he stays hard this long under these circumstances, I can't imagine what he'll be like when we're alone, with no distractions. I might not survive. "What's so urgent you need to break into our room?"

"Susan is back on property," she states seriously. "Accompanied by an official-looking woman with a clipboard. And they are both demanding to see you."

"And it's gone," Hudson says, standing up unimpeded.

"Sorry to ruin the mood."

"It's fine," Hudson says, throwing on his shirt. "Can you tell her that I'll be there in a minute."

"Oh, I wasn't volunteering to play messenger," she snaps back, causing me to cover my smirk with my hand. "I have to get Mira here rehearsal-dinner-ready."

"I just need to do a quick rinse," I say, gathering clothes from my bag. "I can be ready in ten."

Vanessa shakes her head. "Tonight's dinner isn't on a river raft. Susan rented a banquet hall at one of those fancy lodges, with five-course meals and gas fireplaces on the patios. It's bougie. You gotta dress to impress."

"I don't count," I counter, doubting I even have a place setting.

"Yes, you do," she quips. "You're just as important as anyone else here. Except maybe Meredith."

"I second that," Hudson replies, standing next to me, running his hand along my arm. And I have to admit it feels nice to be included. “Why don’t you go get ready, and I’ll meet you by the Jeep in thirty?” he says, giving me a kiss on the cheek. Although we just partook in more outlandish displays of affection, this simple expression is enough to make my skin tingle.

“Make it thirty-five,” Vanessa says, pulling me out the door.

26 HUDSON

I give myself five minutes to brush my teeth, splash cold water on my face, and change clothes before I make my way up towards the main cabins to deal with my mother. Riddled with pent-up energy, I jog up the gravel path.

"You can't just take over like this!" Meredith declares, fighting with my mother on the main lawn. Meredith's voice is raw and raspy, her vocal cords having gone through the wringer this afternoon. But at least the swelling on her cheeks and eyes has subsided.

"Someone had to," my mother replies, dismissive. "This entire event's been one disaster after another. I might not get a say in *who* my son marries, but I'll be damned if I don't get a say in *how* he gets married."

Across the lawn I spot a fleet of trucks in the parking lot, as men unload wooden tables and chairs underneath a giant clear-top tent that's been erected in front of the pond. I knew Susan could be a steamroller, but this is a whole other level of takeover.

"I think we can both agree yesterday wasn't the best," Grant says, stepping protectively in front of his fiancée, "but this is still *our* wedding."

My mother instantly turns sweet towards Grant, using her soothing voice. "I know that she convinced you that walking around barefoot and picnicking in the sunshine is romantic, but it's not a suitable way for a son of mine to marry."

"Good thing I'm not your son," Grant corrects, his voice on the edge.

"I hate it when you say that," Susan replies, grim-faced. "Now, if you two could go back to your room and peruse the clothing I had the planner organize for you, I'd be very grateful."

She assesses the cream crochet dress Meredith is wearing with disgust.

"And choose something appropriate for dinner later."

"You're unbelievable," Meredith says, storming off to her cabin. Grant hangs back for a moment, and I wait for him to fight back, to cause a scene, but he just shakes his head before following his fiancée into their cabin.

"Can you believe how ungrateful she is?" my mother says to George, who is scrolling on his phone. "I bring in couture and she still has something to complain about."

My mother is dressed for an evening at the Ritz, in a sleek black dress, golden hair pulled back in a gold clip, and a string of pearls around her neck. It's standard attire at the fundraiser events and non-profit galas she attends. Completely devoid of personality and only distinguishable by the price tag.

"Amelia," Susan says, reaching to grab the attention of a dark-haired woman in a black jumpsuit, who I can only assume is the wedding planner. "Please tell the beauty team that Meredith's heading back to her cabin. And to make sure they make her look dignified."

Amelia's chic bob stays pin-straight when she nods, checking something off on her clipboard.

"And now I'll deal with you," my mother says, turning her attention towards me. "Do you know you missed the rehearsal?"

"I'm sure I can walk a straight line without needing to practice," I reply, forgetting that my mother does not care for snark.

"That's not the point," Susan snaps. "You left Katherine all alone!"

I open my mouth to respond but she hasn't finished. "But let me guess, you were off playing in the park."

She says *park* like it's a dirty word, the catalyst of most of her and my father's fights. I remember quite a few evenings where he'd come home from work and she'd accuse him of loving the park more than her.

"I made sure Katherine recovered from the bear spray incident before I left."

My mother scoffs. "I'm not so sure about that, she could have been blinded."

Of course her concern doesn't extend to Meredith, who received the brunt of the spray.

"Honestly, Hudson, of all the people here, I thought you'd be the one to take this wedding seriously," Susan continues, giving me a once-over. "I mean, you're not even dressed properly."

"I just got back."

"I swear, sometimes you're just like your father," she huffs under her breath. After being divorced for almost two decades, she still holds him responsible for my disaffection towards her, not that she made much of an effort with our relationship.

"Did I hear my name?" Katherine asks sweetly, interlacing her arm with mine. Susan immediately brightens in her presence.

The dress she's wearing is a deep maroon, falling just below her thighs, exposing tanned legs, artificially colored with the self-tanner that always stained my shower. Her dark hair is swooped back at the nape of her neck, held in place with a silver hairpin Susan gifted her last year, and her lashes are dark, caked with mascara to distract from her red-rimmed eyes.

"Yes, dear. Just telling Hudson that it was completely unacceptable for him to leave you all alone this afternoon. We're going to make sure that doesn't happen again, right?" she asks, her eyes falling to me.

Amelia glances at her watch, a worried expression on her face. "Susan, did you still want to get to the venue a bit early for final table approval?"

"Yes. I want to make sure that they didn't sneak in any carnations."

"Why don't you take Katherine with you?" I suggest. "I'm sure she'd love to help you with the table arrangements. Make sure everything is perfect for Meredith and Grant."

"I'm sure Susan has everything handled. Her parties are always immaculate," Katherine gushes. "And anyway, I really wanted to get some quality time with Hudsy. We've barely seen each other all week," she coos, putting on a show. She knows that I won't show my hand in front of Susan, not when I have two more days to get through. But I still have a few cards of my own to play.

"I thought you'd want to chat to Mom about the Franklins," I suggest. "Since they've been giving you so much trouble."

Katherine grits her teeth, and I swear I hear a hiss escape.

Susan's tone softens. "Oh, honey. Is that deal not completed yet? I thought they loved the last property."

"These things drag out. People need time to decide between Venetian marble and butcher's block for their kitchen."

For the few brief years my mother worked, she was a realtor. Very low-level, middle-class families, but that work experience made her just empathetic enough to counsel Katherine.

"Why don't we give them a call? Try to figure out what it'll take to have them make a deal."

"I couldn't possibly. You have so much going on."

"Oh, please. It's no bother. I'd love a distraction from all this," Susan declares, waving her hand. "Come with me to the car; I'll put them on speakerphone."

My mother heads towards her SUV, already digging her phone out of her bag.

"Let me just say goodbye to Hudson," Katherine calls, waiting until my mother is out of earshot before she turns on me.

"Are you kidding me right now? Pawning me off on your mother?"

"I would have thought you'd want to distract her, considering she's taking a proverbial sledgehammer to Meredith's wedding right now."

"What are you talking about?"

I pull her to the side, pointing towards the men still working tirelessly on the lawn. "Do you not realize that she's completely taken over? Meredith is distraught, Grant's pissed, and I'm sure that banquet hall is going to look like a goddamn cotillion."

"And that's my concern because . . . ?"

Katherine crosses her arms, and I see the truth. This lie. This scheme. It never was for Meredith and Grant. It's always been for her.

"God, I've been a fucking idiot," I laugh, in an attempt to keep from completely losing it. "I put my whole life on hold for you. I let you stay at my apartment. Hell, I've been sleeping on that fucking couch you picked out for months because I thought you were actually having a hard time."

"I am," she pleads.

"Only because you have to keep up this facade of perfection. You can't be single. You can't live in an apartment without crown molding or chic appliances. You can't be seen as not having it all together. Well, newsflash, most of us don't have it together. We are all struggling in one way or another and you can't keep using that as motivation to throw yourself pity parties."

"That's harsh."

"It's the truth," I say, turning my back to her, seething. All these months, all these missed opportunities with Mira because I didn't want to be an asshole. But instead I've been a chump.

"And this," I say, motioning between us. "This whole thing between us, the fake dating, the playing nice. I thought we were doing this to protect Meredith, to make things easier for her. But now that she's getting absolutely steamrollered by Susan, the only thing you seem to care about is keeping up this charade. And for what? Because you think we're going to get back together?"

Katherine's lip quivers as Susan shouts from the passenger-side window. "Katherine. I have the Franklins on the line and they're ready to make a deal."

She doesn't argue. She plasters on a fake smile, one I've come to recognize, and makes her way towards my mother.

And as I watch their taillights fade into the distance, I know that I'm done pretending.

27 MIRA

Outside I find Hudson's leaning against the Jeep, arms crossed as he stares into the distance. He's wearing tapered tan trousers and a mossy green sports coat that complements his freckled complexion. His auburn hair is unruly, in that just-woke-up way I love, and his stubble is more defined, landing in that sweet spot between beard and five o'clock shadow. And his undershirt is a vibrant paisley print of gold and burgundy. He takes a moment to notice me, but when he does, he offers me a dimpled grin and it takes every bit of willpower I have not to grab him by his bolo tie and pull him in for a kiss.

"You look . . ." He trails off, his eyes tracing along my curves with desire, and heat rushes to my cheeks. "Incredible."

"Thank Vanessa, she did all the work," I say as he removes my bag and slings it over his shoulder.

After blowing out my hair, contouring my face, and applying a shimmery powder to all my exposed skin, she sent me out the door to Hudson like a fairy godmother.

"Her dress?" he asks, biting his lip in appreciation.

The gold dress hugs my curves in all the right places, creating a Grecian ruching all down my body. There is a slit up the side that makes it completely impractical for work, but with the way Hudson is staring, I'd wear it every day.

I nod, smoothing out the silky fabric beneath my palms. "She really should start a rental service. I think she'd make a killing."

"Ask her how much it would be for me to buy it."

"Why? Want me to wear it on date night?" I ask playfully.

Hudson matches my smile and presses his lips just below my ear. "Just in case I end up ripping it off you later."

The comment sends an instant pulse between my legs. If Hudson had been this confident in the bar, Finn would have had to install protective glass for all the people who'd have thrown themselves at him.

"Get a room, you guys," Vanessa says, coming around the corner, Adrian trailing behind her.

"We had one but you barged in," Hudson says, resting his hand on the small of my back. I'm glad we don't have to hide in front of them.

"I told them they could ride with us, since they missed the shuttle," I explain, and Hudson opens the back door for Vanessa. Always the gentleman.

Once they're settled, he helps me climb in, a feat in this dress, and waits until we're all buckled to start the engine. Noah Kahan plays on the radio as we ease onto the main highway. The drive into town is idyllic. Long stretches of quiet roads, baby-blue skies, and actual tumbleweed blowing across the deserted streets. Hudson's hand burns against my thigh. Every few miles, I catch him smiling to himself.

Being here, with him, invokes a sense of belonging I hadn't known I was missing. Even when things between Phoebe and I were at our best, I always felt as if I needed to keep parts of myself hidden for fear of rejection. But Hudson never makes me feel as if I need to be anyone other than myself. He never judged me when I sang out of tune on karaoke nights or mixed my metals on my fingers. He didn't care that I let my curls stay unruly or had a second helping of chicken wings. And he is the only person who brought me back from my grief, even if he had no idea I let a piece of myself go.

"I can't believe the sunsets are so late here," Vanessa says, the sky barely melting into a haze of pink and purple.

"I like it," Adrian replies, scooting forward in his seat to be heard over the wind. "I feel like I'm actually taking advantage of the entire day."

"Because you're normally in bed with a book by now," Vanessa argues.

"It's how I decompress."

I breathe in the crisp Wyoming air. This is one of those memories I wish I could bottle, to open on rainy days, and then I remember that I can preserve it another way.

Reaching down, I unzip my camera bag, removing the smaller of the two bodies and attaching the wide-angle lens. Bringing the viewfinder up to my eyes, I take the photo. The background is a bit blurry, Hudson's smile a little off-center, his arm cut off on the frame as it reaches once more for my thigh. But it's perfect.

I'm about to put my camera away when I see movement against the horizon. Massive, dark brown behemoths, gliding across the grassy fields. "Are those—?"

"Buffalo," Vanessa says, as we all turn to look.

"Bison actually," Hudson corrects.

"But they are basically the same thing though?" Adrian asks.

"Buffalo tend to live in warmer climates, while bison have thicker fur which allows them to survive the harsh winters," Hudson explains.

"Can you pull over?" I ask, moving my viewfinder to my eye to find the perfect frame.

Hudson eases the car onto the shoulder. I unbuckle and stand up on my seat, holding the roll bars of the Jeep.

I'm in no danger of falling, but I don't mind the way Hudson keeps a hand on the back of my calf, keeping me steady.

The animals move in a herd, the littlest lagging behind as I wait for the shot. I wait until there's equal distance between them, the animals taking up the entirety of the frame before I click the shutter. I check the image on the back of the LCD screen when I catch Hudson staring at me.

"I can't wait to see that one," he beams.

And for the first time since Phoebe's wedding, I'm actually excited to be holding my camera.

28 HUDSON

"This is definitely an upgrade from the Majestic," Mira says when we pull into the Deerview Lodge and Spa, a valet waving us forward. The sprawling four-story building resembles a castle, with a stone facade and gas lanterns lining the walkway. Lush shrubbery and colorful flowers create a protective barrier between the parking lot and guests sipping cocktails on the patio.

"Your mom must have thrown serious money at this event, last minute and all," Vanessa says, stepping onto the stone path.

"Probably not more than a single dividend check, since George boasts how he bought Microsoft stock before the internet was even a thing," I say, regurgitating the anecdote my stepfather shares anytime someone asks how he amassed his fortune. As if being born into generational wealth and having a financial advisor in high school didn't help.

Relinquishing my keys to the valet, I make my way over to help Mira. After watching her struggle to get in the car earlier, I can only imagine how difficult it must be to get out in that dress.

"Here, let me," I say, offering her my hand.

She's windblown, with pink cheeks. Paired with the shimmery powder on her shoulders and the golden dress that's gathered around her curves, she looks as if she just stepped out of a Renaissance painting, one where a knight might be kneeling in front of his maiden. And I would lie down at her feet right now, in front of everyone, if she asked.

I don't realize how long I've been staring at her until Vanessa's voice breaks through my thoughts. "You guys coming?"

"In a minute," I reply, watching the fabric slide down her bare legs. I never thought I could be jealous of fabric and yet, here I am, wishing I could be the thing wrapped around her. I wait until Adrian and Vanessa are a few paces ahead of us before I guide her back towards the vine-covered banister, my hands tangling in her hair, pressing my lips to hers.

"Stop," she breathes, her hand pressing hard against my shoulder, and I freeze.

"Did I do something wrong?" I ask, hoping I haven't overstepped.

Her eyes dart back and forth, the relaxed, carefree woman from the lake retreating. She moves away from me. "Someone could see."

"I don't care," I say, wrapping my arm around her waist, but she shakes her head, pained.

"But I do."

The words leave me with a lingering chill, like a blanket being ripped off on a cold winter morning, and I'm desperate to be warm again. After everything we've gone through to get here, I don't want to give it up, not even for an evening.

"Mira, I can go in there and tell them the truth," I plead. "I want to. I don't want to hide. Meredith is your friend, too. I'm sure she'd be happy for us."

"But would Katherine? Or your mom?"

"Fuck 'em."

She scoffs, unbelieving.

"I'm serious. I've put so much time and energy into pleasing those people, and for what? They don't care about me. And I'm tired of putting in the effort, especially if it means not being able to walk in there with you."

I grab her hand, thankful when she allows my fingers to intertwine with hers. But I can tell she's not convinced.

"I don't want to cause a scene," she says, untangling her hand from mine.

I want to honor her wishes, but I have no idea how I'm supposed to go in that room and pretend that I don't know how soft she is underneath my fingers, or the way she tastes like candy and sunshine when I lick along her thighs, or the sounds she makes, desperate and breathy, when she comes.

"I just need everything to go smoothly—this is my job—and then I'm all yours."

I want to hold her and tell her that whatever she's afraid of, we can handle it together. That I'd endure the brunt of the judgment waiting for us if it meant I could sit beside her all night, listening to her laugh, stealing an extra dessert off the buffet knowing that she always likes something sweet around midnight. But her resolve is impenetrable and I know I won't win this fight.

I move my hand to rest against her cheek, nudging her chin up so that her hazel eyes meet mine. "I understand."

Leaning forward, she allows her lips to touch mine ever so lightly and bends down to pick up her camera bag.

"Now, go in. Say hello to your family. And I'll come in a few minutes later."

"Mira, that's ridiculous," I sigh, hating even a few feet of separation when she's feeling like this.

"Just do it, please."

I squeeze her hand before I make my way up the stone path and into the lodge. There's a wary smile on the hostess's face as she greets me, leading me through the restaurant floor towards my party. Unlike the Majestic, whose brand is more adventure center than resort, this place caters to the ultra-rich. I pass plates of steamed broccolini and filet mignon. Metal signs adhered to the walls indicate which direction to go if I want to visit the spa, cigar room, and wine cellar, but we pass by all of them, stopping in front of a set of mahogany doors.

"Right through here," the hostess says. The room is bustling, everyone standing around with champagne flutes and crystal wine glasses. Long tables are adorned with tapered candles and gold place settings, and vases of white roses are scattered throughout. The upscale, gaudy decor is worthy of a gala, but it isn't right for either Meredith or Grant, who would rather be roasting s'mores around a bonfire, knocking back a few beers, and joking with their friends.

They stand together, visibly uncomfortable; Grant in a tailored black suit, and Meredith in a structured white dress that looks more appropriate for a Labor Day party than a rehearsal dinner. They absentmindedly chat with their guests, all the while shooting pointed stares at Susan, who is beelining for me across the room.

"Finally," she says, pulling me towards the top table, where I'm to take my place beside Katherine, who I can tell is already a little tipsy from the slew of empty champagne flutes in front of her. "We've been waiting for you."

"For what?" I ask, grabbing my own glass from one of the trays floating around.

"To start dinner," she replies, as Amelia ushers Meredith and Grant to their seats.

"Why do I need to be here to start dinner?" I ask, genuinely confused.

"Because you're giving the welcome speech."

I practically choke on my drink. "I'm sorry, what?"

"Amelia and I thought it would be nice if you said a few words tonight since Derrick is speaking tomorrow."

"A speech isn't something you can spring on a person at the last minute," I argue. "I mean, they're literally called prepared remarks because you're supposed to get time to prepare for them."

"He's your brother." Susan waves at the caterers as they bring over a tray of salmon puffs. She snatches one, popping it in her mouth and swallowing it before anyone can see her actually consume it. "You can't tell me you need a study period to find something nice to say about him."

Considering I couldn't think of anything besides "Congrats" to write on his card, trying to find words to fill a whole speech is improbable. We've never got along. Not really. Even when we were kids, I remember Grant ignoring me every chance he got. Slamming the door and staying in his room the summers I was forced to visit thanks to the custody agreement. So unless Susan wants me to go up there and recount the night Grant got so mad he threw one of his baseball trophies at me, giving me the scar on my shoulder, I don't have much to say.

I turn towards Katherine, who hasn't looked at me since I arrived. "You're giving a speech too, right?"

She holds up her phone, displaying paragraphs of text.

"Want to join forces?"

She laughs, still mad from my earlier declaration. Of all the times for her to actually hear me, this is the worst moment.

"Are you not speaking tomorrow, dear?" my mother asks, clicking her tongue against her teeth in disdain.

"Meredith asked Vivianne to do the honors," Katherine explains, as Amelia clinks a knife against her glass, grabbing the attention of the crowd.

"If you could all take your seats, please. We're going to have our first speaker of the night. Grant's brother, Hudson Hayes."

A cacophony of heels clicking against linoleum and chairs being pushed aside fills the room, as all eyes turn to me. I thought

I would have more time, that Katherine might have jumped at the chance to go first, but she's clearly relishing my downfall.

I down my glass of champagne as Amelia hands me the microphone.

The room goes silent. I've been to enough weddings to know that whatever I say is supposed to be heartfelt. A poignant yet charming tribute to the bride and groom, strung together with personal anecdotes and well wishes, but staring at the happy couple of honor my mind goes blank, completely devoid of original thought.

My palms begin to sweat, and there is a dry, scratchy cough building in the back of my throat. And when I move the microphone too close to my mouth, reverb blasts through the quiet room, causing guests to cover their ears.

Is this what it's going to feel like addressing the employees at Elite on Monday? Will the Slack channels be filled with private messages discussing my inadequacies?

I try to shake off my insecurities as Grant grabs my arm. "Dude. Say something."

"Thanks for coming," I say, at a loss at what to say next, until Mira steps in front of me, camera in hand, offering me a confident smile. She's absolutely stunning in the candlelight, glowing like a campfire, and staring at her, I find my words.

"Welcome, everyone, and thank you so much for coming out to celebrate Grant and Meredith this week," I say, my voice steadier now.

Light applause rings out from the crowd, the loudest coming from Derrick, who is fisting an entire bottle of champagne. "Wooo! Fuck it up, Hayes."

"Thank you, Derrick," I chuckle as Grant pats his best friend on the shoulder, his other arm draped around his fiancée.

"As you all can see, it's pretty obvious that these two are crazy about each other. From not spending more than a few days apart since they started dating, to traveling to a new state or country every other month, it's safe to say that these two can't get enough of one another," I say, motioning towards them.

"They found each other at one of Susan's parties, funnily enough," I say, pointing to my mother, who delights in the attention. "It's also funny to think how one day, one moment, one decision was all it took. Meredith could have stayed at home that night. Grant could have gone to a basketball game. But instead they met on a boat in the middle of Lake Norman.

"But how did they know they were right for each other? It's the question we all ask ourselves after that first encounter, questioning if those butterflies fluttering in your chest are momentary or forever. Growing up, I always believed that love was about sacrifice; this idea was based on characters I'd read about in books or seen in movies. I thought that to show ultimate devotion you had to give up parts of yourself for the person you cared about the most. Like how Wesley gave up years of his life to protect Buttercup, or how Arwen relinquished immortality for Aragorn."

As I move my eyes around the room, I see expectant faces. And I'm ready to bare all. "But recently I discovered that love isn't about sacrifice at all. It's about showing up. It's about being honest. And it's about endlessly giving yourself to another. Whether it's staying up a few minutes later because you don't want the night to end, or remembering to order extra bao buns because they are her favorite. It's laughing at a terrible TV show you have no interest in watching because she loves it or making her coffee in the morning because you want to make sure she's caffeinated enough to get through the day."

Mira stops shooting, her camera in her hand but far enough away from her face that I know her attention isn't on capturing this memory but being a part of it.

"And so the question becomes how do you know if you've found that person. The one you can give your time and energy to. The one who is not only deserving but who will give it back. As someone who recently stumbled upon such a person, I can attest that when it happens, you won't be able to miss it. It's like spotting a rare flower in the forest or stumbling upon a first edition of your favorite book at the thrift store. It's so unexpected, wonderful, and exhilarating. But there's another part that makes it so terrifying. Because you can't help but wonder if you deserve this."

Tears well at the corner of Meredith's eyes and she wipes them away with a napkin, and there's a softness to Grant that gives me pause. But it's Mira, who's staring at me from across the room, that makes me keep going.

"I used to be so afraid of never measuring up, of never being enough, of not making the right sacrifices, but now, I'm ready. Ready to step up. To live every day for the people I love, and to ensure those people feel that love every day."

And as the words leave my mouth, the truth within them radiates through my chest. Taking over Elite, standing up for myself, being my authentic self. None of these challenges seem as daunting now that I have Mira. It's as if all the anxious static in my brain has subsided and I can finally hear the music clearly. And it's fucking beautiful.

"And so, I hope that you continue to show up for each other, believe in each other, and remember that the only sacrifices you should be worried about making is who gets the last slice of pizza," I say, raising my glass. "To Meredith and Grant."

29 MIRA

Applause erupts throughout the room, glasses clink in celebration, and the happy couple lean in for a kiss. But I don't move. I barely take a single photo, as Hudson's words override my instinct to capture the moment.

I'm pretty sure he just declared his love for me in front of his entire family. Of course, they were all unaware of who he was talking about, especially since Susan kept glancing over at Katherine in hopeful admiration, but Hudson's gaze never moved from mine. And when I see Adrian slide a twenty over the table to Vanessa, who proudly stuffs it into her bra, my hypothesis is confirmed.

I want to run over to him, kiss him, or slap him for publicly declaring his love, but I'm reminded I still have a job to do as he hands the microphone over to Katherine. If she is rattled by his speech, she doesn't show it. Instead, she plasters on a smile and takes her place in the spotlight.

"I'm so happy to be here with all of you, celebrating the love between Meredith and Grant. I know I haven't known you as long as some of the people here, but my love for you both is boundless," she says. I move around the room, snapping photos.

The top table is placed on the far-right side of the room, backed up against the wall, meaning I have to stand in the center of the hall to capture not only Katherine but also the guests' reactions to the speeches. Most of whom are still weepy from Hudson's words. Words directed at me.

Every time I think about them, I get dizzy. All those nights I stayed late at the bar, all those texts we shared in early mornings and mid-afternoons, they meant just as much to him as they did to me. To know that what I've been feeling is more than a childish crush grounds me.

I move around to get another angle, stopping besides Hudson's chair. I try to focus on Katherine's speech. She's muttering about Pilates and girls' nights spent at the local wine bar, but her words are lost as I focus on the way Hudson's finger grazes against my calf, trailing up the exposed skin, while I click the shutter aimlessly. I know I should move, capture more of the guests' reactions, but I stay put—not willing to part from Hudson yet.

It isn't until Katherine raises her glass that I focus, snapping photos of the hug Meredith offers her best friend as she wipes away tears. I hate to admit that watching them together makes me wistful. Even if I have Hudson, it doesn't erase what I've lost; it can't overwrite the grief still heavy in my heart.

I sit with it for a moment as waiters float into the room, carrying trays of salad plates as dinner service begins.

Since Susan arranged this soiree, I know there won't be a place setting waiting for me, a fact confirmed when Amelia passes by and says, "There's a vendor meal waiting for you in the parlor."

Grateful for a few minutes of solitude to collect my thoughts, I scuttle to the corner, set my camera down and sneak out of the room.

I only make it a few feet before Hudson pulls me towards an empty hallway. His mouth is against mine in an instant and it takes all my mental resolve to break away.

"You have to go back in," I tell him, knowing his absence won't go unnoticed.

"One more minute," Hudson breathes, his teeth biting the sensitive skin of my collarbone, then my neck, then my lower lip. There's nothing but the wall and his sturdy arm keeping me upright. His lips move up my jaw and towards my ear, his voice barely a whisper when he says, "Do you have any idea how hard it is for me to keep my hands off you?"

"You did a pretty good job of it at Finn's," I joke.

"That was before I knew that you wanted this too," he says, his fingers trailing up the slit of my dress, stopping just below my hip. "Before I knew what you felt like."

I don't know if it's the champagne or the declaration, but I'm thoroughly enjoying this new emboldened Hudson.

"It would be so easy, wouldn't it? If I just moved my hand . . . here," he whispers, and I shudder at the closeness of his skin, the scratch of his stubble against my neck.

He curls a finger underneath the fabric, my nerve endings on high alert as he runs a knuckle upwards. I lean forward, resting my chin against his shoulder, before we hear footsteps coming down the hall.

My heart is racing. I move away from him, readjusting my dress.

"It's just Derrick," I say, watching him carry a bottle of bourbon down the hall.

"I can't stand that you've kissed that asshole," Hudson fumes. "I should have set that fire the second I saw him sit beside you."

"You set the fire!"

A familiar blush crawls up his neck and into his cheeks.

"Smokey Bear would be so disappointed in you."

"I think he'd give me a pass this once," he says, brushing his lips against the tender skin of my neck. We waste another few minutes in the hallway until I hear the clink of glasses coming from the dining hall.

"If we miss any more of the evening we'll both be in trouble," I say, moving away to straighten my dress.

"You go in first," Hudson says, leaning back against the wall, and I make sure to walk as slowly as possible.

Inside, waiters are placing second courses in front of the hungry guests. The scent of prime rib and Mac and cheese makes my stomach rumble.

"Mira, over here," Vanessa calls, scooting out the chair beside her. "We have an extra seat."

"Who died?" I joke, knowing that Hudson's mom isn't the kind of woman to miscount.

"We were supposed to be sitting with Grant's great-aunt and uncle, but I think they bailed after the boat ride. No one's seen them on the property since," Vanessa says, sliding a plate over to me.

"Their loss is my gain," I say, reaching for the roll on the plate, tearing off a piece to pop in my mouth. It's delicious, warm, and buttery, and it melts in my mouth. "I'm absolutely famished."

"Multiple orgasms will do that to a person," Vanessa jabs, and I almost choke on my roll. "What? You were gone for like thirty minutes, and your lips have that extra, just-got-fucked pout about them. So, unless you snuck out for a quick Botox session, I'm assuming you ran off with Hudson?"

Instinctively I bring my hand to my face. "Oh God? Do they?"

Vanessa chuckles as the door opens, Hudson making his way into the room, his cheeks flushed and the green of his irises flickering like gemstones as his eyes cut through the crowd to find me. There's a subtle smirk on his face, similar to those shared between children sneaking ice cream for dinner, as he takes his place at the top table.

Taking another bite of my roll, I feel my phone vibrate in my bag. I sneak a glance at Hudson, wondering if he's sending me dirty texts from across the room, but the anticipation burning in my belly is snuffed out when I read the notification.

Your review has been removed by poster.

I read the message again, stunned by the words on the screen.

Your review has been removed by poster.

Removed by poster. That would mean . . . Phoebe.

My stomach tightens as I grip the phone, opening a browser and searching for my business name. The sinking two-point-five rating has been replaced by a perfect five stars.

I wait for the joy, elation, peace, that I thought would come, but all I feel is hollow. My phone buzzes again, messages and emails coming in, but there's one that stands out among the rest.

New Message from Planning by Phoebe

My finger hovers over the notification.

What could she possibly have to say to me after all this time?

Will this be a heartfelt apology? A plea for forgiveness? And if so, do I even want to hear it?

I'm still deciding what I want to do when I hear a shrill voice behind me say, "What do you think you're doing?"

Susan is glaring down at me, making me feel like a student who got caught checking her phone during class. How could Hudson be a product of this uptight, overly judgmental woman?

"Typically, people don't want photos of them eating," I explain, putting my phone away.

"And so what? You think you can just take a break? I'm paying you to do a job, I expect you to do it."

"Mom," Hudson says, voice stern as he rushes up beside me. There's fire behind his eyes and I know he's ready to defend me, but I shake my head, telling him to stand down.

His lips tighten into a scowl.

"Hudson, go stand with your stepfather. I'm going to get my family photos."

Quickly, I gather my camera, taking a few test shots as Susan places everyone against the far wall, but I can't focus on placement or lighting choices—all I can think about is Phoebe.

"Are we all here?" I ask, bringing the viewfinder to my face.

"One second." Susan holds a finger up towards me. "Katherine. Come join us. You'll be family soon enough if this one knows what's good for him."

It's one thing to hear how much Hudson's mother adores Katherine, but to see it in person makes me feel inadequate. She's effortlessly chic, with a clean girl aesthetic that makes her seem as if she's stepped off a page of *InStyle*. As she slips in beside him, even though Hudson's hands stay at his side—his body is stiff, a fake smile plastered on his face—I can't stop wondering what's going to happen when we start dating for real. How will he explain our relationship to his family, who are under the impression that he and Katherine are so in love they're on their way to getting engaged? Will they think I stole him from her? Will they judge me as harshly as Phoebe's friends did?

Fear and anxiety prickle my skin, but my body goes on autopilot, snapping photos as Susan reorients the group, removing one person and adding another. Click. Flash. Move. I react accordingly, checking the LCD screen for proper lighting but not really looking at the image.

Without that review standing in my way I can go back to my regular life, I can go back to weddings, to my business, to stability.

Susan directs everyone into groups of two. Meredith and Grant. *Click.*

Her and George. *Click.*

Katherine and Hudson. *Click.*

I do it over and over again until she's satisfied. And I can't help but wonder if I actually want this career anymore.

30 HUDSON

Watching Mira taking orders from my mother makes my stomach roil. If anyone treated Mira that way at the bar I'd escort their asses out faster than Lilah could pour a Guinness. I want to tell my mother to stand down, that we've gotten enough family memories for the evening, but protesting would only lead to more questions, and Mira made it clear she didn't want to cause a scene.

She's handling herself like a champ though, taking punch after punch from my mother, but I can tell that her resolve is beginning to fray at the edges when she suggests that Katherine and I get a few shots together. Since Katherine's still pissed about our fight from earlier, she keeps her distance as we stand like awkward pre-teens at a middle school dance.

"Get closer," my mother orders, moving Katherine so that she's standing in front of me.

"Let's just get this over with," Katherine sighs, throwing an arm through mine, throwing on a smile. I grit my teeth, making sure to never break eye contact with Mira through the lens.

After she's satisfied with the family photos, Susan drags Mira around each table, forcing her to capture a photo of each guest with the couple. She hasn't even bothered to learn Mira's name, referring to her as "the photographer" each time she needs her attention. I keep a watchful eye, making sure I can step in if I need to. I don't think I've ever seen my mother thank, tip, or appreciate anyone who has ever waited on her, and tonight is no different.

She orders Mira around for the rest of the night, only letting up after the tables are bare and the candlesticks blown out.

I move towards Mira, eager to help her pack her bag and get out of here, when Katherine blocks me.

"So you're with *her* then?" she asks, the sharpness of her words catching me off guard.

"Derrick saw you two making out in the hallway," she clarifies, as hurt radiates off her. "Is that why you wanted her to stay in our room? So you two could . . . what, hook up in secret?"

"No, of course not," I reply, appalled. Even though we were broken up I would never be that much of an asshole. "I didn't know she was going to be here."

"Were you going to tell me? That you were together?"

"Would you tell me if you were seeing someone else?"

"But you're in love with her," she says, a sheen in her eyes.

It takes me a moment to realize it isn't a question but a statement. And I can't deny it anymore.

"Yeah. I think I am."

Katherine dabs at the corners of her eyes, before taking a deep breath and running out of the room.

"Is she okay?" Mira asks as I grab her bag from her hand.

"I'm more worried about you? I'm so sorry about Susan."

"It's fine," she says, waving off my apology. "But as someone who's dealt with so many Momzillas in my day, your mother takes the cake."

"She's not really meant to be outside a five-mile radius of her country club."

She laughs and I feel the pressure release from my chest.

"I should have fought harder about all those photos with Katherine."

"It wasn't a big deal."

"Then why do you look so upset?"

"I guess I never stopped to think about how this is going to work," she says, gesturing to the space between us. "I think I'm just worried about how your mother's going to react when you show up to the next family gathering with the photographer by your side?"

"I don't know if you've noticed but I'm not really close to that side of the family. I never have been," I admit.

"Still. She's your mom."

I shrug. "Technically. But she never wanted to be. She doesn't want to be now. It's shitty but I really thought, these last few years, that she wanted to get to know me. That she wanted to actually be a mom. But it was all an act. A performance to look good in front of her friends, in front of Katherine. It's part of the reason I agreed to the whole fake-dating ruse to begin with," I say, the trauma spilling out of me. "I was afraid to know if my mother's feelings towards me would change when she found out she wasn't going to get the daughter-in-law she wanted. But if this week has taught me anything, it's that those feeling didn't exist in the first place."

"Hudson," Mira replies, squeezing my hand, and I've never been more grateful for a touch.

"It's okay, really," I assure her. "I have my dad and that's enough. We're sort of the male version of *Gilmore Girls* if that show occurred in the woods instead of suburban Connecticut."

"I'd watch that," she laughs, slipping her arm through mine. "I'd need a field guide to understand all your nerdy nature facts, but I could see it becoming a hit."

"I'd love for you to meet him, my dad. After dealing with all this," I say, gesturing towards the room. "It'd be nice to show you the other side of the family. We could even go up to his cabin in Asheville."

"Do we have to hike to get there?"

"Nope," I say, with a coy smile. "And there's a hot tub."

"Mmmm," she coos, and I'm already imagining us snuggling up on the couch, watching the leaves fall from the window.

"Please tell me Susan's gone," Meredith asks, resting her head on Derrick's shoulder, passing him a bottle of bourbon. Besides the party posse, the only people left in the room are the cleaning staff, who vacuum over the gold carpets and break down tables and chairs.

"I think you're safe," I say, checking my watch. "She has a strict ten o'clock bedtime on weekdays."

"Guess the game is over," Angie sighs.

"What game?" Mira asks, walking over to their table.

"We were taking shots every time Susan bossed around a server."

"I'm surprised the bourbon lasted that long," I reply, looking at the half-empty bottle.

"This is our second one," Derrick says, before Meredith snatches it from him.

"Here," she says, handing it to Mira. "After the way she treated you tonight, I think you deserve the rest."

Mira smiles, taking a swig. I can't help the way my eyes track the hollow of her throat, and I can't wait to get back to the ranch to finish what we started.

"You ready to head out?" I ask, placing a hand at the small of her back.

"Yeah, just need to run to the restroom first," she says, excusing herself.

"How are you guys getting back?" I ask the group, knowing the shuttle already departed.

“I volunteered as designated driver,” Jocelyn says, holding up Grant’s keys. “I knew someone was going to have to get the posse home.”

“This is why I love you,” Angie coos, wrapping her arms around her girlfriend. Following them out, I take Mira’s bag and make my way into the night air, the quiet of midnight approaching as I flag down the valet.

31 MIRA

In the bathroom, I take a minute to decompress. I run cold water over my hands and try to breathe out all the frustration I'd been holding in all evening. Between Susan watching my every move, and Hudson showering me with attention, I haven't had a moment to read the message from Phoebe, a message that has been consuming my thoughts ever since it pinged into my inbox.

Hiding in one of the stalls, I open the email. The message loads, the text filling up the screen. I try to focus my eyes on the words when I'm interrupted by the sound of footsteps over the marble floor.

Underneath the stall I see two sets of shoes, and Grant's voice reverberates against the tile walls. "Are you sure about this?"

I hear a breathy reply. "Yes, please. God."

"When I'm done with you, you won't even remember why you were upset," Grant says, his voice hungry and deep with need as I realize what's happening.

Meredith and Grant have snuck off for a quickie, and I'm crashing their party.

I sneak out of the stall as quietly as possible, keeping my head down as I tiptoe towards the exit. I'm only a few steps away when I see the scene reflected back to me in the full-length mirror. Grant on his knees, with a pair of legs wrapped around his shoulders, legs that belong to Katherine.

I close my eyes in hopes that this is just an optical illusion, but when I open them to find she's still there, her fingers locked in his hair, calling out his name, I can't believe it. I try to sneak away but the automatic toilet flushes. Katherine's eyes go wide in panic as she taps Grant on the shoulder, shoving her dress back down below her knees.

Tears build at the back of my eyes, my heart pounding in my chest, the heavy thump, thump, drowning out all other sounds as I rush out of the lodge. Outside Hudson's waiting for me, sitting in the driver's side of the Jeep as I climb in, slamming the door behind me.

"Drive," I command, but he doesn't move.

My hands shake in my lap, as he reaches for me.

"Are you okay?" he asks, concern flooding his voice, but my eyes stay locked on the floorboards.

"Mira, talk to me."

I shake my head, unable to look at him. "I just need to get out of here."

He gently lifts my chin to meet his gaze, but I can barely hold it for longer than a second.

"Did something happen? Are you hurt?"

I take a breath. Then another worry constricts my lungs. Will Hudson believe me if I tell him what I saw? Will he call me a liar like Phoebe did? Will this entire mess start all over? Am I trapped in some fucked-up version of *Groundhog Day*?

"Yes. No. I don't know," I reply, panicked.

"Mira, talk to me."

"Did you ever wonder why I was able to take this wedding on such short notice?" I ask, my breath shaky. "Why I've been spending my weekends at Finn's instead of at work?"

Hudson shakes his head, confused.

"It's because I'm a terrible person."

"You're not."

I shake my head again. "I am. I ruined my best friend's wedding. I ruined our friendship. I ruined my career."

"I'm sure that's not true."

"It is. All because I let my guard down for a second," I cry, the familiar sting of tears building at the back of my eyes. "I thought he was just being friendly. I had no idea that . . ." I trail off.

"No idea what?"

"That he would kiss me."

"Who kissed you?"

"Phoebe's fiancé," I say, letting the words hang in the air. It's the first time I've said them aloud. The first time I've admitted what happened outside of that bridal suite. And I ready myself for judgment.

The memory replays in my head, as it has a million times before, as I think of everything I could have done differently.

"I should have done more to stop him."

"Stop him?"

Tears stream down my face, the heavy weight of it too much to carry. I haven't allowed myself to cry about my breakup with Phoebe, or about what actually happened that day. Instead I compartmentalized it, focused on fixing my reputation, on hustling my way into a paycheck. And yet the heavy shroud of shame was always there, suffocating me.

"He was wasted," I say, wiping my face, black mascara coming off on my fingers. "He usually was. He was a big drinker, which was one of the many reasons I never thought he was good enough for her. But I knew better than to tell someone that their fiancé was an asshole. And I knew she wanted us to get along. So, I did what best friends are supposed to do. I laughed at his terrible jokes. I asked about his fucking day as if I cared about his earning reports. But that day he was so gone. I sent his groomsmen on a coffee run, to help sober him up, and when I came back to check on him, he was struggling with his tie."

I clench my fists, remembering the smell of Scotch on his breath and his punchy cologne in my nostrils.

"I reached for the tie, to help. And I made some comment about how his shirt wasn't buttoned. I think he missed one or something, and he stared down at me, with these eyes I'd never seen before. They were dark and hollow. And the next thing I knew he'd pushed me up against the chest of drawers and was all over me. I tried to push him back, but he was so strong."

I stare down at the floorboards, picking at a loose thread on the stitching of my dress.

"It wasn't until the wedding planner walked in, a member of Phoebe's team, that he pulled away. She ran straight to Phoebe of course. I told her what happened, that Cliff came onto me, but she didn't believe me. She told me I was jealous of her happiness. That I wanted to ruin her relationship because I couldn't find one of my own. I hid in my car, until the ceremony was over, waiting until I could go back in and get my belongings. But I swear, I wasn't coming onto him. I genuinely thought I was helping him. Putting in an effort because Phoebe asked me to. But she was my best friend, I would never—"

I take a breath, the tears falling harder now.

"After the wedding community turned on me, I started to believe that maybe I had been in the wrong. That maybe I had given him some sign. That I was the bad guy after all."

"You weren't the bad guy, he was," Hudson tells me, reaching for my hand.

"Then why does Phoebe hate me? Why did everyone stop talking to me."

It is the question that has circled my thoughts for longer than I care to admit, and now doubt creeps in. If I was really the victim, wouldn't she have heard me out?

"Mira, you were violated. And you lost someone you thought you could trust in the process. It's fucked up. And I'm so sorry that happened to you. But none of it is your fault. You have to believe that."

"I want to. I really do. But every time I think about it, of Phoebe choosing him, it hurts all over."

"I know." Hudson wraps an arm around me. "But I'm here for you, okay. You're safe. And I believe you. I'll always believe you."

I sink into him, burying my head in his chest. He rests his chin on my head, stroking my hair, repeating it over and over. "I believe you."

And for the first time the weight that's been pressing down on me finally feels a little lighter.

32 HUDSON

Mira's tears sink into my shirt, but I don't care. She can stay here and cry until I'm completely soaked through, because after the story she just told me, I'd do anything for her to feel safe. I've never been one to hold onto anger, but finding out that Mira feels so guilty after some asshole assaulted her, and her so-called best friend had the gall to make her the villain rather than face the fact that she was about to marry a grade-a douchebag, makes my blood boil. And to know that she's been holding onto this, letting it eat away at her for months, makes me squeeze her tighter.

Seeing her this vulnerable, this raw, is new, and I'm glad that she feels comfortable enough to show that side of herself, that she can trust me not to let her fall. But I can't help but wonder why this is all coming up now. I know that trauma doesn't have a timeline, but something must have triggered this, right?

I want to ask her, but the answer comes to me when I hear Grant's voice boom from the entryway.

"Mira?" he calls, and my fists clench with irritation.

"What did he do?" I ask, pulling away just enough to see her face. "I swear, if he touched you . . ."

"Not me," she says, as I catch sight of Katherine, stumbling out behind him.

I'm already out of the car and rushing at him before he knows what's happening. Grant may have five inches on me, but I use his intoxication to my advantage as I shove my weight against his ribs, knocking him off balance. He barely has time to steady himself before I pull back and punch him right in the face.

The sound of bone against bone echoes into the night and he falls back onto the concrete.

"What the fuck, Hudson?" Katherine shouts, hunkering beside Grant to assess the damage. From here I can see that his eye is already swelling, the thin skin of his cheek inflamed.

Adrenaline pulses through me as I stare down at my stepbrother. I've wanted to punch Grant for years. From the first time he bullied me so badly I slept in the woods in an attempt to get away from him, with nothing but my book and a flashlight. Or the day I found out he purposefully asked the girl I liked on a date, only to stand her up. But through all those events, I kept it together. I gave him the benefit of the doubt. But knowing that his actions have hurt Mira breaks my resolve.

Grant groans when Katherine helps him off the ground.

"As soon as we get back I want your shit out of the apartment," I shout, anger coursing through me. "Hire a moving company, send me the bill. Because I'm done."

Katherine stands there stunned, her eyes glued to me as I walk back to the Jeep. Mira has her knees pulled into her chest, her eyes still swollen from crying, as I pull out of the lot and onto the road. We make the drive in silence, my hand never leaving hers.

I park the car in front of the Big Barn but neither of us move to get out.

"I can't go back to that room," Mira says, and I nod my head in solidarity.

"My mom's cabin is empty," I offer. "I can run in and grab our things."

She nods, and I quickly make my way inside, tossing our stuff into our bags, and hauling them back to the Jeep.

The cabin is dark as we make our way inside before Mira clicks on the lamp by the couch. I set down our bags and slip off my suit jacket, wincing when my swollen hand catches on the fabric.

"You need ice," Mira says, wrapping her fingers against my bruised knuckles.

"I'll be okay," I promise, but it doesn't stop her from going to look inside the freezer.

She hands me a towel full of ice, and I place it against my knuckles, the tendons already tightening. She leans against the wall across from me, her eyes heavy with exhaustion.

"Do you mind if I go upstairs? I think I just want to go to bed."

"I'll go with you," I say, picking up our bags and following her up the stairs. The bed is still made, the plaid comforter is perfectly tucked in on the sides, and I doubt my mother's head ever graced the pillow.

"Do you want to take a shower? I bet they have hot water."

"I just want to sit here for a minute," she says, leaning towards me and burying her head in my chest. I thread my hands in her hair, massaging the space around her temples until she lets out a soft purr of contentment and safety.

"What do you need?" I ask, willing to give her the world.

"I don't know, sleep maybe," she says, picking at the fabric at her knees.

The dress is stained, little droplets of water or wine dotting the fabric, and she places her hands in her lap. The straps of the shoulders have already left marks against her skin, and I know she can't be comfortable.

"You can't sleep in that dress." I dig through her bag hoping to find pajamas, but I spot a familiar piece of fabric bunched up inside. It's my Shire shirt, the one I gave her to wear the night she came to my apartment. I can't believe she brought it with her. I hold it up, showing it to her as she gives me a sheepish smile.

"I didn't have much time to pack," she says, reaching for it.

The straps of her dress have fallen over her shoulders, the delicate gold fabric glowing against her skin, as she moves her hair to the side.

"Can you?" she asks, turning her back to me.

My fingers glide along the zipper, my knuckles skimming the pale skin of her back, and she lets the dress fall to the ground.

And although I've longed to get her out of that dress all night, watching her slide my favorite shirt over her skin, knowing that her body is pressing against the fabric I've worn my entire life, feels more intimate. Her dark hair falls over her shoulders in heavy waves as she climbs into bed. I lay the blanket over her, tucking it in on the sides. I want to lie down beside her, to feel her warmth, to memorize the sound of her breath, but after everything she's told me, I don't want to overstep.

"I can sleep on the couch," I offer, but I'm grateful when she reaches for me.

"Stay, please."

"As you wish."

She offers me a weak smile before I kick off my shoes and find my place beside her. She cuddles into my chest, her head resting just below my chin, and I wrap my arms around her. I breathe her in, kissing the top of her head as we lie together.

"You didn't have to hit him," she whispers, and her fingertips graze over the bruised skin on my knuckles.

I move a stray hair from her face, tucking it behind her ear. "It was about time Grant learned that his actions have consequences."

"Like hooking up with Katherine?"

I reposition myself so I can see her face. "I'm pissed he did that to Meredith. She doesn't deserve that. But honestly, I punched him because he hurt you. He might not have done it on purpose but . . ." I trail off. "It's one thing to have him inflict pain onto me but I won't have him do it to the people I love."

The word hangs in the air between us for a moment as I wait for her response. I know she heard my speech earlier and we never really had a chance to talk about how she felt about it.

"Love?" she asks, carefully, scooting closer, even though there is no space left between us.

"I think I've been in love with you for a while now," I say, the words tumbling out of my mouth.

"Are you sure?" she asks. "I mean, we barely know each other outside of the bar."

I can't restrain the laugh that burrows out from my chest. "You're kidding, right?"

"Okay, you know my coffee order, but—"

I cut her off. "Mira, we've been talking non-stop for weeks. I know so much about you. For instance, I know you splurge on Chinese takeout every Sunday because you know you'll have leftovers. That you love blasting Midwest emo so loud your neighbors have called in two noise ordinances against you. That you always give the unhoused guy outside a dollar and that you let Lilah borrow that sheer black top for her date. It looks better on you by the way, so I hope she gave it back."

A little laugh sneaks out of her mouth.

"But more than that I know that I wake up every morning excited to see you, that I check my phone the second I wake up hoping there's a text from you. I wish I could be there in that apartment when you're working late, so I could coax you to sleep with good wine or multiple orgasms. Or that every day I go without seeing you, I write down everything I want to share with you on my notes app, so I don't forget a single thing."

Mira diverts her gaze from me, a pretty pink hue building along her cheeks, and I turn her chin back towards me.

"I know that this scar," I say, running my finger along the discolored line on her arm, "happened when you had to hike down Hanging Rock after an engagement session and you vowed to never do a shoot there again."

She lifts her head, her eyes staring up at me. "I never told you that story."

"No, but you told Lilah."

She stares at me quizzically as if trying to place the memory.

"It was my first day," I say, filling in the blanks. "You were sitting there, drinking whiskey and, I dunno, you looked so cool. Like you never needed anyone to take care of you. And I knew I didn't stand a chance. But I listened to your stories, I followed your photography page the day you asked if you could put one of your stickers on the bar. I couldn't help taking an interest."

I take a deep breath, as the butterflies that used to visit me every time she walked into Finn's make a reappearance in my stomach.

"You know it took me a week to work up the courage to ask for your drink order."

"But I always get the same thing."

"I know." I smile, recalling how my hand trembled the first time I grabbed the whiskey bottle for her. "But that was the day you let me in. And I promised that I'd never let myself squander your attention."

"Why did you wait so long to ask me out then?"

"If you haven't noticed, my life, my relationships, my family, it's complicated. But I didn't want to fuck anything up between us by asking you out, or putting too much pressure on us. I thought I could settle for your friendship, even if all I ever thought about was what it would be like to lean across that bar and kiss you."

"So that's your excuse then?" she laughs, throwing her arms around my neck and running her fingers through my hair.

"Excuse?"

"For never being able to make a drink?" she asks, pulling me towards her until our mouths are a breath apart. "Because you wanted to kiss me?"

"I feel like it's a pretty good excuse," I say as she brings her mouth to mine. Her tongue slips into my mouth, and my hand crawls up her back, stopping at the back of her neck, steadying her against me. Our bodies respond to each other as if we are tethered, the push and pull creating a delicious friction before she reaches for the button of my pants.

As much as I want this, to be with her, to know her in this way, I want her to be sure.

"Mira," I breathe.

"Hudson," she says, matching my tone.

"We don't have to do this right now," I say, giving her an out.

"I've had a lot of really shitty things happen in my life lately, but being with you made them feel inconsequential," she explains, her hazel eyes soft in the warm glow from the bedside lamp. "And I know what I need right now, what I want, is to be with you. So unless you want me to stop . . ."

I can't find the words to argue when she bites the delicate skin of my neck. The bruise she left on Monday has almost faded and I'm eager for her to write over it, to brand me, to let everyone know that I'm hers.

My fingers fumble with the buttons of my shirt, quickly going down the line as her nails rake down my chest. The black polish is chipped and faded, her signature look. I grab one of her hands and kiss her palm, pinning it behind her head.

Her hair's been let loose, the deep-brown curls falling around her face, and I weave my fingers through it, guiding her mouth to mine. Her tongue slips into my mouth, and she moves against me with an unbridled passion as if kissing me is the only thing keeping her breathing, and I want to be that oxygen.

There's heat behind her eyes while she watches me discard my shirt on the floor before bending to my knees to taste more of her.

Her body hums against me as I move my mouth along her stomach, up her ribcage, then my hands slide underneath the fabric of my shirt she's wearing, pushing it up over her breasts.

I take one of her taut nipples between my teeth and bite down just hard enough that she arches her back. She moans, the sound an achy whimper when my hand reaches between her thighs, to find that she's completely soaked through. "Birth control?" I ask, highly doubting there are condoms in the bathroom.

"IUD," she replies, peeling off her shirt.

I wiggle myself out of my pants as she reaches for me, tugging at the fabric of my boxer briefs, pushing them down until I've sprung free.

"Come here," she begs, her eyes darkened with need.

I settle between her legs, waiting for her reassurance before I slip inside her. I go slow, my body moving in even, gentle strokes. This isn't something to be rushed, but an experience to be savored. But unlike seeing bioluminescence in Puerto Rico, or the aurora borealis in Iceland, or volcanic lightning in Guatemala, I know that nothing will ever compare.

We work together as she matches me, rhythm for rhythm, pressure building inside me. I can't let go, not yet, not until I hear that coarse sound escape from her lips, the one that lets me know that she's gotten what she needs. I'm on the edge, my head buried in her neck, when she cradles my face in her hands.

"Hudson."

She says my name as if it's sacred, her body pulsing beneath mine.

"Say it again," she demands as I let go.

"I love you," I breathe against her skin, into her hair, over her body. "I love you. I love you."

Each time I say it, the tension in her body releases, tears leaking from the corners of her eyes while she grinds against me, nails digging into my shoulder blades as if she needs to be embedded in my skin.

I don't care that she doesn't say it back. She doesn't have to. Because I'll love her regardless. Whether it's a night, or a year, or a lifetime, I'll love her for as long as she lets me.

33 MIRA

I wake up to the weight of Hudson's arm draped over me, the tickle of his beard against my neck, and the *I love you* I never expected still wrapped around me like a warm hug.

I should have said it back. I wanted to. But there is still a remnant of fear lingering in my chest. To let someone in, to trust completely, is harder than I thought it would be, since the last time someone made promises to me they turned out to be hollow.

Rolling over, I check my phone and remember the email. The one still waiting for me in my inbox.

"Mmm," Hudson groans, sleepily kissing my shoulder as his hold against my stomach tightens, pulling me back to bed. His mouth moves against my bare skin, planting light kisses along my collarbone, my neck, but when he moves to my lips, I hold up a hand in protest.

"I need to brush my teeth."

"You don't need to move from this bed," he says, pushing my hand away and kissing me for real.

As much as I want to lie here and let him have me, I only have an hour to get my gear together, and head to Meredith's to start the getting-ready photos.

"I have to go to work," I reason, before I see the bruises on Hudson's fingers and the memory of last night hits me like a gut punch. In college, Meredith always said that she'd want the truth no matter how bad it hurt. That she'd rather face a problem than tiptoe around it, and I know that I can't let her walk down that aisle without making her own decision, even if it's to my detriment.

"I have to tell her," I say, hoping that Hudson might talk me out of it. That he will offer me an alternative solution. But he nods in understanding.

"We can tell her together," he says, threading his hand through mine, bringing my knuckles to his lips. And the sincerity in his eyes makes me want to shout: *I love you too.*

"I'll back you up. Whatever you need."

My heart leaps at the idea of having him by my side for all the hard moments in my life. And although I'm grateful for his support, I know that this is something I need to do by myself.

"I think it might be better coming from me."

"Are you sure?"

I give him a soft kiss and slip out of bed. I take a long, hot shower, my first of the trip, and put on my own clothes—a pair of black jeans and an oversized black button-down—and head over to Meredith's cabin.

Upbeat, pop music blasts from the Bluetooth speakers as I climb the stairs and peek inside Meredith's room. There's the frantic, pre-wedding energy in the air, with everyone in various stages of undress. Jocelyn is sitting cross-legged on the floor in front of a light-up vanity as she applies foundation to her skin, and Vanessa is plaiting her hair in a loose braid, giving me a bright smile when I make my way into the room. Katherine is steaming the bridesmaids' gowns—mismatched floral dresses with embroidered embellishments. She doesn't look at me, diverting her gaze as she focuses on the fabric in her hand, and I'm baffled by how she can stand in this room right now.

Ignoring her, I head straight for Meredith, who is sitting in a chair by the window. Her hair is pinned up in rollers and there are purple eye masks adhered to the delicate skin underneath her eyes.

"How are we feeling this morning?" I ask in a voice way more chipper than how I actually feel.

"I got my iced coffee. I got my girls. I finally got service on my phone. Life is good."

I stare at her, trying to think of an excuse to get her alone, when she hops up from her chair as if she's forgotten something.

"You need my details, right?" she says, gathering a pair of white espadrille sandals, seashell jewelry, a sandalwood-scented perfume. Her dress, a crocheted two-piece with bell sleeves, hangs on a wooden hanger on the window frame.

"I put my jewelry and some knick-knacks in here," she says, handing me a plastic box. "There's a letter from Grant in there as well. I waited to open it. I thought maybe you could get a photo of me reading it."

My stomach tightens at the suggestion.

"Did he give it to you this morning?" I ask, wondering what excuse he's offered for why he came home sporting a black eye.

"Nope! He had Jocelyn messenger it over from the barn. They're all getting ready over there. We decided to do the whole one-last-night-apart thing. His idea, of course. He's so much more of a traditionalist than me."

All my instincts tell me to keep my mouth shut, to smile and nod, and pretend I didn't catch the groom wrist-deep in the maid of honor, but staring at my friend, I let my courage win.

"You know, Mere. I'd love to get your opinion on bridal party photo locations, since we'll be doing them on site. Do you have a second to run downstairs with me?"

"Totally," she beams, and follows me down the stairs. I wait until the moment we're out of earshot before I rip off the proverbial Band-Aid.

"I have to tell you something."

Her face falls. "Oh God, is it the bakery? They promised me they could make a vegan cake shaped like our dog, but I didn't believe them. The consistency isn't conducive to sculpting, or at least that's what another bakery told me," she says, taking a deep breath. "If it looks like a mutant, maybe we can have cupcakes instead. I'm not really sold on the whole feeding each other thing, but . . ."

"It's not the cake," I reply.

Her eyebrows furrow in contemplation. "What is it?"

"Mere," I say, grabbing her arm to hold her attention. "I hate to do this, today of all days, but I would feel like shit if I didn't say anything. And I get it if you don't believe me, but I have to tell you . . ."

The words come out too quickly, and Meredith stares at me with a concerned expression.

"I saw Grant and Katherine hooking up in the bathroom last night."

I take a wary step back, my nails in my palms, waiting for her response. I expect screaming, crying, or a rare burst of violence. But I don't expect laughter.

I consider that it might be a shock response. I've heard about people who find themselves hysterically giggling in uncomfortable situations with no ability to control it. But then her expression turns serious.

"Oh my God. Mira. No," she says, consoling me. "Grant and I have an open relationship."

The admission is so unexpected that I have to take a seat on the edge of the couch.

"You do?"

She nods, placing a hand on my shoulder.

"Grant asked me last night, before they did anything. That's the rule. We have to ask for permission, but I was with Derrick so . . ."

"Oh," I say, letting the reality of it sink in.

"I'm so sorry. I know that must have been awkward."

"I just . . . I thought . . ."

"I know it's unconventional, but with my background, I think life's too short not to allow yourself the things you want. Sometimes it's dessert for breakfast or flying to the middle of nowhere to get married, and sometimes it's to fuck the hot bartender."

This time it's my turn to laugh.

"I've never wanted to be confined by the traditional ideals of marriage, and Grant gets that about me. He loves me for it. I didn't want to stop living my life to the fullest, and nor did he. We're honest and never take the other person for granted. He will always put me first, and vice versa, and at the end of the day, that's enough."

It makes sense. Even in college Meredith broke a lot of hearts by never wanting to commit. And honestly, I'm happy that she's found someone that understands her lifestyle choices.

"I figured someone would find out eventually. It's not like we're discreet. We go out on dates with other people all the time," she offers, leaning back on the couch. "Honestly, I'm more shocked Katherine got Hudson to agree."

I bite my lip, not sure if this is my secret to tell. Meredith senses my apprehension and points a finger at me. "You know something."

"They broke up."

"Really?" Meredith gasps.

"A while ago."

"How do you know?" she asks, inquisitively.

"Between you and me, I'm pretty sure Hudson and I are dating now."

Meredith takes a beat, eyes widened. "When did this happen?"

"Uh. Technically we've been talking for months, but officially yesterday."

"Wait. So last night. His speech. That was about you?" she asks, realization washing over her.

"Yeah, I guess it was."

"I have so many questions," Meredith says, resting her head on her hands.

"When it's not your wedding day, I'll be happy to answer them," I say, pushing myself off the couch.

"I do want to know the answer to one though." She turns to face me, a quiet reflection on her face as I ready myself to regale her with tales from the lake, or the rehearsal dinner, or Finn's, but she asks, "Why did you think I wouldn't believe you?"

The question catches me off guard as unease works its way through my body. "I had to tell someone a similar truth and it didn't go as well."

"Oh, honey," Meredith says, wrapping me in her arms. "Is that who wrote that review?"

"You saw that?" I cringe.

"I looked up your account the other night to make sure I had the right number. And it popped up. I thought who the hell would say something like that. But if that person didn't want to see the truth, that's their burden. Not yours."

Meredith rests a steady hand on mine, gripping it tightly. "You're a good person, Mira. And an even better friend. You came to me because you care and didn't want to see me make the wrong choice, and that's admirable. That takes strength. I'm so fucking grateful I have you on my side, and here with me this week. I want you to know you can always come to me, okay. About anything. And I'll always hear you out."

Her words simultaneously rip me open and stitch me back up as I fight back the pricking behind my eyes.

"Oh no," Meredith says, standing up to wrap her arms around me. "I didn't mean to make you cry."

"I'm sorry," I sniffle against her cotton robe. "I think I just need a minute. Is that okay?"

"Take all the time you need," Meredith assures me, giving me another squeeze for good measure. "Like I said, you don't have to put on your work face for me. I trust you completely."

I take a minute to collect myself, waiting for Meredith to make her way back up the stairs before I slip outside for some fresh air. The heatwave broke overnight, and even though it's still a balmy eighty-eight, it's worlds better than the triple-digit hell we've been suffering through.

Gripping the railing, I find Hudson sitting on the porch of our cabin two doors over. He's dressed down in a soft brown tee and green shorts.

"How did it go?" he asks solemnly.

"Better than I expected," I say, sinking into his arms. "Meredith and Grant are open."

"Really?" he asks incredulously.

"Yeah. Meredith spent last night with Derrick."

Hudson lifts an eyebrow in surprise. "That guy never takes a day off, does he?"

"He really doesn't," I sniffle.

Hudson uses his thumb to wipe away a stray tear. "So, if things went okay, why are you crying?"

"I guess I'm just processing," I say, reaching into my back pocket to pull out my phone. "Because Phoebe sent me an email last night."

"Have you read it?"

I shake my head. "I tried. But with everything going on, I didn't know if it would help any. But now I think I need to."

"Do you want me to give you some privacy?" he asks, raking a hand through his curls.

"Can you stay?"

"Always," he says, resting his chin on my shoulder and giving me a squeeze.

Taking a deep breath, I open the email with shaky hands.

> Mira,
>
> I know this apology is too late, but I felt you deserved one. I realize now in my haste to cover up my insecurities and fears, I created so many for you. I left that review in a moment of weakness, believing that if I placed the blame onto you, I wouldn't have to face the truth. But I've learned that pushing a problem away doesn't make it disappear. If anything, it eats at a person until they are doomed to face it head-on. Cliff left me a few weeks ago. He said he'd fallen in love with someone else, someone he had been seeing off and on for the entirety of our relationship. Someone I found out about a few days before our wedding. When I confronted him about it, I believed him when he said it was over, that he would never do anything like that again, and that he was ready to start a new life together. I loved this man, and like everyone I understood that people make mistakes. I thought that marriage might be a clean slate for us. So when you came into that room and told me what happened, it wasn't that I didn't believe you. It was that I

> couldn't face it. I wanted it to go away. And so I unleashed my misplaced anger onto you. More than that I knew that I'd never be able to keep our friendship and stay in my relationship, so I chose him. And that was my biggest mistake.
>
> I'd been keeping his indiscretions a secret from everyone: my family, my friends, you. I couldn't bear to have people look at me with pity and concern, to force me to face the reality that the man I loved was not who I thought he was. I didn't want the judgment, the shame of it, so I blamed you. I punished you, and I've spent these last few weeks punishing myself for it.
>
> I want you to know I took down the review. I've also asked all the wedding venues I know to add you as a preferred vendor. I know that you won't want to work together, so I made sure that an associate will be the lead on any upcoming events where we were originally paired. I understand if you never forgive me, I wouldn't forgive me, but I need you to know that the loss of my marriage is nothing compared to the loss of your friendship. I miss you dearly, and I will regret my actions towards you for the rest of my life. I'm sorry it's taken me this long to reach out. And I do hope, one day, we might be able to be friends again.
>
> Phoebe.

I close the message.

"How do you feel?" Hudson asks, as I oscillate from anger to pity to acceptance.

"I don't know," I say, truthfully. "I thought that I wanted an apology, or forgiveness, or reconciliation, but I think I just want to put it all behind me."

Of all the nights I spent hoping to get an email like this, I realize that I didn't want her forgiveness. If anything, I think I was waiting for her permission to move on. For years I let Phoebe dictate my choices. I changed my shooting style, my clothing, and my personality to fit into her world, to serve her clients, and now that I've been freed from those impossible standards I can't imagine going back.

"I think after this I'm done with weddings for good," I state. "I think I want to take some time to fall in love with photography again, my way. Shoot the images that I want. Make real art. Go back to my roots."

After allowing weddings to sidetrack my goals for so long, I'm still thankful for all the things they brought me. That they awarded me a life I never imagined for myself. That they gave me the chance to run my own business, to create art for a living. That they reminded me of where I started, that they brought me back to Meredith and Vanessa, and reminded me of the friendship I'm worthy of. But more than that, weddings are what brought me Hudson. And even after I move on, I'll always be grateful for that.

34 HUDSON

Thanks to my proximity to the Activity Center, I catch up on a few emails, check in with my dad, who has sent me multiple photos of my new shiny office, and message Linda from HR about drafting a position for Content Creation and Photography.

After our conversation this morning, I wanted to offer the position to Mira then and there, to ask her to travel the world with me, to work beside me, and to help turn my father's career into my dream job, but I knew she wouldn't accept it. She said she wanted time to figure out what she wants for herself and I respect that. But after this is all over, I'm going to remind her that the offer will always be on the table.

From the kitchen window I see a crew of fifty milling about the ranch, hauling wooden tables and chairs onto the lawn, and stringing thousands of twinkling lights inside the sprawling white tent. Amelia follows them, clipboard in hand, no doubt making sure everything is to my mother's exact specifications.

Susan hasn't bothered to show her face on the property herself, most likely entertaining a beauty team of fifteen at the lodge. But her absence is probably for the best. Meredith deserves to have a stress-free morning. Sipping a cup of peppermint tea, I consider killing the next few hours reading until I see Vivianne struggling out on the lawn. She's carrying two buckets of flowers down the hill, her shoulders sagging under the weight. I make my way over to her to help.

"Need a hand with that?" I ask as she sets one down.

"That'd be wonderful," she replies, wiping sweat from her brow.

"You didn't pick these all by yourself, did you?"

"No, no," she says, swatting away the idea. "Grant did. Early this morning. He filled about thirty of these buckets too. Guess he wanted to make sure there was enough for the arrangements."

I try to mask my shock. Grant doing anything without personal gain is a new experience for me, but I'm glad to know that he's growing.

"Meredith always told me that he would do anything to make her happy but watching him get sunburnt in that field really proves it."

"Why didn't he bring the buckets down here himself then?" I ask, placing them at the entrance of the tent.

"Oh, we were hiding them at my place. Afraid Susan might get one of her henchmen to sabotage them."

"Makes sense," I reply, sympathetically.

"A little birdie told me you were the one to give Grant that shiner he's walking around with."

"Not my best move," I admit, knowing that Mira's going to have to spend hours Photoshopping it out.

"Perhaps it's what needed to be done," she assures me. "Bottling up emotions like that isn't good for your health."

"I don't think punching him was good for my health either," I say, stretching out my hand.

"Who knows, maybe this was just the thing you needed to move forward."

"Maybe," I shrug, not putting too much stock into her assessment.

“I think this is a new chapter for you,” she beams, taking a few stems from the bucket, admiring them together, before adding another. “I can feel it. Your energy has shifted. It’s much lighter today. As if you’ve let go of what was holding you back. Perhaps so you could move on with a certain photographer.”

I raise a questioning eyebrow at her.

“Oh, don’t look so surprised. It doesn’t take a psychic to see your connection with Mira,” she replies mysteriously. Then adds, “Plus I saw you two sneak in the cabin together last night.”

“Ah,” I say, handing her the pair of shears she’s reaching for on the table.

“It’s okay, dear. I should have warned you that your relationship with Katherine was never going to work. A Virgo and a Sagittarius. Outrageous pairing.”

“What about a Virgo and a Taurus?” I ask, recalling the daily horoscopes Lilah would read for us at the bar.

“Two earth signs!” Vivianne squeals in delight, clasping her hands together, causing her bracelets to clang. “That’s harmony.”

I’m elated to know that the stars are on our side, as Amelia stalks up to us, stress written all over her face.

“What are these?” she asks, inspecting the wildflowers as if we’ve just hauled a herd of livestock to the wedding. “It doesn’t matter. They have to go. We have a shipment of roses coming in momentarily and—”

“Send ’em back,” Vivianne says with a stern authority I’ve never seen before.

Amelia stands back flustered. “But Susan said . . .”

“My niece wants wildflowers for her wedding so she’s getting wildflowers,” Vivianne replies, grabbing a pair of shears from the bucket, wielding them like a weapon. I watch the struggle on Amelia’s face, as if she’s weighing up whether this is worth the fight.

She concedes, rubbing one of the petals between her fingers. "But if Susan asks, I'm sending her straight to you."

Vivianne gives her a solemn nod in return before Amelia flees to the other side of the tent to micro-manage more vendors.

"I don't mind helping if you need an extra hand," I offer, watching as she begins gathering flowers into simple bouquets, cutting the stems and placing them into glass vases on the tables.

"I'd appreciate that," she says, resting her hand on my shoulder. "And I'd also appreciate help with the rest of those buckets."

After I've hauled the flowers into the reception space, Vivianne hands me a pair of scissors and I get to work. We spread the variety of Indian blanket flowers, blue Rocky Mountain columbine, and purple daisies evenly, until the tables are alive with color.

Once we're finished I head back to my cabin to freshen up and find Grant waiting on the steps. He's halfway ready, in dress pants and a button-down, but his hair is wet and his eye is a mess of purple and yellow. I await retaliation, but he just asks, "Can we talk?"

"Sure." I open the door to let him in.

He looks around, assessing the place. "So, you took over the parents' cabin?"

"I thought it was the best option, considering," I reply, letting the events of last night hang in the air.

"About that." Grant rubs at the back of his neck. "It's not what you think."

"I know," I say, taking a seat at one of the barstools in the kitchen. "Mira talked to Meredith."

He's fidgeting, and this nervous energy is making me uneasy.

"I need you to know nothing ever happened when you were together. I know we're not on the best terms but I'd never do that. Bro-code and all. But Katherine came to me last night, crying about you. She said you were over. I shouldn't have crossed that line and I'm sorry."

"I didn't punch you because of Katherine," I explain as the guilt lifts from Grant's shoulders.

"You didn't?"

"No. We've been over for months. She can sleep with who she wants. If I'm being honest I think I'd just been waiting for an excuse to punch you for years."

"I get that," Grant says, taking a seat on the couch across from me. "I've been an asshole to you. And that's not fair. I'm not saying this as an excuse or anything, I know that my actions are my own, but growing up in that house, you have no idea what that was like. You got to go home, but I got Susan twenty-four-seven." Grant's shoulders slump as he takes a deep breath.

"I lost my mom. My best fucking friend. And then within a year, this woman came in and tried to take her place. I didn't want her. I didn't want you. I just wanted my mom back."

His vulnerability reminds me of the glimpses of Grant I used to see. The one I shared popcorn with in the game room when George and Susan were arguing. The one who lent me his Game Boy when mine fell from the treehouse and cracked in half. The one I'd catch sitting up on the roof late at night, staring up at the stars. And as if a glamour's been removed, I see it, the armor he's been wearing all these years, rusted and cracked, worn with age, as it slowly slips off and away.

"It's okay," I say, but Grant shakes his head.

"You didn't deserve a mother like Susan. Neither of us did, and that's a lot to handle. I was conditioned to accept her, because it was all I knew, but you knew there was something better and that's not fair to you."

We sit in silence for a few moments.

"These are probably the most words we've said to one another," I say, trying to recall the last time we had a real conversation.

"What can I say, I've grown up, man."

"I've noticed."

"And it doesn't hurt that Meredith has me going to therapy."

"Really?" The admission catches me off guard. "That's amazing."

"I resisted at first. But Meredith told me that if our relationship was going to work we had to communicate effectively, and I took that shit to heart. I mean, your mom and my dad never talk. She asks for the Black Card and he hands it over. And I didn't want that life. I wanted a real partner."

I remember all the years we endured awkward dinners, Susan chatting to friends on the phone as George typed emails on his phone or read the paper. It definitely wasn't the basis for a healthy relationship by any means.

"And it's nice being able to talk to someone about anything. It made me see a lot of shit differently. And it's really made me and Meredith make a deep connection."

"I bet," I jest, as Grant nudges my shoulder.

"I never thought that anyone would accept me, or understand what's going on in my head, but Meredith does. She listens. She supports me. And most importantly, she calls me on my bullshit. Like how I've been a shitty brother to you." Grant turns towards me, in earnest. "You always put in an effort. You always tried and I never let you in."

"I could have tried harder," I argue.

"You did more than I deserve," he replies. "Like I know you got us that permit for the wedding."

I rake my hand through my hair. "You know about that?"

"Amelia told us. Said that if you hadn't pulled some strings we would be getting married in the backyard here."

"It's not a bad view."

"No," Grant sighs, "but it's not what Meredith wants. And you made that happen."

I've never shied away from talking about my feelings, but talking about them with Grant is like seeing a corpse flower into bloom, a rare phenomenon.

"I get if it's too late, but I do want to say I am sorry for the way I treated you growing up. For taking out my issues on you. For everything really."

There's a tenderness to his words that makes me believe he really means it.

"I totally understand if I was too much of an asshole, but I would really like to be brothers."

I allow myself a moment to process what he's saying. What he's asking for. And after everything this weekend I have to believe in second chances.

"We can still try."

Grant stares at me, disbelieving.

"Really?"

"Yeah," I nod, "I've always wanted a brother."

Before I even know what's happening, Grant hops up from the couch and wraps his arms around me. Grant clears his throat as he pulls away. "Now then, if you wouldn't mind, I'd love to have my brother come and get ready with me and the rest of my friends."

35 MIRA

"Alright, now grab her hand and frolic down the mountainside like you're the main characters in *The Sound of Music*," I direct as we hustle to get photos done before the ceremony.

Although the scenic view Meredith requested is only a half-mile hike like she said, this didn't account for the twenty-minute drive up the side of the mountain to get to the trailhead.

"It's not like they can start without us," she assures me when I mention the time constraint, but I can't argue with her. "Now come on, I can't wait to see you work your magic."

We venture through the grassy terrain, laughing and joking together, as we stop every couple of feet to take more photos. I worried there might be some residual awkwardness between us after the incident last night, but Grant treated me like one of the party posse when I made my way into his cabin to take the groom's getting-ready photos. More shocking though was finding Hudson there, laughing and having a good time. They even took a photo together. And although I had zero time to ask how the hell that happened, Hudson assured me that he'd tell me all about it later.

"Okay, now spin and kiss," I say, clicking my shutter rapidly to ensure I get the shot. Now that I've admitted that this might be one of the last weddings I'll ever capture, I'm feeling nostalgic, eager to appreciate every moment.

Grant follows my directions perfectly, taking the lead as he sweeps Meredith into his arms and dips her backwards, pressing his lips against hers. Although their relationship might be considered unconventional there's no denying there is a genuine love between them. They lengthen their kiss, their hands finding each other's bodies, and I call out another prompt.

"Can you try picking her up?"

"No problem," Grant replies, effortlessly lifting Meredith into the air, and I can't believe she thought he was camera-shy. Grant has been grinning non-stop all day, playing to the camera like he's on a reality TV show. Thankfully Vanessa stopped by his cabin with her makeup kit and did a pretty remarkable job of covering most of the damage Hudson inflicted last night. The purple-and-blue bruise looks like nothing more than a bad night's sleep.

The scenery is stunning, the landscape rivaling that of a mythical fantasyland, as the purples, yellows, and greens meet the blue sky at the horizon. Without the pressure of packing my portfolio with click-worthy imagery I'm able to have fun with it, a feeling I haven't associated with photography in quite some time, and I think of the images I've been most proud of this week.

The lake, the bison, and now this mountainside.

I know Hudson wasn't serious about that job offer, he couldn't have been, but I can't help but wonder what it might be like, to get paid to travel. To take photos of all the gorgeous places of the world, to have financial security, to do more of the things that make me feel alive.

I direct Meredith and Grant in a few more poses before they make their way back towards me, their bodies finding each other for a final portrait.

"You two ready to party?" I ask, putting on my lens cap.

"Hell yes," Meredith replies, as Grant bends down to help her gather the crochet overlay of her dress. We make our way to the ceremony site.

The drive down the mountain is quiet, a rarity for Meredith, and I can tell that the pre-ceremony jitters are finally setting in. Her knee bobs up and down as she stares out the window, a bouquet of wildflowers in her lap. I watch her eyes find a peaceful contentment when Grant rests his hand on hers, moving his thumb over her wrist.

It's the same way Hudson settles me when I'm overstimulated, my brain constantly ruminating on the next problem instead of being in the moment. The way I know that when he's around I can exist without worry. Last night he was amazing in helping me process all the emotions I've kept bottled up for months. He made me feel safe, and loved, and cared for when I was most vulnerable. Even this morning, as he sat by me while I read Phoebe's letter, he gave me the strength to believe in myself again.

And I can't wait to tell him that I love him too.

36 HUDSON

Colter Bay is stunning, a picturesque, serene, rocky beachfront that backs up to the towering Tetons, their snowcapped peaks glistening in the afternoon sun. Thanks to the permit we requested, we've been given a dedicated area for Meredith and Grant to tie the knot, but it has no bearing on the tourists enjoying the crisp mountain water behind us.

"Someone should go say something," Vivianne says, as Amelia and her team erect the wedding arch, the view blocked by the slew of college kids drinking on a party raft behind it.

"Don't worry, I got it," Mira assures Vivianne, taking charge.

After watching her all day, I understand why she's always starving after work—she must burn thousands of calories each shift. Between running back and forth all day, with those cameras hanging from her shoulders, she hasn't sat down for a second. Her stamina is endless and she runs down to the rocky edge, shouting at the group. It only takes a minute before they are paddling in the opposite direction and waving apologetically.

I stand there in awe of her. Here, with a camera in her hand, she's headstrong and tenacious, taking charge and handling crises with ease. It's what has allowed her to succeed for all these years, but I know there's another side of her too. The one who remembers little details, who helps elderly guests walk over rocky terrain, and who is smiling at me.

I can't believe that I get to see all of her. The sour and the sweet. The subtle and the strong.

I want to wrap my arms around her, to push that hair out of her eyes, to kiss her there and then, when my mother's voice rings out over the crowd.

"HUDSON WALTER HAYES!"

And I know I'm fucked.

Despite the rocky terrain, Susan's surprisingly quick in her heels, her determination to cause a scene greater than any fear of turning an ankle. She comes right up to me, her lavish blue dress flowing behind her.

"Did you punch your brother last night?" she asks, pointing an accusatory finger in my face.

"It was a misunderstanding," I explain, but rage flares behind her eyes.

"Seriously?" she says, pinching the bridge of her nose in disgust. It's the same movement she'd make anytime I left my boots on the rug or embarrassed her by reading during her cocktail parties. "You decide this week is the time to work out your squabbles. I swear, we can't get through a single family function without you or your brother embarrassing me."

"Oh my fucking God," Grant says, stepping in between us, irritation lining his face. "Can you go one day without making everything about you?"

"Excuse me?" Susan's mouth pitches open. "Do I need to remind you that I'm the one who paid for all this?"

"You mean, my father paid for all of this," Grant claps back. "Because you haven't had a job since what? 1999?"

She's stunned into silence, a feat I didn't believe was possible.

"What in God's name is going on over here?" George asks, pulling on the lapel of his navy suit jacket.

"Your son is being an ungrateful brat," Susan says, crossing her arms over her chest. And now I understand why she's always been incapable of mothering, because she still acts like a child herself.

George turns his attention to his son. "Grant?"

"What?" he snaps as we both watch George's expression go rigid, his chest expanding in indignation.

"Your mother and I put a lot of time and money into this event—"

"I didn't ask you to do that," Grant argues, not backing down. "Meredith and I told you we wanted to pay for this ourselves. We tried to and then Susan came in and steamrollered our plans."

"What plans?" George asks, annoyed. "I hope to God you didn't plan to embarrass us because that's what you've been doing all week. Putting us up in that sorry excuse for a hotel, torturing us on a boat, starving us to death. Is that what you wanted to do?"

"Just because it's not what you want doesn't mean it's unacceptable." Grant drags a hand over his face. "I know you think that I'm throwing my life away, that I'm still that stupid kid that needed you to clean up my mess, but I'm not. I'm an adult with a solid career, and a soon-to-be wife. I get that you want everything to be perfect but that's not me. And it's definitely not Meredith. I tried for years to fit into that mold, but I finally found someone who accepts me for me," Grant says, his eyes radiating with pure love as he finds Meredith standing a few paces from us, Vivianne by her side. "And I'm going to marry her on our terms. We're going to have wildflowers and a keg at the reception. And we're not posing for any family photos not on our approved list. And you're not going to say a negative word about me or my wife for the rest of the day? Got it?"

Coming up beside him, Meredith links her arm through Grant's in solidarity and their relationship makes sense. Their bond of found family, of cherishing the people who have chosen them, of overcoming childhood trauma, of accepting each other, flaws and all.

"I was just standing up for you," Susan argues, her voice low now that guests have noticed the not so private conversation we're having.

But Grant's voice stays steady. "You want to know why Hudson punched me?"

I stare at him with wide, unbelieving eyes, but he shakes his head. "Because he caught me fucking Katherine."

George puffs out his chest in horror, his skin turning red, and my mother clutches her chest, her glare traveling from Grant, to Meredith, to me, as if she suspects I might punch him again.

"What are you saying?" George asks, frazzled.

"We're in an open relationship," Meredith explains. "Which is frankly none of your business but here we are."

From the lack of surprise on Vivianne's face, I'm certain Meredith has explained her relationship status to her aunt. And, honestly, I'd expect nothing less. They are a family who actually communicates and trusts each other.

"Hudson? You're not a part of this lifestyle, are you?" My mother's eyes turn to me, disgusted, and I know what she's asking. If we are all baring our truths I might as well add mine to the pile.

"Katherine and I broke up months ago," I admit, waiting for her judgment. "And since we're all being honest, I'm with Mira now."

"Who the hell is Mira?" my mother asks, stunned.

"I'm Mira," Mira says, coming to stand beside me.

Grant and Meredith beam at us as we create a wall between Susan and her judgment.

"I hate to break up the fun," Amelia says, coming over, having absolutely no context to the bombs we've just dropped on our parents, "but it's time to start the ceremony."

"Perfect," Grant says, readjusting his suit jacket, "we're done here anyways."

Mira follows Grant towards the ceremony, and Amelia leads Meredith and Vivianne to their starting line. I'm about to move off and find my seat when my mother pulls me back. "Why didn't you tell me you and Katherine broke up?"

There's hurt on her face, an emotion I didn't believe was possible thanks to the Botox and her general heartlessness.

"Considering you already made a wedding binder for us, I wasn't sure how you would take the news."

"What did you think was going to happen? That I'd force you into a betrothal?"

I raise an eyebrow. "I wouldn't put it past you."

"Hudson," my mother replies sheepishly. "I know we don't always see eye to eye, but you don't have to hide parts of your life from me."

"Really? Because if I told you that I left Katherine and started dating a photographer that I met at a bar where I work in the evenings, you would have said . . . what exactly?"

"I don't know. But I at least would have gotten to know the girl."

"Okay, sure," I scoff.

"I'm not heartless. I know I have impossible standards and I'm not easy to please but I'm human too. I understand that relationships don't always work out. I mean, look at me and your father."

There's a rare tenderness in her voice that I haven't heard since I was a child. I think back to those days before the divorce. All the days my father would work in the garage. How they would fight in the kitchen when they thought I was asleep. How miserable they both were. And how happy my mother was when she left.

"I want what's best for you, always. And we might not agree on what that is but I'm not going to dictate who you can love."

I cross my arms, unbelieving.

"I know you might not believe me, but I do love you."

I try to remember the last time my mother uttered those words to me. My tenth birthday, maybe.

"Do you?"

"What kind of question is that to ask your mother?" she asks, taken aback.

"I just haven't felt that from you in a long time."

"I don't believe in coddling."

"No, you don't," I say sourly, "but that doesn't mean you have to be so cold. I mean, take a look around. Grant's getting married today, and have you been happy for him for a second?"

My words must strike a chord because my mother takes a step back. For the first time in my life, she seems lost for words.

"I suppose I could do better."

"That's all I'm asking for. That's all any of us are asking for. For you to try. Because if you don't, you're going to lose us. All of us. And then what's going to be left for you?"

I let her sit with her thoughts as I find a seat beside Vanessa. Adrian is sitting on a stool at the front, strumming an acoustic guitar, playing a rendition of "Flightless Bird, American Mouth." All eyes focus on Meredith as she makes her descent down the aisle, her aunt by her side, smiling with every step. And as much as I try to give her my full attention, I can't help but get distracted by Mira, who is huddled in the aisleway, standing so close beside me I can smell her shampoo. She stands there, eyes glued to her camera, as she swings back and forth, capturing both Grant's reaction to his bride and Meredith's unbridled joy.

Throughout the twenty-minute ceremony, Mira races from one side to the other, squatting down to capture the hand-fasting ceremony, and zooming to the front to catch a tear on my mother's face. She's completely in the zone, and I imagine this is how doctors spring into action when a patient is rushed through the door. She doesn't miss a single moment.

I sit and listen to the officiant share stories of Grant and Meredith's first date, the first time they said I love you, the moment they knew there was no one else in the world for each other. And with everything out in the open, their story feels lighter, more genuine, and I too find myself getting swept up in emotion.

I think back to my own firsts with Mira. The first time I saw her with sad eyes and a guarded exterior, the first time I got her to laugh at a corny joke, the first time she texted me and I swore I'd never go a moment without my phone, the first time she stayed past closing, keeping me company as we dried glasses together because neither of us wanted to go home without the other. I think of how many more firsts are to come, and I can't wait to have them with her.

37 MIRA

Tonight, the Majestic Ranch is truly living up to its namesake, as the reception tent glows on the main lawn. Brass candlesticks line the tables, and hundreds of wildflowers create a dizzying array of color across long linen drapery. White roses sit at the end of each table, creeping up the sides, as the setting sun reflects off golden plates. The tent is lined with twinkling lights, making it shimmer like the stars above.

Meredith and Grant sit at the top table in two rattan chairs behind an intimate sweetheart table. Music plays through the sound system, and I start snapping photos of all the details.

"I helped with the centerpieces," Hudson boasts, as I move to photograph the arrangement.

"Guess I'm going to have to add 'floral designer' to your ever-growing list of hidden talents," I reply.

Vivianne appears, giving me a squeeze. "You were so great out there," she says with a warm smile, fanning herself with a yellow paper fan.

"Wait until you see the photos before you dole out the compliments," I reason.

"I'm sure they're going to be wonderful. Everything you've ever done has been a masterpiece."

"You've seen my work?"

"Oh yeah. Meredith would send me shots you took in college and a few on your socials. It's truly breathtaking stuff. I'm so thankful that you were able to come out here for this."

"It was my pleasure," I reply honestly, and Amelia directs our attention to the newlyweds as they share their first dance. I follow them with my camera, catching every dip and turn and starry-eyed kiss before the song ends and they head straight to the cake table, honoring Meredith's mantra of *Always eat dessert first.*

The three-tiered vegan masterpiece does resemble their dog Rocco. They cut into it, respectfully feeding each other from silver forks. Once they sit down, large platters of food are placed onto each table, as guests pass around entrées. Hudson pulls a chair out for me and it's not until I settle into my seat that I see a place card with my name on it and gratitude washes over me.

"I got you a drink," Hudson says, handing me a glass tumbler, and I instantly recognize it as my favorite: a whiskey sour.

"Don't worry, I didn't make this one," he assures me as I take a sip. It's absolutely delicious.

"This might be better than Lilah's."

"Never say that to her, or you'll be back to wishing I was making your drinks," he says, rubbing his hand along my back. It's such a subtle movement, but the fact we can finally be open about our relationship fills me with pure elation.

"You two are so damn cute," Meredith says, coming up behind us, draping her arms over my shoulders for a hug. Grant's standing beside her, sharing a handshake with Hudson as he offers him his congratulations.

"What else is left on the agenda for tonight?" I ask, pulling out my camera, but Meredith swats me away.

"You've captured all the major moments."

"Yeah, but your contract is for another couple of hours and—"

"Mira, please," she says, cutting me off. "I told you to enjoy yourself this week and that means the entire week. Now put that camera away and have some fun. That's an order."

And who am I to argue with the bride?

38 HUDSON

After filling our bellies with first and second helpings, Mira stretches her arms over her head, and I grab one and lead her out onto the dance floor.

"It may be the first time I've ever danced at a wedding," she says, resting her head on my chest. Even after running around she still smells sweet, like cinnamon and citrus.

"I'm glad I could be the first to ask you then," I say, giving her a little spin. She giggles before falling back against my chest, and I want to record the sound on a loop. To listen to anytime I need a pick-me-up. She threads her fingers through mine as my other hand finds the small of her back, leading her in tiny circles. Her voice is warm when she says my name. "Hudson?"

"Mhmm."

"Were you serious about that job offer?"

"One hundred percent," I assure her.

"And do you think I'm actually qualified?"

"Yes. Overqualified, honestly."

"And I wouldn't have to climb Everest with your team, right?"

"Everest is so 1999," he jokes.

"I'm serious. I'm not built like you. My endurance is more for dealing with uncomfortable family dynamics and too much PDA. Not scaling the sides of mountains."

"You'd have to shoot content on location of course, but you don't have to do the activities. You'd be adjacent to them. And if you're ever uncomfortable then you don't do it."

"And it's a real job? You didn't just make it up for me?" I know she's trying to be stern, but I can't help but find the way her brows furrow in the middle absolutely adorable.

"It's real. The listing is going live on Monday. You can even apply through the website if it makes you feel better. Although I will say that having an in with the CEO will make the hiring process go a little faster."

"Oh, I bet," she laughs.

"It comes with full benefits, a steady paycheck, and you'd get to travel."

"With you?"

"Technically, I'm supposed to be more behind the desk, but I'm hoping to do a little restructuring, be more hands-on than my dad was. So, yeah, we'd get to travel together." I'm already buzzing at the idea. Of traveling the world together. Of showing her my favorite trails. Of trying new food together. Of sharing sleeping bags and hotels on the road.

"I don't want any special treatment."

"Oof, that might be an issue," I say, restraining a smile.

"Why's that?"

"Because I plan on doing things with you I'd never do with anyone else at work."

She swats at my chest playfully. "That's not what I meant."

I kiss her forehead softly. "I want you to know, there's no commitment either. You can leave whenever you want. Or if you prefer you could do contract work for us. It would pay a little less but you could pick and choose the jobs you wanted to take. I never want you to do anything that doesn't make you happy. If you hate it, you walk away, no hard feelings."

"I think I'm going to apply."

"I think you should," I say, excitement radiating through me. "I've been looking for someone to take over this role a long time, and Mira, your images are better than anything that's ever come across my desk."

She grins, and brings her lips to mine. The kiss is polite and docile, appropriate for the setting, but it's still enough to bring me to my knees. I'm ready to rush out of there, to end the night early, but Katherine taps me on the shoulder to cut in.

"Can we talk for a minute?" she asks, and I find myself looking towards Mira for permission.

"It's okay, I need to pack up my gear anyways," she says, giving us space. "Find me in a few?"

I expect Katherine to lead me to the bar or her table, but she slips her hand into mine, bringing me back onto the dance floor. She's in the same green color as the rest of the party posse, but unlike Vanessa's dress, which is layered and long, Katherine's is cinched at the waist, corset-like, with lots of buttons up the back.

"I just wanted to apologize," she says, swaying against me, keeping a respectable distance between us this time.

"For what exactly?" I ask, knowing she has several things to apologize for.

"For everything. For what happened with Grant. But mostly for before. It wasn't fair of me to keep our lives entangled this long. I guess I've just been feeling insecure about everything. I mean, I'm almost thirty, and I'm starting over. I'm single. I'm not great at my job, and my best friend just got married, is moving and growing up without me."

"I get it, I do, but you could have talked to me about it. I would have helped you."

"I know," Katherine replies, turning away for a moment to compose herself. "It's a lot of change at once. And I'm worried that I can't handle it. But that's not your problem."

I soften at her words. Because even after everything, I'm not heartless to her plight.

"Have you thought about going to therapy?" I suggest.

"Meredith gave me a referral, and I have an appointment for later this month."

"I think it'd be good. Just to have someone to talk to."

She nods solemnly. "And just so you know I did hear you. I called a moving company and made an appointment but they couldn't get me in until Thursday. I really tried, but . . ."

"That's okay," I say, willing to give her a few more days. "Thursday's fine."

"I think I'm going to move back to Charlotte for a while. Save some money, and buy a house in a few years, or move out of state. I don't know. But I'll figure it out."

"Where are you going to stay in the meantime?"

She glances over at Derrick, who's finishing off a piece of cake. "Derrick said that he has an extra room. And he's gone most of the week at work."

He gives us a wave, and I have to admit I sort of see them together.

"I really want you to be happy, Kat."

"Thanks," she replies, her voice soft, and slips back into the crowd.

Itching for a change of scenery, I make my way over to Mira. She's chatting with Vanessa and Adrian, who are currently bickering about whether Derrick is going to knock over the cake, when I butt in.

"Sorry to interrupt, but do you want to get out of here?"

39 MIRA

"Where are we going?" Hudson leads me through the wildflower fields, the grass brushing against my legs as we make our way deeper into the property. When he asked if I wanted to leave the reception I thought we'd go for a drive, or hole up in our cabin, but we kept walking past everything until the sounds from the party became whispers in the wind.

"It's a surprise," he assures me, while I relish the quiet. There's nothing out here but the sounds of nature, the crickets chirping, and the croaking of frogs from the pond. It's the same tranquility I felt at the lake, as if there is no one else in the world but the two of us.

"Please tell me you didn't plan an orgy with the adventure guides, because I'm going to have to pass," I joke, trying to discern where we're headed.

"That's not a surprise, that would be the makings of a horror film," he says, as we climb further up the hill.

The sky is an explosion of reds and oranges, like fire shooting up from behind the dark blue mountains, as the last rays of sun crest over the golden mountaintops. It's the first night I've been able to appreciate the sunset, to see it not as the end of another horrible day, but as the opportunity for new beginnings, a chance to start over—and with Hudson by my side that thought doesn't feel as scary.

We climb the last stretch of elevation until the ground levels out and I realize what he's done.

LED lanterns light a pathway towards a tent that's been covered in fairy lights, the same variety from the wedding. Beside it a campfire is roaring. There is also a table set with a bottle of champagne and all the ingredients for s'mores.

"You said that camping would only be fun if there were s'mores and stargazing so . . ." Hudson says, leading me down the path. Peeking inside the tent, I can see it's outfitted with a blowup mattress, a plethora of pillows, and a crochet blanket.

"When did you have time to do all this?" I ask.

"I may have had some help," he replies, grabbing the bottle of champagne from the plastic bucket filled with ice.

"Make sure to thank Vanessa for me," I say, as he pops the cork on the bottle. Foam gushes over his hands and I take the bottle, saving him from himself. "You really can't pour a drink for shit." I shake excess champagne off my fingers before taking a sip.

"Thankfully I have other skills," he counters, moving his hand to my face and bringing my mouth to his. He tastes like champagne and vanilla frosting as I soften against him. In my life I've truly never had much security. I always thought that I needed to be better, to be someone different, to change, but the way Hudson stares at me, the green of his eyes darker beneath the night sky, I know that he'd never ask me to be anyone other than myself.

It was easy to allow myself to believe that love is a myth—that it, like many social constructs, is just a product of the wedding industry, that it's a fairy tale awarded to few. But as warmth spreads through my chest, down my body, I understand that I just never felt it before, real love, true love, the kind that keeps people together for forty years. Because love isn't just passion or lust, it isn't an all-consuming, can't-eat, can't-think proposition; it's problem-solving, listening, and understanding. It's everything that Hudson's done for me and more. Not only this week but ever since the first time I saw him in that bar. He's been taking care of me, in subtle ways that I hadn't realized I needed until now.

"What are you thinking about?" Hudson asks, moving a stray curl behind my ear.

I nod, allowing his steady arms to hold me in place, and I can feel the words I need to say slide to the tip of my tongue.

"That I love you too."

EPILOGUE – MIRA

Two Years Later

"And this is where Gandalf asks Bilbo if he wants to go on an adventure," Hudson says, doing his best Ian McKellen impression. He's dressed in an Aragorn costume, complete with a sword that we had to check through security at the airport, as he bounces from one Hobbit-hole to another.

If Hudson is a ray of sunshine on a normal day, being in the land of his favorite franchise is like dosing pure dopamine as he buzzes up the grassy knolls. I'm all too familiar with the quote, since Hudson made me watch all six parts of the film franchise as well as the extended versions and commentaries to get the full picture. But even though I'll never love the movies as much as he does, I can admit that the village of Hobbiton is quite breathtaking. Colorful flowers of pink and yellow line the cobbled paths, while vines and lush green grasses grow up the sides of the circular windows and doors.

"And Frodo stood right here," he says, glancing inside one of the Hobbit-holes from the movie sets. I love seeing him like this, carefree and unburdened. It's our first official vacation since Hudson took over as CEO, and he deserves the break. Thanks to his new conservation and educational initiatives Hudson has been awarded a coveted 30 Under 30 award from *Forbes* magazine and has already broken ground on two new scholarship-based summer camps.

"Ah. This is so cool," he says, geeking out. "Can you take my picture?"

"Only if I can put it in this month's newsletter," I say, reaching for the camera around my neck.

"Newsletter," he scoffs. "This is going to be my new profile pic on LinkedIn."

After we got back from Wyoming, I applied for the job at Elite Elevation, and Hudson offered it to me about fifteen minutes after I hit send on the application.

Working for a corporation is so different to the wedding world. I don't have to answer emails at two in the morning or edit until my eyesight goes blurry. I never have to worry if I'll walk into a job and get screamed at or ordered around. And, as Hudson promised, I'm never required to go into the office if I don't want to. But I like stopping in, bringing him lunch, or commandeering one of the communal desks to edit, and I got to know the team before we spent a week in the field together.

My first job out was at Acadia National Park and although I wasn't a seasoned hiker by any means, the team made sure to make me feel like part of the family. They let me take my time, showing me tips and tricks on how to survive life in the wilderness, offering me snacks of dehydrated fruits and jerky, and never making me feel less than when I needed help scaling mountainsides or getting an ATV out of reverse. And of course, having Hudson by my side every step of the way was an added bonus.

Because Hudson always made sure to put time in our schedule for me to relax or work on my own creative pursuits, I rekindled my love of documentary photography, spending our off days capturing street vendors in Mexico, sheep farmers in Texas, and fishermen in Maine. Hudson always assured me that I could take breaks, that he didn't want me to burn out again, but capturing content for a brand that was making a positive impact in the world, elevating unsung heroes in the environmental community, and highlighting pioneers in hiking and adventure sports didn't feel like work. It felt like an honor.

I click my shutter again before Hudson waves me over. "You think we can take a photo together? I want to prove that I got you to dress up."

I stare down at the costume I rented for the occasion. The floor-length Galadriel gown is crushed white velvet with balloon sleeves and braided rope embellishments. I've even donned a replica crown I found from a custom designer on Etsy, a purchase I hid in our guest bedroom for weeks hoping he wouldn't stumble upon it. When we got back from Wyoming, Hudson spent most nights at my apartment, while Katherine boxed up her stuff. But even after she moved to Charlotte, the place never really felt like home. Two months after I started working for Elite, Hudson put the condo on the market, I broke my lease, and we ended up getting a place together. A cute little cottage, with garden boxes and a porch swing, and a shed that Hudson converted into a darkroom just for me.

My images are not only anchor images for Elite Elevation but have gone on to win several prestigious awards in nature magazines and have been published in *National Geographic*. And in my spare time I've been able to curate a portfolio for a gallery with exhibitions in New York, San Francisco, Denver, and Asheville—a city we visit once a quarter to catch up with Grant and Meredith. The two of them are thriving, as Meredith's massage therapy business just expanded, hiring two other holistic healers, and Grant was made CFO for the brewery after he helped them expand to four additional locations. Meredith even convinced Vivianne to leave Arizona and open a medicinal tea shop in the River Arts District.

"I'd only do this for you," I reply, placing my camera on the moss-covered rock and setting the timer. Standing in front of the door, Hudson moves beside me as the camera's timer counts down. And even though I know what's coming, I'm still stunned when he drops to his knee, sword held at the hilt.

"Mira," he says, taking my hand, his fiery red hair popping among the lavish greens, making his eyes gleam. "I want to say that these last two years have been everything to me. You guided me along this journey when I was completely directionless. You inspired me to stand up for the things I want and be thankful for the things I'm given."

He takes a breath. "I've said it before and I'll keep saying it to whoever wants to listen, but I'm hopelessly in love with you. There isn't a day that goes by that I'm not grateful that you're here, with me, and I want to spend the rest of my life making you laugh, cooking you pancakes, and never mixing you a cocktail ever again," he laughs, pulling out a ring box from his breast pocket. He flicks it open to reveal a gold ring with an opal that shimmers in the sunlight. "Will you marry me?"

Bending down, I take his face into my hands, bringing his lips to mine. Even after all this time he still kisses me as if it's the last one we'll ever share and I let myself sink into him. His hands wrap around my waist, and he stands up.

"Is that a yes?" he asks, removing the ring from the box and waiting for my hand. Thankfully Vanessa clued me in on Hudson's proposal, since they'd gone ring shopping together. That girl really can't keep a secret, but at least she helped me orchestrate this surprise for him.

"On one condition."

"Anything," he states, and I know I could ask him for the world.

"We elope."

"I'd marry you right now if we could," Hudson says, guiding the ring onto my finger.

"Funny you should say that," I reply, ripping down the Under Construction tape in front of the Hobbit-hole. I knock on the hardwood, and as it swings open, it reveals our friends and family hiding inside. It's a small group: Hudson's dad, Oliver, Finn and Lilah, Vanessa and Adrian, my mom and dad, and Susan, George, Meredith, and Grant.

They are all beaming, and thanks to first-class tickets and a spa package at the resort, Susan's been pampered into placation. Not that she'd have any say over this wedding at all, since I tricked her into believing that it was a family vacation, one she was more than willing to attend since Hudson and her have begun working on their relationship. I wouldn't say that it's perfect by any means, but I can't deny that Susan's been putting in the work, coming to our house for the holidays. She even bought Meredith and I personalized gifts this year. Sure, they were designer handbags we'd never use, but she did get our names embroidered on them, with no spelling errors.

"Oh my God, Mira," he says, peering into the faces inside the Hobbit-hole as if they're a mirage.

"Is that a yes?" I ask.

"Of course it's a yes," he says, sweeping me into his arms and going in for a kiss.

"Hey now. You can't do that until you say 'I do,'" Vanessa shouts.

"There are no rules today," I reply, kissing him back.

"I can't believe you did this," Hudson says, the weight of the moment sinking in.

"We can always wait if you want, but I assumed today was going to be the happiest day of your life, so I thought why not make it mine too."

I remove a wooden box from my pocket.

"Hudson Walter Hayes," I say, displaying the custom forged ring I made for him, with flecks of green embedded in the gold to match his eyes. "I would rather be with you for one life than live through all the epochs of this world on my own."

"Did you just quote *Fellowship* to me?" he replies, mouth agape.

"Mmhmm. I even learned a few Elvish phrases too, but I'll save those for later."

Hudson is practically salivating when Vanessa interrupts us. "Come on you two, you can canoodle later. We flew all the way out here for a wedding, so let's get you hitched."

"I can't believe I'm about to get married in a cloak, holding a sword," Hudson says as we take our place in front of one of the Hobbit-holes.

"Just wait 'til you see who's going to perform the rites," I reply, as the officiant walks over, dressed in a Gandalf costume.

"No!" Hudson shouts, stunned.

"I thought you might like that."

"I fucking love you," he says, squeezing my hands.

"I love you too," I say, before Gandalf, or "Jack," as his name was listed on the website, begins offering us words of wisdom to live by. Our vows are completely unrehearsed, truths spoken from the heart that still embody more *Lord of the Rings* references I actually get now. Vanessa throws flower petals over us as we kiss, and Lilah snaps photos on a film camera. I don't care if they come out blurry, or crooked, because every time I look at them, I will always remember this feeling: of saying yes, of letting go, and marrying the love of my life.

ACKNOWLEDGMENTS

Writing a book is hard. It's so much harder than I ever thought it would be, but the process was made immensely easier by the fantastic people in my life, and without them, I would never have achieved my dream of finally sharing one of my stories with the world.

First off, I have to thank my amazing agent, Susan Velazquez Colmant, who believed in my stories and gave me the chance to share them with all of you. Thank you for falling in love with two of my favorite characters and the city lights that I can't wait to share with the world soon. Thank you to my UK team, Stevie, Bekah, and Arzu, for all your hard work and prompt responses on what was a completely impossible deadline that we smashed out of the park.

To my amazing friends Chloe, Emily, Paula, Arielle, Megg, Madison, Shelby, Zara, Brittany, Leigh, Nicole, Rachel, Megan G, thank you for supporting me, for reading my rough drafts, for listening to my voice notes, answering my anxiety-spiral texts, and indulging me in whatever crazy last-minute ideas I come up with even if costumes are mandatory. You all have seriously changed my life and shown me what true friendship really is. I wouldn't want to celebrate this milestone with anyone else.

To Sylvia, Kasey, and Chloe (*again*), who slept on sidewalks with me to see our favorite band and called it "camping," while

I panic-submitted drafts to agents. I'll never forget those days with the rats.

To my wonderful beta readers, Kirsty, Kerry, Kaylea, Jessica H, Jessica C, and Lindsey, your feedback was absolutely integral to this process, and I appreciate you more than you know.

To my Discord Writers Group: Jay, Elizabeth, Darelle, Sophia, Alyssa, Madeline, Alix, Rebecca, and Taylor, thank you for being my sounding board when I needed a space to vent, to assure me that I'm not the only one spiraling, and for always being there to celebrate my wins. I wish you all nothing but success in your own writing journeys.

Thank you to Vanessa, who was my first Romance friend on Reddit. You made me believe that I could do this. You supported me when I didn't know what a writing community looked like, and I can't wait to see your book on the shelves next to mine one day!

To Roulette, who gave me the gift of parking. I wouldn't be half as productive as I am without you!

To Erica Baker, Nancy Goodwin, Jill Massey, Chris Brockman, Cole Russing, and every teacher who went the extra mile and encouraged me to take risks, keep writing, and who read my stories when they were definitely not getting paid enough to do so, I appreciate every one of you.

To all my wonderful wedding clients I've had over the years, thank you for considering me a friend, for making my job feel effortless, for treating me with respect and kindness, and for supporting me in everything I do. I see you, appreciate you, and wouldn't be here without you.

I want to say the biggest thank you to my mother, Alicia, for raising me to watch and read content that was probably too mature for me, but that shaped me into becoming the storyteller I am today. For sitting through every indie movie, taking me to museums (*even though you hate them and only took me for "the culture"*), for keeping my many parties afloat when I was knee-deep in editing or drafting, for picking me up from Girl Scout camp the first night, because sleeping outside is not for me, and for getting all your friends to preorder copies of my book. You're the Lorelai to my Rory, and I can't wait until we live together *Grey Gardens* style.

And lastly, to my husband Andrew, who keeps me fed and in clean laundry when my ADHD brain can't handle another task. Thanks for taking such good care of me and the dogs. Without you, I wouldn't be writing this right now, and I'd be eating the same chicken and rosemary potatoes recipe from that episode of *Oprah* I watched in fourth grade. I appreciate you and your *NYT* recipe subscription every single day. But seriously, thank you for dealing with my 2 a.m. cleaning sprees, my reading light, my Sunday night spirals, my manic episodes, and finding the positive even when I was certain that this whole writing thing was never going to work out. I love you.

ABOUT THE AUTHOR

Jessica Fowler fell in love with storytelling from a young age, from writing ghost stories in historic cemeteries, devouring gritty YA novels faster than she could buy them, and watching every indie movie she could get her hands on. After earning degrees in Creative Writing and Film Studies from NC State University, she began writing romantic comedies inspired by her favorite vacations.

Jessica lives in Raleigh with her two supervillain dogs, her biochemist partner, and an exorbitant amount of leather jackets. When she's not shooting weddings for her photography business, Three Region, she's probably sipping a mocktail at one of her favorite dive bars, in the middle of a mosh pit, or at the local library.

You can follow her writing journey on Instagram and Threads @jesswritesitoff

Follow the Author on Amazon

If you enjoyed this book, follow Jessica Fowler on Amazon to be notified when the author releases a new book!
To do this, please follow these instructions:

Desktop:

1) Search for the author's name on Amazon or in the Amazon App.
2) Click on the author's name to arrive on their Amazon page.
3) Click the "Follow" button.

Mobile and Tablet:

1) Search for the author's name on Amazon or in the Amazon App.
2) Click on one of the author's books.
3) Click on the author's name to arrive on their Amazon page.
4) Click the "Follow" button.

Kindle eReader and Kindle App:

If you enjoyed this book on a Kindle eReader or in the Kindle App, you will find the author "Follow" button after the last page.